Defying Normal

Normal Series, Book 2

Defying Normal

ELDON REED

TATE PUBLISHING
AND ENTERPRISES, LLC

Defying Normal
Copyright © 2016 by Eldon Reed. All rights reserved.

No part of this publication may be reproduced, stored in a retrieval system or transmitted in any way by any means, electronic, mechanical, photocopy, recording or otherwise without the prior permission of the author except as provided by USA copyright law.

This novel is a work of fiction. Names, descriptions, entities, and incidents included in the story are products of the author's imagination. Any resemblance to actual persons, events, and entities is entirely coincidental.

The opinions expressed by the author are not necessarily those of Tate Publishing, LLC.

Published by Tate Publishing & Enterprises, LLC
127 E. Trade Center Terrace | Mustang, Oklahoma 73064 USA
1.888.361.9473 | www.tatepublishing.com

Tate Publishing is committed to excellence in the publishing industry. The company reflects the philosophy established by the founders, based on Psalm 68:11,

"The Lord gave the word and great was the company of those who published it."

Book design copyright © 2016 by Tate Publishing, LLC. All rights reserved.
Cover design by Joana Quilantang
Interior design by Manolito Bastasa

Published in the United States of America

ISBN: 978-1-68270-822-4
1. Family & Relationships / Adoption & Fostering
2. Fiction / Family Life
16.03.14

This novel is dedicated to the memory of two amazing people who inspired the writing of this series:

John and Lorene Reed
1910–1979 and 1914–1989

Although this is a work of fiction, and no people or events in the book are real, the idea for this story came from my parents.

John and Lorene Reed fostered dozens of children while living on this beautiful piece of real estate. The setting for this novel was real. The ranch was owned by my mother's sister. My dad was the ranch foreman.

These two people (now deceased) were responsible for fifty-two "lives under construction." Many arrived, saddened by their family situation. Some talked about it. Most didn't.

Lorene taught these children the social skills to live in an adult world. John taught them the value of hard work. Both John and Lorene showed each child an unselfish love. Not many people would make sacrifices as they did for children of total strangers.

There is no doubt in my mind that each of these children, now adults, will remember the time they spent on this Angus ranch and with two very caring foster parents. No, they won't forget.

Acknowledgements

I'd like to thank several people who have played a crucial role in my writing career:

Jerry B. Jenkins—author of *The Left Behind Series* and founder of Christian Writers Guild.
Diann Mills—author of over fifty novels in the Christian genre and my personal mentor.
Sandra Byrd—author and mentor in the Craftsman Course at Christian Writers Guild.
Dr. Dennis E. Hensley—author, editor, and mentor, Christian Writers Guild.
Janet Safford Cline—critique partner.
Elaine Heusinkveld Soerens—critique partner

And whoever welcomes one such child
    in my name welcomes me.
                    —Matthew 18:5 (NIV)

Prologue

It seems every time I sit down to this old Remington and start pecking away at my journal, I get interrupted. Usually, it is a good interruption, like my lanky six-foot-two husband, Kirk, sneaking up behind me and planting a kiss on my cheek, or a phone call from one of my teacher friends wanting to chat. But this time, it was an interruption that gave me a bit of a shudder. This one would be more than a temporary interruption to my writing. It would forever alter our lives in ways we never imagined.

I shouldn't complain. I have been blessed with an incredible life. Kirk manages this eighteen-hundred-acre Angus cattle ranch where we live. Uncle Carl Childers is the owner but has given Kirk full authority over the operations of the ranch.

The pastures are beautiful. Streams wind their way down to three large ponds stocked with catfish, bluegill, and largemouth bass. On the east is a wooded area with post oak and blackjack trees, a haven for morel mushrooms in season.

From the beginning of our marriage, Kirk and I had assumed our home would be blessed with children. I remember him saying, "Katie, it's even part of our name."

"Yes," I had said. "I thought of that before I ever took the name of Childers."

We waited for a first pregnancy, but it never came. I understand now how God had a somewhat different approach to satisfy our longing for children. It was a TV commercial showing the need for foster parents that led us to apply. After six weeks of evening classes, we were certified in the state of Oklahoma. Fostering seemed right at the time, and we understood it might provide an avenue to eventual adoption.

My husband's salary doesn't allow for many luxuries, but the joys of country living far outweigh a huge paycheck. God has been good to us, and we are careful to count our blessings.

A house is the umbrella that covers a family with not only shelter, but a base camp for laughter, love, and even an occasional tear. The ranch house is unique. It is a huge lodge-type structure with foot-thick walls of solid rock. The big main room is some thirty feet by sixty feet. On one end, a massive rock fireplace towers up to the peak of the twenty-five-foot cathedral ceiling. On either side of the fireplace are built-in bookcases with a small ivy-covered window above each. In the center of the room hangs a six-foot round wagon wheel chandelier over our big oaken farm table that can seat ten. To its right is a wonderful farm kitchen with my hundred-year-old Elmira wood cookstove, which I use during the winter months. Thankfully, I also have a contemporary gas range. At the back of the house are three bedrooms and two baths. A spring-fed creek trickles year-round on the north side of the house, just deep enough to get the feet wet. Fuzzy moss-covered rocks protrude here and there—a beautiful image screaming for a canvas and brush.

I remember one Monday morning, I received a long-awaited phone call from a Mrs. Sawyer with the Department of Family Services. Seven-year-old Brandon would be our first foster child.

What a joy he has been. We fostered him for two years and, after many disappointments along the way, eventually were allowed to adopt him.

Kirk and Brandon were bonded in a way I didn't know was even possible. The ranch became the playground for the two. Brandon shared Kirk's love of hunting, fishing, and even the farm chores. The two guys spoke a language so foreign to me, I was often left scratching my head, trying to decipher their guy talk.

But now, back to the interruption that left me a bit numb. The phone rang, and I recognized the voice of our sweet caseworker and my friend, Betty Sawyer.

At that moment, it was quite an odd feeling. Somehow, I knew that phone call would impact our lives in a dramatic way. I just didn't know how.

I put the dustcover back on the old Remington because my real job was just beginning.

1

Nine-year-old Thorne Barrow had walked seven of the eight blocks from school. A glance down at the Alien Queen digital watch on his wrist showed 4:00 p.m. *Stupid detention hall.* His untied high-top Converse sneakers—two sizes too big—slapped the broken pavement to the rhythm of the death metal tune booming through his earbuds. Rounding the corner of Elm and First, two police cars lined the street where he lived. An ambulance sat backed up in the front yard. In his neighborhood, it wasn't unusual to see police cars, but this was his house. *What the…*

Two medics rolled a gurney out the front door. A sheet covered a body, forming a big hump on the stretcher. In front of them, two policemen escorted Big John Barrow, handcuffed and cursing, toward one of the cop cars. Surprising, not because he was handcuffed—nothing new there—but he was supposed to still be in jail.

The EMT in front lifted the gurney over broken-up sections of the sidewalk. The bone-white sheet covering a body on the gurney dominated the scene.

Thorne cringed at the sight of a woman marching toward him. The burly female in a police uniform grabbed his hand. He resisted the woman. Her strong grip on his small wrist fueled the fire in him. "Get your hands off me, you stupid woman! That's my dad. And who's that under the sheet?"

"Honey, you need to come with me. You don't need to see this. We'll get to the details later. Tell me your name."

"Let go o' me! I'm not tellin' you." He tried to pull away, kicking at the woman's legs.

She gripped his arm even tighter. "Honey, you do need to tell me. You said that was your dad with the handcuffs, right?"

"Yeah, why's he here? He was already in jail. So why is he being carted off again?"

"Okay, I'll make a deal with you. You tell me your name, and I'll answer your question about your dad."

He glared at the woman. Any woman, especially one in a police uniform, couldn't be trusted. But what was going on? She would know.

"My name is Thorne." Her vise-grip hold tightened. "Hey, you're hurting my wrist. Let go!" The woman smelled like she'd just poured a whole bottle of perfume over herself. Disgusting!

"Well, Thorne, your dad is going back to jail for something he did."

"Where's my mom? I wanna see her."

Still holding on to his pencil-thin wrist, the officer knelt down in front of the child. "Honey, that's just not possible right now."

Thorne watched as his dad was shoved into the backseat of the patrol car. Then the EMTs caught his eye as they rolled the gurney up to the rear doors of the ambulance. The front overlapped the floor of the ambulance, and the metal legs folded up. With a quick shove, the whole thing slid inside. One guy slammed the doors shut. Both of them walked around to the cab, jumped in, and the EMSA logo on the back grew smaller as the vehicle sped away.

Thorne jerked away from the female officer's grip, stared at the house next door, and flipped his middle finger in the air. "How you like that, you crazy old bats?"

Eighty-year-old Emma Knutson watched the scene next door unfold from her front porch. She had seen the boy quarreling and struggling with the policewoman. "He's just like his dad—and his dad's dad before him."

Emma's neighbor sat next to her on the porch swing. "I'd say. If you ask me, it's bad blood. The whole family is meaner than two shades of sin! I've lived just across the street for nigh on forty years now, and the whole lot of them Barrows ain't never been worth a dime. John's been in and out of jail, and I hear the oldest boy's headed to the pen."

She stuck her pointed index finger toward her friend with an on-the-spot theory. "Emma! You don't s'pose that was John's wife there under the sheet, do you?"

"I wouldn't put it past that old buzzard. The gunshot we heard just may have been aimed at poor Lana Lou. He's always treated her like a dog. I don't know why she didn't leave him years ago!"

"I'm tellin' you, Emma, I'll be glad if that family ever moves outta this neighborhood. Yep, they're nothin' but bad blood!"

Freedom had been fleeting for John Barrow. At six feet four inches, two hundred fifty pounds, he stretched out on the familiar bunk in the exact same cell he had occupied for the past six months. Less than a full day of freedom. Venom coursed through his veins while he stared up at the bottom of the top bunk. Lana Lou had accused him of child abuse the first time. *Child abuse! Them boys had to be disciplined! That woman never knew nothin' about discipline.* Assault on a police officer had landed him in jail the second time. Equipment he'd stolen from a job site had bought him a meal ticket behind the familiar bars the last time. With each stint, his court-appointed lawyer had finagled a minimum sentence for him. But this time was different. There would be no short sentence. No parole. No going back home—such as it was.

John Barrow recalled how he had walked back into the battered old bungalow earlier that morning, the home he had inherited from his grandfather. The old house was quiet. The kids were in school, or at least the youngest, nine-year-old Thorne, probably was. Hand-me-down furniture in the cramped living room sat just as he had last seen it when cops entered the house six months ago, handcuffed him, and hauled him off to the county jail. Except…

A badly scuffed pair of once-black biker boots sat in the corner by his sagging and form-fitting brown recliner. His ashtray spilled over with unfiltered Camel butts—not his brand. He walked into the kitchen. Dirty dishes spread over the length of the countertop. Trash spilled over from the plastic trash can on to the floor in the corner.

Was that a whisper coming from the bedroom? "Lana Lou, you here?"

If it was a voice, it stopped suddenly. The only other sound came from a northern mockingbird, sitting high in the maple tree just outside the open kitchen window, the one that had never shut completely. The sunlight streaming in through the window showered the air with dust particles, accentuating the stillness.

Then another whisper—baritone for sure. He took the Glock from the top of the fridge, walked down the hallway, and threw open the door to their bedroom.

Lana Lou ducked under the covers. The bearded biker sat up—and the Glock fired.

Lana Lou Barrow was left again with the boys, no income, a thirty-year-old Ford pickup with a busted engine, and John right back in the county jail, charged with murder. The boys—nineteen, seventeen, and nine—would be no help to her. The oldest would soon start serving one year in the state penitentiary for his part as an accomplice in setting fire to a local church. The belligerent seventeen-year-old had no respect for her and was failing again in all subjects. For him, school had become part-time. The truant officer had already visited the Barrow house. Lana Lou's baby boy, nine-year-old Thorne, had started to live up to his name. Her neighbor had asked her why she had agreed to curse him with that label. "You're setting that child up to be a thorn in your flesh for the rest of his life," she had said. "You can't just slap a tag like that on a child and expect him to ever be worth a hoot. He'll drag that banner in the dust forever."

But John had insisted. And who was she to argue?

Thorne Barrow was a cocky little out-of-control brat who ruled the rest of the Barrow brood. He hated his father, rebuffed his mother's on-again-off-again attempts at discipline, and had become the backyard bully to younger kids in the neighborhood.

2

Betty Sawyer pulled up to the address she'd been given. At first, the house appeared to be abandoned. The dandelion-infested yard hadn't seen a mower in weeks—probably months. She stepped around the rusted Mongoose BMX bike lying across the broken and uneven sidewalk and stepped up on the weathered wooden porch. The blaring rattle of sound effects from a video game penetrated the walls. Pounding on the aluminum frame of the storm door brought no answer. She pulled it open and found the old wooden door unlocked. "Hello, anyone home?"

Pushing the front door open produced an eerie squeak. She walked in, and a teen traipsed out of the room, holding on to his oversized pants. A smaller boy sat in front of the TV, furiously controlling his game, ignoring the visitor. For a few seconds, Betty stood and watched the entranced boy thumb away at the controller, and still he didn't acknowledge her presence. She reached for the remote lying on top of the TV.

When the screen went blank, the boy's head shot up. "Hey, what'd you do that for?"

"We need to talk." Betty knelt down beside the scrawny kid. "What's your name?"

"Who are you, lady?"

"I'm Betty Sawyer with the Department of Family Services. Is your mother here?"

The boy looked around to see if his brother would answer. "No, she ain't here."

"Is she at work?"

"No, she don't work. I don't know where she is. We ain't seen her in like a week."

"Was that your brother who left the room as I came in?"

"Uh…yeah, I guess. Why?"

"I need you to go get him. I need to talk to both of you."

"Hey!" the boy yelled. "The lady wants you back in here."

The brother clopped back into the room, took one look at Betty, and said, "So what do you think you need to talk about?"

"First off, pull up a chair and sit down so your pants don't gravitate to the floor." That brought a scowl from him and a snicker from the younger one, who was still clutching the video controller. "Okay, guys, tell me about your parents. You can start by telling me their names and where they are now."

The older boy frowned at her, making it clear he had no intentions of cooperating. With a prickled string of obscenities, he ended by saying, "So you just need to march your—"

"Look, young man! We can make this easy, or we can make it difficult. I prefer to make it easy, but you need to cooperate with me. If you want to make it difficult, I've got police backup on the way now."

A long silence filled the room.

Betty waited.

"My name's Josh, and that's my brother, Thorne." His voice squeaked out a falsetto. "Dad's name is John Barrow."

"Is he at work?"

His falsetto had given way again to lower tones. "Nope, he's back in jail now for murdering my mom's boyfriend."

"Your mom's name is…?"

The older boy slumped in his chair, rolled his walnut-brown eyes around the room, mumbled a couple of curse words, and then came back to a steady fixation on Betty. "I don't know why you think you need to know all this. It's none of your business."

Betty pointed a finger at him. "Young man, it is in fact my business. Now, you start talking—without the obscenities—or I'll have the police deal with you when they get here."

The boy plopped down in the nearest chair. "Name's Lana Lou. We don't know where she is."

"She left right after the cops came and took Dad away," the younger one said. He then reached for the power button on the front of the TV.

"Hold it, sonny! We're talking. Leave that TV off."

Now in her fifties, Betty had been a caseworker for sixteen years. Her graying hair hinted at the wisdom she'd gained in dealing with kids who had never been taught the social skills needed to survive in an adult world. Her experience in dealing with young pimple-faced ruffians helped her to pull a bit more information from the boys.

Their oldest brother had recently been jailed for his involvement in arson. These two younger ones had been alone in the house for several days. There was no food left, and the city had turned off the water to the house.

A police car arrived and assisted Betty in getting the two boys into her Buick, along with a few of their clothes, the video game, a boom box, and several CDs. Two slices of moldy white bread had been tucked in between a couple of Godsmack T-shirts.

Back at the office, Betty looked again at the updated listing of approved foster homes in the city. All were at capacity, except one. She knew the number.

3

"Katie, this is Betty. I need your help. I've got a nine-year-old boy who needs a home."

Katie held the phone out a bit and stared at it. They had fostered several children prior to adopting Brandon. Some were sweet kids and a joy to have around. Others were difficult and required her full attention. Physical and mental handicaps took much of her time. Dealing with anger, loneliness, and social ineptitude required even more. Were they ready to foster again? Kirk would say yes.

Her hesitation made for an awkward moment.

"Are you there?"

"Yes, I'm here." She closed her eyes and sucked in a long breath of air. "Go ahead and tell me about this little boy."

"Hon, this kid will probably try your patience. He most likely will upset your home and create havoc every chance he gets. He's not like Brandon—not one bit."

After an uncomfortable silence, Katie managed to say, "What's his name?"

"Thorne—Thorne Barrow."

"Thorne!" She touched her now-cold coffee mug. "Well, I guess the name fits." Her finger circled the top of the mug. *Thorne! What was his mother thinking?*

Telling the caseworker no probably should be out of the question. But why bring an unruly kid into their home? Brandon was a jewel of a child and had made them proud. What kind of an influence would this one have on him?

"Hon, this kid will be a handful compared to Brandon. I found him and one of his two brothers abandoned in a house over in the Carbon Flats area with no food, no water in the house, and no adult supervision. His oldest brother had been caught at the scene with a group of hoodlums setting fire to a church, and he is now in jail. I had to take the next youngest, a seventeen-year-old brother, to a group home. I learned he'd been stealing food from a convenience store just around the corner from their house. A belligerent kid, he appeared to be strung out on drugs. His baggy pants were about to fall to his ankles.

"As you know, we try to place siblings in the same home, but I knew this one would splinter your nerves, and there were no other homes open that were willing to the brother. The group home was my only choice for him. Of course, that will be temporary. He's seventeen now, and when he turns eighteen, he'll be of age and on his own."

Katie listened quietly. This could open the door to a turbulent atmosphere in the otherwise tranquil ranch life they had come to enjoy.

Somewhere, a cricket chirped.

"Katie?"

"Yes." It was barely a whisper.

"Katie," Betty said, "I'm getting the impression I may have caught you at a bad time. Should I call back in a few minutes?"

"No, I'm okay. This is just catching me a bit off guard. It sounds like this kid is very different from Brandon. I'm just not sure—"

"I know Brandon is one big smiley face for you two, and anyone can see the transformation you guys have done with him. That kid has certainly been blessed with your brand of love. But now I'm calling about another child who could use your help. Are you telling me you're not interested in taking on a foster child at this time?"

"No." She swallowed the lump in her throat, and her voice grew stronger. "Kirk says we need to continue to foster. These kids need us. I guess I was just feeling a bit selfish. But we need to do this—we really do. If we don't, who will?"

"Katie, you scared me for a minute there. It sounded like you might back away on this one."

"Sorry. I guess I did come off a bit reluctant."

"I'm thinking Kirk will be a good influence for this kid. I see what he has done with Brandon. Every boy should have a dad like Kirk! Brandon seems to be well-grounded and should be a good influence on this child too, as well as good company for him.

"So…if you and Kirk are okay with it, I'll bring him on out to the ranch. He will probably test your patience, but if I know you two, you'll be able to steer him in the right direction."

"Okay, we'll see you in a bit. Remember, the gate code is 742."

"Got it. I should be there in less than an hour."

Katie was still clutching the disconnected cell phone and staring at the blank wall when Kirk walked in. "Okay," he said. "That can't be good news. Do I wanna hear about it?"

"Probably not. I've just told Betty we'd take another foster child—a nine-year-old boy."

"Doesn't sound so bad to me. What's his name?"

"Thorne." Katie laid the phone down and shook her head. "Betty says he'll probably live up to his name."

Kirk laughed. "Thorne, huh? Well, I won't let him get under my skin. How about you?"

Katie ignored his attempt at humor, looked up into his denim-blue eyes, hesitated, and then said, "We'll see."

4

Brandon was the one to open the front door, even before Betty had a chance to knock.

Betty stood there with her hand on the boy's shoulder. "Hey, Brandon, I think you've grown a couple of inches since I last saw you."

"Yeah, Dad says I'm gonna be as tall as him—and he's six two!"

"Brandon, I'd like for you to meet this young man. This is Thorne."

With a dish towel still in her hand, Katie walked over and stood behind Brandon. "Well, hello there. Come on in. I was just finishing up the dishes. Have you two had lunch?"

"Yes, I stopped and grabbed us some burgers about ten miles back."

Katie looked at the scrawny kid with coal-black hair all but covering those big walnut-brown eyes. Not nearly as tall as Brandon and very small for his age, Thorne looked to be no older than seven. "So your name is Thorne? How do you spell that?"

The boy stood there with his hands on his hips and looked straight up at Katie. "It's spelled t-h-o-r-n-e." He slung his head to one side to flip the mop of hair from over his eyes. "Kids make fun of my name. They like to call me a little prick."

Katie grinned. "Well, I personally think Thorne is a very cool name for a boy. I'll bet you won't ever run across a girl with that name. Come on in, guys. I want to show Thorne his room. It's right next to Brandon's."

Thorne didn't move. He stood there with both hands in his pockets. His eyes wandered all over the room, first up to the wagon wheel chandelier high above the big dining table, and then to the huge, towering rock fireplace on the north wall. Then he touched the inside rock walls, sliding his finger along the mortar between the rocks. "Is this place a castle?"

Brandon gawked at him. "No, it's a house! It's where we live." A strangely insolent tone blurted out from the otherwise humble guy. "You should know there are no castles in Oklahoma."

Thorne's eyes were still roaming around the big room. "I've never seen a house like this." He looked toward the big farm kitchen on the south end of the cavernous room. "Wow! Your kitchen is right in the living room! In our house, the kitchen is tiny and at the back of the house. This is awesome!"

Betty smiled. "He also thought the horses up by the gate were awesome."

Thorne jumped right in. "Yeah, they were standin' right there by the road. Betty punched in a number, and this big gate opened. We drove through it. Then she stopped the car so we could get out and pet the horses."

"That little paint is mine," Brandon proudly announced.

"Paint?" Thorne looked confused. "What are you talkin' about, bro?"

"Yeah, you mean the one with the black-and-white-spotted coat? That kind of horse is called a paint. I named her Puzzle because she looks—"

"Yeah, dude, she looks like a bunch of puzzle pieces. I can see that."

"Brandon," Betty said, "while you're showing Thorne his room, I'll go out and get his clothes and things." She turned to Katie. "I hope you'll have room for all his stuff. He brought a pencil drawing of a mangy-looking dog staring down a kitten. It is very cute and unbelievably good artwork. I asked him who drew it. He told me he did, but I'm not sure about that. You know these kids often tell some whoppers."

She walked toward the door. "My backseat is full of stuff. This kid claimed about everything that was left in the house they were in." Then she whispered into Katie's ear, "Including a couple of moldy slices of bread."

While Betty and Katie were putting Thorne's things away, Brandon grabbed his new friend and headed out the back door. After Katie heard the door slam, she glanced at Betty and said, "This kid doesn't seem like he'll test our patience. He seems like a good kid. He just needs a haircut and some good-old farm food to put some meat on those bones."

"Trust me. This one will be a handful. When you get to know him, you'll find him to be an arrogant and defiant little toot—thinks he knows more than any adult he's ever come in contact with."

"Hey, maybe that's been true, up until today." Then she became serious. "Where are his parents?"

"The house the two boys were in looked like no adult had been there in weeks. I questioned them about their mom—there's rarely a dad still around in these cases—but I found out Dad is in jail awaiting his trial for murder."

"Murder!"

"Yes, the boys said he came home one day and found his mom in bed with another man. He shot and killed him." Betty's right hand flew up to her mouth. "Oh gosh, I shouldn't be telling you that. I could get in big trouble."

"Betty, you've known me a long time now. What you tell me stays right here—always has."

"Thanks. I've always felt I could trust you."

"Besides, I think I may have heard that on the evening news a while back. So what happened to the mom?"

"That's the thing. No one seems to know. The boys said she just left. So I don't know if it's a case of abandonment or maybe there was foul play involved. I checked with the police, and they didn't seem to know anything about her. No one had reported her missing. They did say she was there at the house the day of the murder, and they had questioned her then.

"Neither boy was going to school. The truant officer showed up at their house, and that's when he called us."

Brandon was excited to take Thorne and show him the ranch. First, he took him to the milk barn and explained how he would usually help out there with the milking and separating the cream. Then he took him to the pigpen and explained what had happened to him when he ignored Kirk's warnings and fed the hogs from inside the pen. "Trust me. You don't want one of those Big Mamas to get after you. They'll have you down in the muck faster than you can holler for help."

Thorne's eyes wandered from the big barn and back to the two sows just beyond the fence. "Hey, I could outrun them big old slugs any day. They're so fat, they waddle. I ain't scared of them!"

"You better be! I know from experience."

Brandon promised Thorne he'd show him the horses and take him to the big pond later. "But first, let's go back and get something to eat."

When they got back to the house, Thorne jumped on the ATV and said, "Where's the keys to this bad boy?"

Brandon stared at him in disbelief. "You can't drive that. You're not old enough!"

Thorne squeezed the handlebar accelerator, tried to turn on the lights, spewed out a nasty little swear word, and said, "I'll have this thing up to seventy in no time."

"You're really dumb! It won't even get up past forty!"

"Watch me!"

Brandon rolled his eyes. *Oh brother!* "Come on. Let's go grab something to eat."

Inside, the boys scarfed down their PB&Js and drank their milk. Thorne held his glass up, looked at it, and said, "What's this?"

Brandon twisted his mouth and nose into a half snarl. "It's milk! What hole did you just crawl out of?"

"This don't taste like milk."

"Well, Thorne, this milk comes from our Jersey cows," Katie said. "It's very rich in butterfat. You won't find any skim milk in this house. We like our milk better than the watery stuff you get in the store."

Thorne downed his glass and asked for more. "Yeah, I like it. I just didn't know milk could be good. When we used to have milk in our house, it sometimes had chunks in it and tasted sour."

The rest of the day was more of the same for the two boys. A trip to the big pond, back up to visit the horses, and down to the hay barn revealed the true side of this cocky young boy.

Thorne was determined to convince Brandon of his great knowledge and superiority. Brandon was not impressed. He had a plan. If he could get Thorne to follow him back to the house, he could sneak out and head for the milk barn to help Kirk with the chores. The first leg of his plan worked. The second one didn't. Brandon was halfway down the lane, heading toward the barn. From about a hundred yards back, Thorne hollered, "Hey, dude! Wait for me."

Brandon snapped his fingers and whispered to the wind in his face. "Man! I almost made it." Thorne soon caught up.

Without Thorne right there to bug him, Brandon usually finished milking his one cow well before Kirk was finished with the other two, but not this time. Thorne had a dozen or more comments about the milking process. He tried to persuade Brandon there was no need for him to sit there next to the cow while the machine was pumping. Brandon kept his eyes on the milker attached to the cow's udders. "You don't know squat! I have to make sure it doesn't come loose and fall on the floor because I'd have to sanitize it all over again."

"It's not gonna come loose!"

"It could—and it has! A fly could be bugging the cow. When she kicks at it, that milker's comin' off!"

"Not if you put it on good in the first place."

Brandon's irritation peaked. "Shut up!"

Thorne went out and jumped on the ATV. Kirk followed Brandon into the cream separation room. "How's it going? Did you teach Thorne anything?"

"No. You can't teach that goober anything. He thinks he already knows it all." Kirk had parked the ATV just outside the barn. "I hope you didn't leave the key out there."

"No. I'm already one step ahead of that boy." Kirk opened the door and motioned for Thorne to come in with them. "He needs to learn what we do here in the separating room."

Brandon grinned and shook his head. "You just wait. He'll try to tell us how to do our job."

"Don't worry, I can handle that too."

Thorne wandered through the door with his thumbs tucked inside the waist of his jeans and looked up at Kirk. "Whatcha got, Daddy-o?"

Kirk stared at him for a second, reached down, put his hand on the shoulder of the frail boy, and said, "Let's get one thing straight. My name is Kirk. I'm told your name is Thorne. From here on, we'll go by those names only."

"Uh, sorry."

"No problem. You didn't know, but now you do." He grabbed the liquid detergent bottle off the countertop and stuck it in Thorne's hand. "Thorne, you're in charge of cleaning up the separator equipment today. It's gotta be sparkling clean for tomorrow's use. Brandon can show you how it's done if you need."

Thorne looked at the detergent bottle and set it back up on the countertop. "Since you're not gonna need it again 'til tomorrow, I say we wait to clean it up then."

"No, Thorne, we clean it up immediately after each use. If we wait until tomorrow, the milk residue will dry and be caked on. That'd make it pretty difficult to clean up."

"If it dried, we could just brush it off. That'd be easier."

"Okay, Thorne, we'll do it your way today. Tomorrow you will do it my way."

"Dad, if he waits and lets it dry, it'll be coated on like glue, and he'll never get it clean."

Kirk winked at him. "Naw, he says it'll just brush right off. I put him in charge, so it's his job to have it clean before the next use."

Brandon grinned and shook his head. He left the dirty equipment on the countertop and walked away.

Since neither boy had a helmet, Kirk told them they would have to walk back. He crawled on the ATV and looked at Thorne. "I'll buy you a helmet Monday."

Brandon glanced over at Thorne and saw a disgusted look on his face. Gravel flew as the ATV sped away toward the ranch house.

Kirk kicked off his boots at the door, and Katie tiptoed up to him for her usual kiss. "Where are the boys?"

"Neither one had a helmet, so I told them they had to walk back."

"So how did Thorne take to the milking chores?"

"The boy has his own ideas. He told Brandon there was no need to sit there and keep watch on the milker. He knew it wouldn't come off. Then he told us there was no need to clean the separator equipment today since it wouldn't be used again 'til tomorrow."

Katie smiled. "Yeah, I think he may need a course in Farm 101."

It was bedtime for the boys. In the past, Kirk had made it a point to join Katie and each of their foster children for prayers before bed. This was going to be no exception, but Thorne apparently thought otherwise. He informed them he thought bedtime prayers were silly.

"You may think that is silly," Kirk said. "We don't. In our house we all participate in bedtime prayers. So that means you too."

Thorne bowed his head reluctantly and then mumbled, "I don't know why we have to do this."

"You don't have to know why, and you don't even have to know how," Kirk said. "Brandon can go first, and you'll see he just talks to God in his own way. You can do the same."

Kirk bowed his head but watched as Brandon started to pray.

Thorne's head tipped down a bit, but Kirk could see the boy looking over at Brandon. When it was his turn, he managed to say one simple sentence: "God, help someone find my mom." Then he looked up to Kirk as if he needed affirmation he'd done it right.

Kirk put his arm around the skinny boy. "That was perfect. You can pray that prayer every night if you want to."

Sunday morning, Brandon went to Thorne's room. "Get up. We gotta go do the chores before church."

Thorne opened one eye. "Huh?"

"Come on, you gotta go clean the equipment you let dry. You should do it while Dad and I are milking. Then we've got church after that."

There was no response.

Kirk stood at the door, listening. He walked over, grabbed the covers, and with one quick yank, pulled them toward the foot of the bed. "Get up, Thorne. You've got work to do."

Thorne moaned and curled himself into a fetal position.

"Come on, get your clothes on. You gotta go brush off the milk and cream residue from the separator equipment. Remember, you said it'd be easy."

An hour later, Thorne was still trying to scrub off the pasted residue from the equipment. Finally, he asked Brandon to help him.

"Yeah, I'll help, but you gotta start listening to us." Brandon picked up the top bowl of the separator. "We know more about these chores than you do, so stop trying to act like you know it all."

Church was another thing Thorne Barrow knew nothing about, but he asked questions about it instead of trying to convince them he understood it all. That didn't last long. After the service ended, the pastor greeted Kirk and Katie just outside the church. "Who do we have here today?"

"This is Thorne," Kirk said. "He'll be staying with us for a while until his family situation can be taken care of."

Thorne looked to the side, refused the pastor's handshake, and stuck his own hands in his pockets. Then with sarcasm written all over his face, he looked up at the pastor. "You coulda said what you did in five minutes. You just didn't know when to shut up, did you?"

The pastor laughed, Katie turned purple, and Kirk's hand quickly covered Thorne's mouth. "And you, sir, haven't learned to shut your own mouth. Now go jump in the truck."

Kirk turned to the pastor. "I'm sorry. The boy has a few things to learn."

The pastor thought for a second. "No, I think he was right. I could have delivered the entire sermon in five minutes." He grinned. "Maybe I'll try that next time." He shook Kirk's hand and grinned. "Kirk, you've got your work cut out for you. I'll be praying for you."

5

Even though Katie had to drive in town to enroll Thorne, he said he wanted to ride the bus with Brandon. So she dropped the boys off at the gate and waited for Mr. Simpson's bus to arrive before she drove away.

Previous school records showed him to be in third grade, but Katie guessed he had been passed on to third in spite of not being ready. The third grade teacher at Luther said she remembered how Katie had worked with Brandon to quickly bring him up to reading and math level, so she suggested they keep him in third, even though it might be a struggle at first. Katie agreed. "A nine-year-old doesn't belong in second grade. It would be humiliating for him. I'll do what I can to catch him up, but I'm not sure how long he'll be with us."

"Katie, if anyone can do it, you can," Mrs. Dalton said. "You worked miracles with Brandon."

While the boys were in school, Katie went to Thorne's room to make his bed. She would see to it that this became part of his morning chores starting tomorrow morning. She lifted his pillow to pull up the sheet. There lay the moldy bread that had been tucked inside a T-shirt when Betty brought him to the ranch. A tear formed in her eye. The poor kid had been starving. *Surely he knows he'll have plenty to eat here.* She took the once-white bread, now turning green and blue, and tossed it in the kitchen trash. Taking a fresh slice of bread, she dropped it in a sandwich bag, went back to his room, and placed it under his pillow. *I'll keep doing this each morning with a fresh slice until he asks me to stop.*

She rummaged through the books in Brandon's room, moving the easiest ones to Thorne's room. The problem with the easier ones was they were too juvenile in theme for a nine-year-old. That evening, Thorne rebelled. "These books are for babies!"

"When you can read these to me," Katie said, "we will move out of the baby stage and into some more appropriate for your age. Work with me on this, and you'll soon be reading more grown-up books."

Brandon picked up *Dexter the Tough* by **Margaret Peterson Haddix**, a book she knew he loved but with words that were not easy for a second or third grader. He handed the book to Katie. "But, Mom, you should read this book to Thorne. He'll like it as much as I did."

"Yes, I remember the book. It's about a boy who tried to cover his fears as a new kid in town by bullying. Then he made a friend and found out there was no need to bully other kids."

"Yeah, but you should read it to him. It's got some really hard words." Brandon set the book on the bed and headed toward the door. "Right now, I gotta go help Dad."

Thorne pitched the book down on the bed and snarled at Katie. "I can read that book. I don't need you to read it to me."

After the morning chores were done, Brandon said, "Dad, I'm glad Thorne was busy with schoolwork and not bugging us today. We've got our routine down, and we're always able to finish up just in time for supper." Brandon climbed on the ATV behind Kirk to head back to the house. "Was I a little know-it-all like Thorne when I came here?"

"Yeah, you were a scared little boy, just like Thorne is. When we're scared and unsure of ourselves, we sometimes try to hide it with a cocky attitude. That's only natural. He'll lose his arrogance once he sees he's safe here, and we care about him. We'll be patient with him. It didn't take you long to lose your swagger. Maybe it'll be the same for him."

"I hope so, 'cause I'm gettin' tired of his cocky ways. Sometimes I think he's dumber 'n a bucket of rusty nails."

"Come on. You didn't know it all when you arrived on this ranch either. You were a city boy, remember?"

"Yeah, but I didn't try to tell you how to do your job."

"Give him time. He deserves a chance, just like the rest of us."

Although the first day of school seemed to have gone without incident, Tuesday was an entirely different story. Mrs. Dalton called Katie that evening and reported that Thorne had been extremely disruptive in the classroom and had started a fight on the playground, even breaking a classmate's nose. "As you know, Katie, a second incident like this will be cause for a three-day suspension."

"Oh, that is not good news, but I think I'll let Kirk handle this one. I don't want to lose my influence working with him in his reading sessions. I need to keep that noncombative. Kirk will be better suited for that battle."

The incident wasn't mentioned at the supper table. Katie had told Kirk about it, but they both agreed mealtime was not an appropriate place to address an issue like that. She watched as Thorne quickly finished his plate and asked for seconds. She looked at the scrawny boy and said, "Thorne, slow down. There's plenty of food for everyone. Take time to savor that good Angus meatloaf. I'll even make more next week if you like."

He didn't answer, but before the meal was finished, he had taken a warm buttered dinner roll and placed it on the chair between his legs. Later, she walked into his room to pull back the covers. The roll was inside the plastic bag under his pillow, along with the fresh slice of bread.

The fifteen minutes allowed for video games was up. Kirk grabbed the TV remote, punched the power button, and ran his hand through the straight sooty-black hair falling over Thorne's eyes. *I've got to get this kid a haircut soon.*

The boy looked up with sarcasm written all over his face. "Hey! I wasn't through with my game!"

"The clock says you are," Kirk said. "Come on, I need you to go with me to the stables. I've got something I wanna show you." Kirk removed his belt and tossed it over on the couch. He glanced at Thorne. The boy was backing away with his eyes as big as giant marbles. Kirk rubbed his own stomach and said, "I do believe I ate too much of Miss Katie's meatloaf and potatoes. My belt was way too tight."

As he was driving up to the stables, he looked over at Thorne. The kid sat motionless. *He must know I was told about his behavior at school.* Kirk brought the pickup to a halt and got out.

Thorne just sat there.

Kirk motioned for him to get out and come on. The pickup door opened slowly.

Inside the barn, Kirk flipped on a light, sat down on a bale of hay, and touched a rigid finger to the next bale. The boy slung his head in typical kid fashion to flip the mass of black hair out of his eyes. When he finally glanced up, both defiance and fear filled his face. He quickly turned and looked the other way.

Kirk put his hand on the boy's knee. "You know, Miss. Katie got a call from your teacher this afternoon."

Thorne maintained his silence, his eyes never meeting Kirk's.

"Katie and I are both disappointed. You wanna tell me what happened out there on the playground?"

Thorne shook his head no.

Kirk said nothing for a minute, but continued to stare down at the boy. "It will probably go easier on you if you open up and come clean about it."

"Okay, so I got in a fight. So what?"

"Thorne, lose the attitude. Tell me how that happened."

"This punk called me a loser—told everyone I was nuthin' but a mistake in my parents' bedroom."

"Oh man! That was mean. What did you say to him?"

"I didn't say nothin'. I just punched him in the snoot. It's what he deserved."

"Yeah, Thorne, he may have deserved it, but you were wrong to punch him. Save those punches to defend yourself physically. You know you broke his nose?"

"Yeah, and next time I'll break more than that!"

"Hey! That kind of talk solves nothing. You can't fight your way out of every bad situation."

Thorne looked the other way.

"Since you punched him first, the school sees it as you starting the fight. That happens again, and you're suspended."

"So what if I am? I hate school anyway."

"Well, it's our job to see you change your views on that. Miss Katie's gonna get you reading well, and she'll have you doin' those math problems as fast as any of your classmates."

"That ain't gonna happen." He was looking down between his knees. "My last teacher told my mom I was a nonreader."

"Well, Miss Katie's gonna change that, pal." Kirk placed a finger under Thorne's chin to tip it upward. "And it's my job to see that you learn to solve your social problems with a bit more dignity. You see that tack over there on the wall?"

Thorne stared at the wall. "What tack? I don't see no tack."

"No, not like a thumbtack." Kirk laughed. "Tack is what we call the equipment used for riding horses." He stood up and touched the bit. "See this bit? It goes in the horse's mouth. And see the reins that are attached to the bit? The rider pulls on those reins to steer the horse in the direction he wants it to go. It's my job to steer you in the right direction."

He gave that time to soak in a bit and then continued. "You'll see when I'm riding a horse, I rarely, if ever, yank hard on the reins. All it usually takes is a gentle pull to persuade the horse to turn. That's the way I want it to work with you and me. I don't believe in beatings—whether it's a horse or a child. But you have to work with me and allow me to show you the way to deal with your problems in life."

"So you're not gonna beat me?"

"No, I won't do that. I'm here to help you, not beat you. Now, promise you'll work with me, and we can be civil about it."

"I will."

"Good, now let's talk about your attitude in the classroom. You and the rest of your classmates are there to learn. Mrs. Dalton said you were very disruptive most of the day. You know what that tells me?"

Thorne picked at the loose hay. With blatant arrogance in his voice, he mocked, "What does it tell you?"

"It tells me you are a scared little boy. Know how I know that?"

Thorne shook his head no and brushed the loose hay off the bale.

"I know because when we have no fears, we are content, not disruptive and abusive."

The boy shook his head violently to the side again to flip his long sooty-black mane out of his vision and looked up.

Kirk grinned. "Man, we have got to get you a haircut soon."

"Mom cut it last time—that was before she left us."

"You miss your mom, don't you?"

Thorne looked down for a few seconds, then back up at Kirk. A tear had formed and was about to be expelled from his eye. "Yeah. I'm afraid I'll never see her again."

"Can you tell me about her?"

Another flip of the head, then he said, "She was good to me— called me her baby boy. My brothers both gave her fits, but I tried to help her. My dad would come home drunk and beat the crap out of her.

"One time, Dad threw her clear through the wall. The hole is still there in the living room. Mom always had bruises somewhere on her. I hate him!"

"Well, it sounds like he is where he needs to be now." Kirk picked up a straw and stuck it in his mouth. "Did he ever take his anger out on you or your brothers and beat you too?"

"Oh yeah! We were always glad when he left. He had a belt—just like the one you were wearing—and we knew when he started unbuckling it, we were about to get it."

"Well, that won't happen here. Let's just talk it through when you find yourself in trouble. That doesn't mean I don't believe in discipline, but I promise I don't discipline with a belt. I have other ways."

Thorne stood up, reached toward Kirk, started to put his arms around him, and then shook his hand instead. "Thank you. I promise I won't let you down." Then he quickly pulled his hand away from Kirk's. "I think I would've liked my dad if he'd been like you."

Kirk brushed the straight black mane from Thorne's eyes. "That's a nice compliment, pal. But you gotta promise me you'll stay out of trouble. And when you're in class, you pay attention to the teacher and mind your own business. Is that a deal?"

"Deal!"

6

Friday after school, Katie called Mrs. Dalton to see how the week had gone. "Did you have any more problems with Thorne?"

"Katie, he has been a perfect gentleman all week. He even went up to the kid he punched in the nose and apologized. I wasn't right there, but one of the other students told me about it. She said the other kid told him he was sorry he had said what he did to Thorne."

"Well, that's more like it. Remember I told you I was going to leave that battle up to Kirk? Well, he took Thorne to the stables. Kirk said they sat on bales of hay and had a good long talk. Thorne told him he was missing his mother and was afraid he'd never see her again."

"I applaud you and Kirk for what you are doing with these kids. It's deplorable what some of them go through at home. If I had more parents like you two, I might be able to teach my class something. Instead, I spend my time disciplining, breaking up fights among the boys, and listening to the petty tattletales of some of the girls."

"I've gotta run," Katie said. "But call me if you have any more problems. We want to know about it."

When she hung up the phone, she went to Thorne's room. His bed was made—not the neatest—but acceptable in the Childers house. She pulled back the top quilt, reached under his pillow, pulled out the plastic zip bag, and again replaced the previous day's bread with fresh slices. *I wonder if he has ever noticed.*

Kirk had met the boys after school and took both to the barber shop. Katie heard a knock at the front door. She froze. Kirk would still be in town with the boys. *Who…? How did they get through the gate? Kirk would have just come on in.* Katie left Thorne's room and went to the living room.

She walked into the great room and cautiously opened the door. It was Ronnie, Kirk's part-time helper. "Ronnie, you startled me. I didn't know anyone else had the gate combination."

"Sorry, Mrs. Childers. Kirk gave me the combination last week when I was helping him with the cattle."

"Ronnie, drop the Mrs. Childers thing. I heard that enough when I was teaching. I'm just plain Katie."

He grinned. "Okay, Katie, the reason I came up here was to ask if you and Kirk might want to sell the camp trailer that's been parked up by the barn. The way the grass is grown up around it makes it look like you guys haven't used it in a long time."

"You're right. We haven't. But I'm hoping we will find time to take the boys camping before winter sets in. I don't think either boy has ever been camping."

"Well, that's just wrong!"

"Yeah, I know. Kirk has been aiming to ask you if you might be able to do the milking some weekend so we could get away. Problem is I don't know where a good camping spot is. You got any ideas?"

"Sure. I'd go over to Eufaula. There's a really cool place over on the Arrowhead State Park side of the lake. I could give Kirk directions. My folks have been going there for years. Fishing's good, and there's this general store. It's got anything you'd want, from camp supplies to fishing tackle—there's even a café. They've got the best biscuits and gravy. Oh, and their blueberry pancakes are served with some of the best maple syrup there is. Owner's name is Dorothy. Tell her I sent you."

"Well, that sounds good. So does that mean you'd be willing to pinch-hit for us some weekend with the milking?"

"Hey, no problem. Just have Kirk get with me on the dates. I spend most weekends up at my sis's house in Guthrie, or my mom's in Chickasha. They're both probably getting tired of doin' my laundry and feeding me, so I'm thinkin' they'd be glad to get rid of me once in a while."

"Well, if you'll do that for us, I'll do your laundry for you when we come back." She grinned. "But you know the offer is a one-time arrangement. I'm not agreeing to do your laundry forever."

"Oh man! I thought I was about to make a sweet deal."

"I think I just heard Kirk drive up. Why don't you go tell him about this camp spot and talk about a time when we might be able to get away."

※

Brandon came bouncing in the door. "Hey, Mom, you gotta see this! Thorne's got a new look."

"Well, I see you got a haircut too. So where is he?"

"Noah's barking his fool head off at him—chasing him around the back of the house. I don't think he recognizes him with all that hair gone."

"Brandon, before he gets in here, I want to tell you about the conversation I had with Mrs. Dalton a while ago. She said Thorne has been a gentleman and given her no problems since Kirk had his little talk with him last week."

"Yeah, he even lost his cocky attitude. Dad asked him how he wanted his hair cut, and he told Dad to decide."

"What! You've gotta be kidding!"

"Yeah, like he's always been the one to give orders around here. What do you make of that?"

"As you know, your dad has a way of putting boys in their place. I think he's done that with you a time or two."

"What are you talkin' about? He's never had to do that with me. I never do anything wrong."

"Oh yeah? What about the time he had to talk to you about smarting back to me when I asked you to clean up your room? Or the time you tied the helium birthday balloon of yours to the kitten's tail?"

"Yeah, that cat was walking on just his two front legs. Even Dad thought it was funny."

"Well, anyway, my point was you should lighten up on Thorne as long as he's trying to do what's right. Quit calling him a know-it-all. If you call a child stupid, he'll think he is stupid. If you call him a know-it-all, he'll think he does know it all and will make sure everyone else gets that too."

Thorne ran in, slammed the door, and looked at Katie and Brandon. "I'll bet you two are talkin' 'bout my new haircut. So what do you think?"

Katie couldn't hold in her shock. "I like it. You've got that spike thing going on. That's pretty cool. I hardly recognize you."

"That was Kirk's idea—and I thought it was truly cool."

"*Truly*, huh? That's a new word for you. Where did you hear that?"

"It was Mrs. Dalton. She said I was truly a gentleman today."

Katie smiled. "Well, she may have been truly right. We talked earlier on the phone, and she did say you have been on your best behavior this week. I'm proud of you."

Just outside the window, they could see that Kirk and Ronnie were facing each other.

Katie picked up her glass and turned back to Thorne. "So what's Kirk doing out there?"

Thorne looked out the window. "Oh, he's talkin' to that long-haired hippie."

Katie almost choked on the water she was drinking. "That long-haired hippie is Ronnie. He is Kirk's part-time helper here on the ranch. Up until today, you held that title."

"What, part-time helper?"

"No, long-haired hippie."

"Yeah, but mine wasn't in a ponytail like his."

Katie grinned. "Okay, go to your room and pick out the book you want to work on. I'll be in there in a few minutes."

7

It was the Friday before Labor Day weekend. While the boys were still in school, Kirk backed the pickup to the camp trailer and hitched it up. He pulled it away from the weeds and grass that had grown up around the tires and towed it to the ranch house. He was giving it a good wash job, inside and out, when Katie came out with a sack full of grocery items from the house. "Kirk, let's take some firewood so we can have a campfire."

"Got it. It's already in the pickup bed. You got some marshmallows and graham crackers? Brandon's never had s'mores, and I'll bet Thorne hasn't either."

"It's all in the sack, along with wieners, buns, mustard, and pickle relish. You know, we should have done this a long time ago. We've had Brandon for almost three years, and we've never taken him camping. When I mentioned that to Ronnie, he said, 'Well, that's just wrong.'"

"Yeah, I agree. I just hated to ask him to cover for me, but he sounded like he was glad to get to stay out here on the ranch for a weekend. He loves this place as much as I do. He is really a big help with the cattle. Sometimes another set of muscles is needed when a young heifer is having trouble birthing. There're times I can't do it by myself, and I hate to call a vet. I've been thinking about talking to Uncle Carl to see what he thinks about allowing Ronnie to move into the white house up there by the barn. That way, he'd be right here when I need him. I think he'd jump at the chance to move out of the crowded apartment he's sharing with two other guys and ditch the monthly rent."

"That's a good idea." Katie grinned. "The long-haired hippie—as Thorne called him—would be a great asset to you. Sometimes I think you depend on Brandon too much for help around here. He's just a kid."

"Yeah, a kid who loves it. No, I think Brandon will want to remain my sidekick, and I'm hoping Thorne will too."

"Well, it's about time for the bus. Go on and pick up your two sidekicks. I'll finish the wash job on this tiny Swiss chalet."

"Okay, but I've gotta go in and get helmets."

"Helmets?"

"Remember, the truck is hooked up to your chalet you're going to finish washing. The ATV is the only option." His voice trailed off as he was walking away. "We really need another set of wheels."

Both boys were up early Saturday morning. Brandon was ready to go help with the milking.

"No, Ronnie's doin' that for us this morning so we can get an early start," Kirk said. "We've gotta stop and buy fishing license somewhere on the way."

Two hours later, Kirk was backing into a camp spot at the edge of Lake Eufaula. "You know, Ronnie was right. This is a great place to camp. Nice big trees, unlike most in Oklahoma. And we're within walking distance of the lake. Look at this place! Can't you just see a plume of campfire smoke slowly climbing upward and filtering through the foliage?" A gray squirrel shimmied up a tree trunk nearby. "You know, Kate, you should get out your oils and paint this scene."

"It's all good," Katie said, "except I saw the restrooms. They were a good ways back. I guess we'll get our walking in that way. After all of those hot dogs, chips, soda pop—oh, and those s'mores—we'll all need the exercise."

The boys were already grabbing the fishing tackle out of the pickup bed and heading down to the water. Kirk popped up the camper. The top sprang up to form an A-frame with a skylight in the slanted roof. There was a bed on one end, a bench with cushions that flipped out to a bed on the other end, with a tiny wannabe kitchen in between—no refrigerator, just a little two-foot-cube icebox built into the cabinets. A tiny wall furnace took up the space at the end of the cabinets.

Katie grabbed the makings for sandwiches and took four sodas from the tiny icebox. "You know, Kirk, this is cozy and pretty functional, but I'd hate to have to call it home for any length of time."

"Yeah, you wouldn't even have a place for that old typewriter of yours. And my boots would take up the whole space by the door." Kirk ducked his head to exit the make-believe cabin, but it wasn't enough. He touched his forehead and brought back fingers smeared with a trace of blood. "Man! I think this camper was made for midgets. My six-foot-two frame's got its disadvantages."

"Come on back in. I packed some Band-Aids and antibiotic ointment."

"Sure, just make it quick. I want to go back down to see what the boys have caught."

"Hey, I thought you guys would be ready for lunch."

"Naw, it's way too early. If I know Brandon, he's too engrossed in Act I of *A Fish Tale* to think about eating."

A trail leading through the blackjack trees and post oaks took Kirk down toward the water. The boys were talking to a man wearing a red flannel shirt and a Cardinals baseball cap. The man glanced up as Kirk approached.

"Dad, come on down. Thorne's already pulled in a fair-size bass."

Thorne held the smallmouth bass up, and Kirk took his cue. "Hey, that's probably at least a two-pounder." Thorne's face lit up like a July fourth night sky. Kirk held the bass up, trying to guess the weight. "You sure you ain't a professional fisherman running with all the tournaments?"

Thorne beamed. "Nope, this is only my second fish!"

"Well, I'd say you did really well. You guys catch a couple more like that, and we'll have us a big fish fry tonight."

The man who had been talking to the boys was walking away without saying a word. After he'd disappeared into the trees, Kirk asked the boys, "Who was the guy talking to you?"

"I don't know," Brandon said. "He just showed up all of a sudden and started talking. He's a real nice guy."

"Yeah," Thorne said, "he touched my hair and said he liked my spike."

"Dad, he asked us if we ever did any night fishing. What'd he mean by night fishing?"

Kirk bristled! He turned toward the trees where the guy had disappeared. "Hang on, guys, I'll be right back." He ducked under a blackjack tree. The lowest branch scraped the area of his forehead where Katie had placed the Band-Aid. He scouted out the entire path leading back to the camper, but the guy was nowhere in sight.

Katie was sitting in a folding lawn chair, reading a novel by her favorite author.

"Kate, I'm goin' back down and stay with the boys."

Katie looked puzzled. Then she saw the blood. "Kirk, your head is still bleeding!"

He had already turned to head back down the trail with his voice following him. "It's okay. I'll tell you about it later."

Back at the water's edge, Thorne was baiting his hook, and Brandon had just cast his line about ten yards out into the lake. "What's up, Dad?" Brandon said. "You shot outta here like a jackrabbit being shot at."

Kirk put his arm around Brandon. "I didn't like what that guy said to you. I don't trust him. You guys stick together—at all times! And I don't want you to ever come down here past dark."

"Why?" Brandon said.

"He thinks the guy was some kind of pervert," Thorne said. "Right, Kirk?"

"I'm not sure. I just know it was a bit weird for him to ask if you guys would be back down here at night. I don't like that."

Thorne was still looking at Kirk. "Well, we'll be roastin' marshmallows around the campfire tonight with you, so you got no worries—"

"Set that hook, Thorne!" Kirk yelled. "You got another one on your line." Then he jumped over the tackle box and grabbed the net. "Bring him in, pal. I'll net him."

Thorne looked down at Kirk squatting there with the net. "Yeah, I got another good one. I can tell he's a fat one!"

Thorne reeled his catch in, and Kirk netted it. "Yeah, pal! This one may be bigger than the first one. Way to go! You may have found yourself a honey hole."

Kirk picked up his own Shakespeare Ugly Stik that Katie had bought him last Christmas. He reached down in the minnow bucket and baited his hook, stood up, and slung it over his shoulder to cast. The hook stuck in a post oak sapling behind him. Brandon bent over laughing. Thorne started to laugh but was interrupted by another tug on his line. An hour later, the guys had reeled in a total of five smallmouth bass.

"Guys, reel 'em in and gather up your gear. It's time to head back to the camper. Mom's got sandwiches ready."

"Dad, it's your turn to clean the fish this time," Brandon said.

"No, I think Thorne needs a lesson in fish cleaning, so you and I will be the instructors."

The campfire took the chill off the evening air. Katie had forgotten the wiener-roasting forks, so Kirk hiked back down the darkened footpath to the lake, where he found a willow tree. He cut four small branches off to take back and whittle into green sticks to hold the wieners and marshmallows over the fire. Just as he turned to head back, something caught his eye—something just inside the tree line. Was it the back of a person bent over to duck under the trees? If it was an animal, it had to be a very large one. Bears? Not in this part of the state. Way too big for a raccoon. There was a rustling in the underbrush. Someone had to be hiding. And close by.

He pulled out the penlight from the holster on his belt. Nothing moved, and the light revealed nothing. Whatever it was, it was holding perfectly still. An encounter with man or animal in the dark underbrush was not something he wanted to tackle. He trekked back up the trail to the campsite.

Brandon and Thorne both fell in love with the s'mores, cleaning out the bag of marshmallows. After the fire died down to embers, Kirk told the boys to use what water was left in the six-gallon container and extinguish the fire. "After that, you guys run up to the restrooms and refill the water. There's a faucet on the outside of the building."

"Dad!" Brandon objected. "I don't think we can carry that with six gallons of water. That'd be pretty heavy."

"Okay, you're right. I'll go with you. Next time we come here, let's make sure we get a spot right across from the restrooms. It's a good three hundred yards up there."

The moon was hidden behind a thick layer of clouds, and there were no lights along the way. "This is creepy," Thorne said. "I didn't even see lights from those campers back there. Everyone must have gone to bed already."

The water container was filled. Kirk set it down outside the building and walked in the restroom. The guy with the red flannel shirt stood in front of the sink, looking in the mirror at himself. The man looked a bit startled as his eyes met Kirk's.

"Hey," was all he said. He pulled the bill of his cap down over his face and quickly walked toward the door, brushing against Brandon on the way out.

Back at the A-frame camper, Kirk set the water container just outside the door. Katie had pulled off the bolsters from the bench, slid it out into what was a poor excuse for a bed, and was spreading out sheets and a blanket for the boys. Kirk reached down and grabbed a couple of pillows from the storage underneath. "Babe, I'm sorry. I should have asked if you needed to go up with us to the restrooms."

"No, I walked up earlier. I knew I wouldn't want to traipse up that dark road tonight. You know, this is pretty inconvenient being this far from any facilities and having to carry water from there. Plus, we're out here all by ourselves. Privacy is one thing, but I think I'd prefer to be a little closer to some other campers, especially on a dark night like this."

"I agree. Maybe we should pick a spot next time that's not quite so isolated. When I pulled in here, I thought the solitude would be nice."

Ten minutes after everyone was in bed, Katie bolted upright, bumping her head on the low slant of the camper roof, and whispered to Kirk, "What was that?"

"Well, I think it was your head hitting the roof."

"No. What was the scratching noise before that?"

"Scratching?" Kirk laughed. "Were you scratching those chigger bites you got out there by the campfire?"

"There it goes again. Don't you hear that?"

"It's okay, babe. I think we have a guest, probably a raccoon."

Just then there was a frantic clawing on the metal roof, then a second of silence. Kirk sat up in bed and hit his head on the slanted roof. "It must have gotten to the skylight and found a better foothold."

Seconds later, there was more clawing near the peak of the slick roof. Then they heard the thing slide all the way back down, followed by a thump on the ground below. "Hey, that coon found his ski slope right here on top of our little Alpine chalet." He looked toward the other end of the camper. "Looks like both boys slept right through it all."

"Yes," Katie said, if they can sleep through that ruckus, they can sleep through anything.

As soon as the sun came up, Kirk woke the boys. "Hey, guys, get up and get dressed. I need you to go out and gather some twigs and dry leaves for some kindling so I can get a good fire going. Katie tells me we're out of propane, so we cook on a campfire. We're gonna fry some bacon and eggs and get some coffee brewing."

Katie was searching through the food box. "Kirk, I thought you packed the coffee before we left."

"No, I thought you did."

"Oh great—and it looks like we left the cast-iron skillet out on the campfire last night. That thing's gotta be scrubbed before I cook anything in it."

Kirk hollered at the boys. "Hey, guys! Forget it. We're going up to the café for breakfast."

They all dressed, piled in the pickup, and as they pulled up to the café, the Closed sign unwelcomed them. Attached to the sign was a Post-it note: *Closed for funeral.*

"This camping trip is a bust," Katie said. "I'd rather be back at home, where I feel secure and have the things I need."

"Maybe they'll open up later. We can try them again for lunch. Right now, I'm goin' back to grab some cookies and milk."

Thorne reached up and tapped Kirk's shoulder. "Uh, I don't think so. Me and Brandon drunk it all last night."

Katie's eyes rolled. "You mean Brandon and I *drank* it all last night."

"No, you were drinking soda pop. It was me and Brandon."

The café remained closed throughout the day. Last evening, Katie had found the icebox in the camper had leaked all over the floor, so she had transferred what was left of the wieners, more deli meat, bread, four hamburger patties, and the melting ice to a cooler chest, setting it just outside the door next to the step.

Kirk saw it as soon as he pulled up to the campsite. The cooler chest was turned on its side with the lid open—empty. He laughed. "That raccoon probably thought he'd found himself a four-star restaurant. Hope he enjoyed our grub."

Katie flashed an anguished look his way. "Let's get out of here and go back home, where we have a fridge full of food and comfortable beds—and water!"

He convinced her they might as well stay the night since the spot was already paid for. "Look, we'll drive into town and buy some more food—oh, and coffee!"

The streets in the town were fairly empty. They searched for a grocery store or convenience store, with no luck. But there *was* a Kentucky Fried Chicken and a Taco Bell sharing one building. "What kind of town has fast-food restaurants and no grocery store or even a convenience store? This is crazy," Katie said.

Supper that evening turned out to be a bucket of KFC around the campfire, along with a bag of Cheetos the boys had stashed away.

The fire was nothing but wet ashes. Kirk was helping Katie pull out the bed for the boys. Brandon was lying on their bed alone. "Where's Thorne?" she asked.

"He's out there in the truck playing with his Game Boy. I think he's still pouting because I wouldn't let him go back down and fish by himself earlier. Brandon had started the book he's reading now and didn't want to pull himself away."

Fifteen minutes passed, and Thorne hadn't come inside. "You should go out and get Thorne. It's almost ten o'clock."

Kirk ducked as he walked out the camper door. He stumbled over the empty cooler chest on his way toward the truck. The squeaky pickup door broke the evening silence. Slamming it shut, he hollered, "Thorne!"

The only sound was a cricket somewhere in the distance. Then he hollered again, "Thorne!"

The camper door opened, and Katie stood there in her pajamas. Kirk searched the darkened area all around the truck. Then he pulled out his flashlight and beamed the light into the trees and on the gravel road behind the truck.

Katie was saying something. He looked back at her. "What'd you say?"

"I said we should have left this morning when I wanted to."

Kirk pointed the beam of the flashlight up the trail toward the other campers. The silence was broken by the rustle of dry autumn leaves as a squirrel jumped from one tree to the next. He turned back to her and threw up both arms in a where-could-he-have-gone motion.

"Kirk, do you think he would have gone up to the restroom?"

He was reaching for the truck keys in his pocket. "I told those two to never go anywhere alone!" He opened the creaky door and jumped in.

Katie hollered, "Is his Game Boy there in the truck?"

He never heard her because he had already started the engine and was backing out. Then he put the truck in first gear. The truck tires sprayed gravel as he raced up the road.

Kirk rolled his side window down, watching and listening as he barreled toward the restrooms. The area around the restrooms was unlit, and the moonless night left the area in total darkness after he cut the lights off. He was pulling the keys out of the ignition when he heard it.

"No! Leave me alone!"

Kirk bolted toward the men's side of the building, jerked open the squeaky metal door to the restroom, and saw the man, still wearing the red flannel shirt, with Thorne in his grasp. "Turn him loose, you sorry—!"

The guy loosened his grip, and Thorne ran toward the door. Kirk stepped to within inches of the man, his shoulders all but touching the short man's face. He grabbed that flannel shirt in both of his hands and said, "You touch the boy again, and I'll stuff this smelly shirt down your throat."

In an attempt to exonerate himself, the guy said, "It's okay. I was just trying to help the boy."

"Oh really? Well, I'm gonna *help* you outta here—and I better not ever catch you hanging around here again." Kirk let the front of the man's red flannel shirt go, moved behind the guy, and grabbed both sides of the man's belt to give him a shove toward the door. It was then he felt the encased knife attached to his belt.

The guy was reaching for it just as Kirk snatched it from the holster. "You try anything like that, and I'll have you mopping up this filthy floor with your tongue." Then he hollered at Thorne, "Get in the truck and lock the doors."

The pudgy guy probably knew he was no match for Kirk. "Hey, no problem here. Just give me my knife back."

"I don't think so." Kirk rammed his boot into the guy's backside, slamming him hard into the metal door. "Now get outta here, you freakin' pervert!"

The man ran out and disappeared into the darkness. Kirk pulled out the truck key remote, unlocked the door, and jumped in, his heart drumming out a fast and steady rhythm. He started the engine, relocked the doors, and just sat there staring at Thorne.

Thorne broke the silence. "He was trying to get me to—"

"I know, buddy. You gotta understand there are weirdoes out there. That's why I told you and Brandon not to go anywhere alone."

"But I had to pee."

"You should have come and got me. And I probably should have never allowed you to remain in the truck alone."

Kirk put the truck in gear and started forward. In the dim illumination of the dash lights, he could see Thorne's face. "Kirk, I was really scared. I don't know what I would've done if you hadn't come when you did."

"You could have punched him below the belt where it hurts the most. Then when he doubled over, just ran like a scared rabbit."

When they got back to the camper, Katie met them at the door, her eyes full of questions.

"It was that red flannel shirt guy—I knew I couldn't trust him. I had a bad feeling about him the first time I saw him down where the boys were fishing. Looks like I got there just in time."

Katie sat down on the bed beside Thorne. "Kirk, let's get out of here. I have never felt safe here."

"Babe, it's late. Can't we wait 'til morning? In fact, I think I need to report this pervert—at least to the camp manager."

"What camp manager? I haven't seen anyone in charge here. We're out here all alone."

"Okay, then a ranger. We can go in town tomorrow morning and ask how to contact one."

"No, I want to go now! We're not spending another night here. I'll help you tear down this camper and hook up. Come on. The boys can sleep on the way home."

8

Kirk pulled up to the electronic ranch gate and rolled down his window to tap in the code. From the backseat, a bone-chilling scream erupted. "No! Leave me alone!"

Kirk put the truck in park, turned around, and saw Thorne sitting upright with both hands pushing against the back of the seat. "Thorne!"

There was only a whimper.

"Thorne, wake up, pal. You're having a dream."

"Oh," and then he groaned slightly.

Katie reached around and patted him on the knee. "Thorne, it's okay. We're almost home. It was just a dream."

But it was more than a fleeting dream. Monday, Labor Day, Thorne seemed lethargic, sat around most of the day, and wouldn't eat. Noah tried to get him to play, but he pushed the dog away.

Wednesday evening, Katie got a call from Mrs. Dalton. "Katie, I'm trying to figure out what is going on with Thorne. He seemed lethargic all day. I asked him what was wrong, and all he would say was that he'd had a bad dream."

"Yes, he did—"

Mrs. Dalton cut in. "Yesterday, he seemed sluggish, but today, he was the slugger. Apparently, he started another fight. This time it was in the restroom and witnessed by two other boys."

"What! Oh no!"

"Remember, I said the last time this happened, the next time would mean an in-school suspension. I'm afraid it has come to that."

"I thought we had him on the right track. I can't imagine what has gotten into him, unless… So when will he be allowed to return to his regular classroom?"

"Not 'til next Tuesday. But we won't let him get behind during his suspension. In-school suspension, as you know, means he will simply be separated from his regular classroom. We are such a small school and can't afford to hire a full-time teacher for these kids, so we often use substitute teachers or even volunteers. He won't be allowed to talk and will have a strict schedule of work lined out for him. For lunch, he will be separated from the other kids."

"Should I send a lunch with him?"

"You can if you like, but the cafeteria food will still be available to him."

Katie's disappointment was evident in her closing words to Mrs. Dalton. "Kirk will have another talk with him. I thought his last heart-to-heart with him did some good, but I guess it didn't last. We took him camping at Lake Eufaula over the Labor Day weekend, and he was attacked by some pervert in the men's room. Now I'm wondering if that may be a factor in this recent behavior."

"Katie, I don't know, but you might want to get him in to see a counselor. How bad was the attack?"

"Kirk said he got there in the nick of time and walked in just as the guy was holding Thorne. I know it really scared the boy. He has even had a couple of nightmares since then."

"As you know, a foster child has access to a psychologist at no cost to the foster parent. I believe I'd make an appointment."

"I will, but first we'll try to deal with this last school incident."

Katie met Kirk at the door and filled him in on the conversation with Mrs. Dalton. "It looks like it's already time for another guy talk between you two."

"Not another fight at school! I thought we had that settled."

"Honey, don't be too rough on him. I have a feeling this may have something to do with how he was traumatized up at the lake."

"We'll talk. I think I understand. Just let me handle it."

Thorne remained silent at the supper table. It was as if he knew he'd been exposed. After he'd finished less than half his plate, he announced that he wasn't hungry, jumped up from the table, and headed toward his room. Kirk caught up with him, tapped him on the shoulder, and said, "Come back here. We don't just jump up unexcused while everyone else is still eating."

"But I'm not hungry."

"Well, we are, and we'd like your company while we enjoy our meal."

"That's just stupid! Why should I have to sit there and stare at you guys stuffing your stupid faces?"

"Hey! That will do, young man! There's no need for you to be rude. Now sit down!"

After they had finished their meal, Kirk stood up and glared at Thorne. No words were necessary. All it took was Kirk's finger pointing to the door, and Thorne must have known he was headed to the horse stable for another lecture. Once there, he ran ahead of Kirk and quickly took his place on the hay bale. Then he looked up at Kirk and patted the adjoining bale.

Kirk grinned. "Looks like you're getting the hang of this."

Thorne planted both elbows on his knees, ducked his head, and ran his fingers through his gelled and spiked hair. "Let's get it over with. I know I got it comin'."

"You wanna start by telling me what happened at school today?"

"No, sir."

"Well, guess what. You're gonna tell me anyway, whether you want to or not."

"Okay, so I got in a fight."

"Yeah, I knew that much. How about furnishing me with a little more information than that—like how, when, where, and why?"

"There's no point in telling you all that. You're just gonna tell me I was in the wrong."

"So you know you were in the wrong. Then why did you do it?"

Thorne stared down between his knees at his feet and said, "Look, it's no use trying to make me something I'm not. I've got bad blood in me. My daddy is bad, and my brothers are bad. Everyone tells me I've got bad blood, and that's just the way it is. And my mom…"

"Your mom, what?"

"My mom…she ran off, walked away, and left us all alone. I'll never see her again!"

"Hey, pal, let's not criticize her without knowing all the facts. Maybe she had no other choice. Sometimes life leaves us with no good choices—or none we can clearly see."

"Well, I'm not buyin' that. She left because she didn't wanna mess with us anymore. I hate her!"

"I don't believe that. You may be disappointed in her, but you don't hate her. She gave birth to you. She cared for you when she could. And you can't be so sure you'll never see her again. This world is a lot smaller than you think. Please don't burn any bridges between the two of you."

"Well, look at my dad! He's always goin' to jail for something. And now he's even killed a man! That's some bad blood. I can't get rid of that. I am who I am."

"No, you're wrong! You don't have to fall into the footsteps of your father or anyone else. You are Thorne Barrow, and you are special in God's eyes. He made you just the way He wanted. I'm telling you, He did not make a mistake. Now, you can go your own way and believe that you have bad blood, and there is nothing you can do about that, or you can become the man God meant you to be. It's your choice."

"Look at my brothers—they're all bad eggs. One's already in jail and another was too bad to even put in a foster home with me."

"But they had a choice. They chose to be bad. Don't ever believe you have to be like them. See, you get to decide who you wanna be."

"Then why do I get in fights?"

"I think it's a matter of not controlling your temper. We all struggle with that from time to time, but some of us have learned how to resist the urge to blast out at others—and you'll learn that too."

Thorne finally disclosed the how, when, where, and why of the altercation, and Kirk walked him through an alternative reaction he could have used. Thorne's head was still buried between his knees. Then he looked up at Kirk and said, "Why does Brandon never get in trouble, but I do? Who was his dad?"

Kirk couldn't help it; he grinned and said, "I am."

"No, you adopted him. So what was his old man like?"

"Good question, although I don't like the term *old man*—that's disrespectful. I don't care how bad a father is, a son should never refer to him as *old man*. But I'm glad you asked that question. Brandon's birth father committed suicide when Brandon was very young. After that, Brandon lived with his mother and her boyfriend for the next couple of years, and the guy was a thief, a drunk, a bully, an adulterer, and he is now serving a life sentence with no possibility of parole for killing a woman. And as for his birth mother, I guess you could say she's now a respectable citizen—maybe. But she chose a lifestyle of wealth over her son. Now you tell me, does that all sound like tainted blood to you?"

"Tainted?"

"Yeah, bad blood."

"Sounds pretty bad to me."

"Yep, you're right, but Brandon decided he wanted no part of that lifestyle. He chose to take a different path—and you can too!"

"Well, I'm not sure. Somethin' comes over me, and I just can't help myself."

"Yes, you can. Count to ten before you lash out."

"That don't work. I tried it."

"So our little talks up here, they don't help either?"

"Nope, I still wanna beat the—"

"Stop! You don't need to express yourself with cheap words. And if our talks don't seem to help, let's see if this does."

Thorne looked up.

"There will be no more Game Boy for the next two weeks. What's more, you will help me repair some fences after school tomorrow."

Thorne grinned. "I would've helped you do that anyway."

"Good, I'm glad to have a helper."

The negotiator came out in Thorne. "I'll make a deal with you. Cut the Game Boy ban down to one week, and I'll help you for two days."

"No deal! It stays—two weeks!" Kirk put his arm around Thorne as they walked back to the pickup. "You know, buddy, you could probably make a good car salesman when you grow up."

"Why's that?"

"You're a deal maker—you know, you drive a bargain."

"So does that mean we got a deal?"

"Nope, I ain't buyin' today."

9

"Kirk, I've made an appointment for Thorne with a psychologist at the Brimm Institute."

"Same one we had before?"

"Well, I did talk to her, but she referred me to a male psychologist. In the case of sexual abuse, they always place a child with a counselor of the same sex."

"Okay, I can see that, but the lady was good at her job. The innovative way she had so gently broken the news to Jason about his mother's murder was awesome—and with a picture book, of all things."

Kirk picked up Thorne early from school. "We feel you may need to visit with a professional counselor about that awful night at the campground when you were attacked. If you'd rather, I could wait outside the room while you two visit."

"Why would I want to tell that again? He scared me, and I don't wanna ever talk about it again."

"Okay, but this will probably be the last time you'll have to. Just tell the counselor what the man did to you and how it made you feel."

"I want you to stay with me."

"No problem. I can do that."

A ten-pound largemouth bass jumped at an antique spinner bait in the center of a large diorama behind the psychologist's desk. The background was aquamarine paper that looked amazingly like splashing water droplets. Dried seaweed formed the bottom with cattails on either side. The three-dimensional art piece was framed in weathered barnwood. A tangle of fishing line draped down one side. Thorne's eyes were glued to the piece.

The psychologist immediately formed a friendship, first talking about the diorama. The psychologist asked Thorne about school and then the ranch where he was living. Then Thorne told him about the fish he'd caught there on the ranch pond and also at Lake Eufaula. With a little background information earlier from Katie's phone conversation, he was able to move on to the camping trip and the attack in the men's room. "So, were you really scared when the man grabbed you?"

Thorne ducked his head. "Yeah, he was a lot bigger than me, and I thought I had no one to help me get away from him."

"So then Kirk came and rescued you, right?"

"Yeah, he beat the—"

The counselor cut in. "Oh, so he slugged the guy?"

"The guy tried to pull a knife on Da…Kirk, and Kirk got it away from him and wouldn't let him have it back."

"It sounds like the guy didn't deserve to get it back. You really do like Kirk, don't you?"

"Yeah, Kirk is the best…person I know."

The psychologist was quiet for a few seconds. "You know, Thorne, Kirk probably wouldn't mind if you want to call him *Dad*—right, Dad?"

Kirk leaned over and touched Thorne's shoulder. "I would be honored for you to call me Dad, but only if you want to. I'll try to live up to that name for you…*son*."

After some pretty tough questioning, the psychologist asked Thorne to go out and see the receptionist. "She's got a book to give you. I think you'll enjoy it. And be sure to ask her for one of her special oatmeal cookies she keeps in her desk. She makes them herself. I sneak one for myself every chance I get."

After the door was closed, he turned to Kirk. "I don't believe any real harm was done to the boy. It seems to me you got there just in time. I believe him when he says there was no physical sexual contact, other than the one nasty demand—and that's when you walked in. If he has any more nightmares, just reassure him he is safe now, and he'll never see the guy again."

Kirk reached for the psychologist's hand, thanked him, and walked out to the front desk, where Thorne was stuffing a cookie in his mouth.

"See," Kirk said, "that wasn't so bad, huh?"

"Yeah, and I really liked that 3-D picture behind his desk. But the blue in the water wasn't quite right."

Before heading back to the ranch, Kirk stopped at Maggie Moo's for Oreo Cookie Cupcakes—ice cream and chocolate cake, topped by an Oreo cookie and fudge.

"Cool! I've never been to Maggie Moo's."

"Yeah, these ice cream cupcakes are my favorite, and I think it might become yours too."

On the way back home there was very little talk, but each time Kirk put his elbow up next to the side window, Thorne did the same. While stopped at a red light, Kirk moved his leg over and rested it on the center hump. Thorne did too.

As soon as they walked in the door, Katie looked at Thorne, put her hands on her hips, and pursed her lips. "You guys went to Maggie Moo's, didn't you?"

Thorne gawked at her. "How'd you know?"

"That news story is written all around your mouth. You've got chocolate smears that spell out Oreo cupcake. Didn't they have any napkins there?"

Kirk grinned. "I would have brought back two more for you and Brandon, but I knew they would look like a couple of mud puddles by the time we got back."

"Oh, don't worry. We know how to get back atcha."

10

Katie picked up the boys at the ranch gate. As soon as they got home, Brandon took her aside and gave her the news. "Thorne showed up on the bus with a twenty dollar bill, and he was flashin' it around for everyone to see."

"Where did he get twenty bucks?"

Brandon's shoulders lifted, and he exhaled noisily. "Who knows—probably stole it!"

"Okay, thanks for letting me know." She started to hang the truck keys back on the hook by the door. Then she changed her mind. "Come on, I'll run you up to the milk barn. I need to talk to Kirk about this."

"I can tell you right now, Thorne will be mad at me for tattling, but I thought you ought to know."

"Thanks. I do need to know. Go ahead and finish up the milking. I'll wash up the equipment for you, and you can run on back to the house and do your homework while I talk to your dad."

It didn't take Brandon long to milk his one old Jersey cow, and then he darted out the door toward the ranch house. Katie turned off the cream separator just as Kirk walked in and saw her. "Where'd Brandon go off to?"

"I told him I'd finish up for him. I needed to talk to you."

Kirk leaned back against the countertop and crossed his arms. "This can't be good."

"Well, you're right, we've got a problem. Maybe I should have just gone ahead and handled it myself, but I thought I'd talk to you, get your input. I don't want Thorne to get angry with Brandon for telling me."

"Telling you what?"

"He said Thorne was flashing around a twenty dollar bill on the bus. I assume you didn't give it to him, and I sure didn't. So it looks as if he may have stolen it."

"Probably right." Kirk turned around, picked up the dish towel, and started drying off the equipment as Katie handed it to him from the wash water. "So what are you saying we should do about it?"

"Well, we obviously have to have a talk with—"

Kirk laid the dish towel down on the counter. "I know what my dad would've done to me, and it sure wouldn't have been sitting down with me on a bale of hay in the stable and talkin'."

Katie laughed. "No, we talk, maybe take away some privileges, and make him return the money to the rightful owner." She handed him the last piece of equipment to dry off. "That's not the problem. The problem is how do we do this without him knowing Brandon snitched on him?"

Kirk stood there for a second and set the piece of equipment back on the counter. "You wanted me to grill some burgers this evening, right?"

"Well, yes, but if you're too tired—"

"No, that's perfect."

"Kirk, your eyes are trying to tell me a story. I can tell. But I just can't read you."

Kirk winked. "I've got an idea. Just don't say anything to him and follow my lead. I think I can get him to expose his thievery, and Brandon doesn't have to enter into the picture."

"Good luck with that."

Kirk kicked off his boots on the flagstone floor by the back door. Katie went to the kitchen and started supper. After Kirk had washed up, he walked by Brandon's open door. There he was on the bed with a book. Thorne's room was empty. He walked into the big room and looked around. "Where is the little rascal?"

"I thought he was in his room."

"Nope—just checked."

"Is he outside playing with Noah?"

"Nope. Noah's lying on the back doorsteps, asleep."

Katie pulled some beef patties from the fridge and said, "Maybe he guessed Brandon had ratted on him, and he decided to hide out. He probably knows he's headed to the stables with you again for another guy talk."

Nope, not this time. I'm gonna start out doing it a different way this time."

"Kirk! We can't spank him. DFS rules won't allow that."

"Babe, I know that. Even if DFS was okay with it, I'd probably never spank the kid. It's worked so far without resorting to spanking." He grinned. "I don't think those spankings I got as a kid ever did me any good—just made me avoid my dad."

"So what are you planning?"

"Just watch."

"Well, first you gotta find him."

"Nope. He'll show up eventually."

"This is not sounding good. I don't like not knowing where he's hiding out."

"Don't worry. I know how he's been stuffin' his face after school. He'll show up soon, especially if he smells those burgers on the grill. That'll bring him in for sure."

An hour later, Kirk carried in four burnt offerings on a platter and set them down on the kitchen table.

Katie's back was to him. The air reeked with the smell of the scorched meat. "You burned them?"

"Yep. I kept thinking the aroma would bring in the little thief, so I got started playing Frisbee with Noah and forgot about the burgers."

Katie took the platter of crispy blackened beef patties and set them on the cabinet next to the sink. "Okay, so now all we've got is leftover potato salad and some naked buns."

Kirk grinned. "Naked buns?" He reached down and hugged her. "I married a comedienne!"

Brandon took over half the cold potato salad and fished out three dill pickles.

The back door slammed, and Thorne burst in. "What's for supper? Somethin' smells good!"

"If you like burned hamburgers, be my guest. They're on the counter over there, ready to go in the garbage disposal."

Thorne walked over, took one look, and pinched his nose shut. "What else we got? I'm starvin'."

"Well, I thought I might make some banana pudding."

Ah! This was Kirk's chance. He went back to the master bedroom, took out his wallet, and laid it on the dresser. Then he came back into the kitchen and said, "Thorne, how about you and I run up to Mama Cassie's Café up on the highway and have her cook us up some of her famous dollar-ninety-nine burgers."

"You guys had better bring back a couple for me and Brandon."

"Will do."

"Hurry, Thorne. Run and jump in the truck," Kirk said. "I'm starved too. I'll be right behind you."

With Thorne out the door, Katie gave Kirk a what's-going-on look.

"Follow my lead, babe."

Brandon said, "Dad, I'll go with you."

Kirk turned to Brandon and grinned. "Naw, you're full of potato salad. Thorne and I will go." He flashed a slight wink at Katie.

As soon as they pulled up to Mama Cassie's and got out of the pickup, the smoky aroma of the greasy spoon's grill infiltrated the evening air. Thorne sniffed. "Now that's some burgers done right!"

They went in and seated themselves at the nearest red plastic-covered booth. A cute high school senior took their order and hurried back to the kitchen. Kirk tapped his fingers deliberately on the red Formica tabletop in a nervous pattern. "Man, I'm starved! I'm sure glad Mama Cassie was open."

Thorne echoed, "Yeah, me too. I can't believe you burned our burgers. I skipped lunch today, so I'm super hungry!"

After a fairly lengthy wait, the cute girl brought their burgers. Kirk pushed the plastic platters away. "Oh, I forgot to tell you, we need 'em to go."

"Well, I should have known you two weren't gonna eat all four of these. I'll get them boxed up for you and be right back out."

A couple of minutes later, she brought the burgers out in a sack along with the bill for the food. Kirk stood, reached into his rear jeans pocket, looked at Thorne, and feigned surprise. "Oh man! I forgot my wallet."

"You had a bunch of coins in the truck last week—mostly quarters."

"Yeah, but I used them in the carwash. I guess we'll have to just forget the burgers and go back home and eat those naked buns."

Thorne laughed. "Naked buns?"

"Yeah, that's what Miss Katie called 'em. You know—no meat or anything."

Kirk took the sack to the payout counter, where Mama Cassie was closing the register for the evening. "Sorry, Miss Cassie. I forgot my wallet. Guess we'll have to just leave these here."

As Thorne was eyeing the gum ball machine, Mama Cassie said, "Kirk, you can pay me later—"

Kirk winked and shook his head at her. Then with a louder-than-normal voice, he said, "No, if I can't pay for them, we aren't gonna take 'em."

That got Thorne's attention. "What! We're leavin' the burgers here?"

"Look, I told you I don't have any money with me, so we can't just walk out without paying for our food."

Thorne reached in his jeans pocket. "I could loan you some money." He pulled out the twenty and handed it to Kirk.

"Thanks, buddy, you saved my neck."

Nothing more was said during the trip back to the ranch house. Thorne grabbed the burgers and bounced in, eager to dig into one. Kirk was right behind him. Thorne set the sack down on the table and started to open it up.

Kirk placed his hand on top of the sack and glared at Thorne. Without breaking his long-drawn-out stare into Thorne's eyes, his deep baritone boomed. "Where'd you get that twenty?"

Kirk sat down and patted the bale of hay beside him. "You know the routine. This bale of hay has your name on it."

Thorne plopped down with a muffled thud on the hay bale, hung his head downward between his outspread knees, and was quiet.

Kirk gently slapped Thorne on the knee. "Start talkin'."

With his head still dipped downward, Thorne mumbled a garbled couple of words.

"Hey, pal, you'd better speak up, or we're gonna be here all night."

He still didn't lift his head. "What's there to say?"

"You can start out by telling me where you got that twenty. I think I asked you that back at the house."

"I stole it."

"Okay, that's a start. Who'd you steal it from?"

"My teacher."

Kirk finally managed to pull out a few more facts. Thorne had seen his teacher place her purse in her desk drawer, so when she went to lunch, he snuck back in and took the twenty while no one else was in the room.

"Weren't you supposed to be in the cafeteria too?"

A belligerent streak came over the little thief. "All right, I already told you I didn't eat lunch—remember, up at the café, I told you I was starvin'—and you was gonna walk out of there and leave them burgers 'cause you conveniently didn't have any money!"

"Thorne, lose the attitude. I think you may be forgetting I'm the adult here."

Thorne started to raise his head. Then he quickly ducked it and whispered a perfunctory, "Sorry."

"Okay, that's better. Now you tell me, what should we do about this?"

The demon came out again. "You're the stinkin' adult! You—"

"Stop it! I already told you to lose the attitude. You don't wanna see the *stinkin'* attitude that's about to come out of me! I'm not gonna put up with that kind of talk from you. We can be civil about this, or you'll be sorry." Kirk touched the underside of Thorne's chin and tipped his head up. "Look at me! I'll ask you again, what should we do about this?"

Their eyes met for the first time. "I guess you could beat me like my old man used to do."

Kirk shook his head. "I think you know me better than that." He put his hand on Thorne's shoulder. "First, you will return the money to your teacher and tell her you were wrong to take it. Ask her to forgive you."

Thorne quickly glanced up at Kirk, ducked his head again, hesitated, and then muffled out an, "Okay."

"Then you will ask her if there is anything you can help her with, like cleaning the chalkboards, straightening the desks—you might even ask her if you can do an extra assignment in math."

Thorne turned his head toward the door and groaned.

Kirk reached down and tipped the boy's head back up again. "When someone is speaking to you, it is rude to look away. You would do well to remember that. It'll come in handy as an adult."

Thorne started to get up. "We through?"

"No. Sit back down! I'll let you know when we're through."

Thorne groaned again.

"Look, pal, I take this theft very seriously. You're not gonna get off the hook with a simple apology to the teacher and returning her money. I'll be watching you like a hawk over the next month, and I'd better see a change in you."

Thorne stood up, turned his back to Kirk, and blurted out, "Don't you get it? I can't change! I am who I am. You forget, my old man's in prison for murder, my brother's in jail for settin' fire to a church, my mom's a no-good—"

"Stop it!" Kirk hooked his finger in the belt loop of Thorne's jeans and urged him back down to the bale of hay. "Listen to me. You are not bound by the genes passed down to you. You can be the person you want to be. If you find that difficult, then you need to have a talk with Jesus about it. He'll guide you on to a happier path."

"What makes you so sure about that?"

"Because that's what I did, and it worked for me."

"Yeah, but you probably didn't have parents like mine."

Kirk put his hand to his chin. *Should I tell him?* With deliberate turtle speed, he eased forward and stood, put both hands in his pockets, and ducked his head toward the boy. "Thorne, my dad was an alcoholic—and violent." He looked up and took in a deep breath. "The man beat me and my brother with his belt about every day. We could never do anything right in his eyes.

"But what really turned me against him was the day he threw my mom down the stairs. I was in the kitchen, heard them arguing, and just as I glanced up toward them at the top of the stairs, the man picked up my mom and threw her down the stairs. I wanted to kill him, but instead, I ran to Mom and helped her to the couch. She was hurt really bad. By then the bully had vanished. The fall probably was what eventually killed her. She never was the same after that. He never spent a day behind bars for it.

"I hated him, so I ran away—was caught shoplifting a bag of peanuts from a convenience store. They tried to return me to my dad, but he couldn't be found—probably was on another of his three-day binges. So I was placed in foster care. I was seventeen, embarrassed that I needed a foster parent. I was a belligerent teen who knew nothing about love and nurturing—hadn't seen any of that with my family."

"Wow! That sounds like me. So how'd you get to be like you are now?"

Kirk sat back down on the hay bale, leaned back against the wall, stretched his six-two frame out, and propped his left boot up on a sack of oats in front of him. "I'm glad you asked. You see, the one year I spent in the foster home was the best thing that could have ever happened to me. My foster mom was a beautiful lady—and I don't mean physical beauty." He laughed. "She was a short chubby woman, no more than four eleven and probably weighed well over two hundred pounds, but she had a heart of gold. There was never a doubt, she loved kids—even surly teenagers—and I knew she loved me. She and my foster dad would make me go to church with them on Sundays—I hated it at first."

Thorne sat still, and he kept his eyes fixed on Kirk.

"My foster dad was the one who convinced me to make a decision to accept Jesus into my life. He said Jesus would turn my life around—put some joy in place of the anger I often displayed for the whole world to see. I wasn't sure how that was supposed to happen. He explained to me all I had to do was tell Jesus I was sorry for all the bad things I'd done and ask Him to forgive me. Then—here comes the important part—he told me I had to try to do my very best to always do the right thing."

Thorne was silent.

Kirk placed his hand on Thorne's knee. *Here's my chance.* Now that Thorne was listening, stopping now was not an option. "That same day, the man gave me a Bible and showed me some places to read. I did read them, and I asked Jesus to change my life. I told Him I'd been a real scoundrel and had done a lot of things I shouldn't. I asked Him to take away my anger and forgive me. I promised Jesus I'd do my best to stay out of trouble from then on."

"So did you?"

Kirk smiled. "I do my best. I still have a little goof every now and then. An angry thought sometimes surfaces, and I'll almost say something I shouldn't. None of us are perfect. But my life has turned around a hundred and eighty degrees. God has given me a love in my heart. He's blessed me with the most beautiful and caring woman any man could ever ask for. He took away my anger and replaced it with a love I didn't know was possible. He can do the same thing for you."

Kirk paused. "That's why I can look at you when you've been a real hooligan, and I can see possibilities."

Thorne wasn't moving, not even blinking.

"I see a future for you. God has a plan for you. Just accept Jesus into your heart and, as Brandon puts it, make him your friend."

Thorne jumped up. He turned around and just stood there looking straight at Kirk. "I'll think about it."

Kirk pulled off his baseball cap and slowly ran his fingers through his thick copper hair. *Well, that's a start.*

Thorne walked outside the horse stall, stuck both hands in his pockets, and looked up toward the sky.

Kirk put his hand on the boy's shoulder. "Come on, man. Let's go see if they left us any of that banana puddin'."

Katie pulled out the bowl of banana pudding with whole vanilla wafers decorating the top, spooned out some for Thorne, and walked back to the master bedroom. Kirk followed her. She pulled back the covers on their bed, tossed the pillows aside, and a sheepish grin appeared on her face. "I just want to know one thing, big guy. Did you burn those burgers just so you could pull off your scheme to expose the little thief?"

Kirk raised an eyebrow, and his denim-blue eyes twinkled. "Now, Kate, would I waste our good Angus beef like that?"

11

"So where's Brandon?" Thorne slammed his passenger door with gorilla force. "Your perfect son never showed up to get on the bus."

"Thorne, what's your problem? You get in the truck, and anger spews outta your mouth like a busted fire hydrant!"

"It's just that you think Brandon can do no wrong."

"Yep, he's a pretty good kid—most of the time."

"Well, this time your little darling screwed up!"

"How's that? I'm sure you're all too willing to tell me."

"First off, he didn't show up for seventh hour PE. Then I see him and this redheaded bozo walkin' away from the school, just as Mr. Simpson is pullin' away."

"Thorne, stop the name-calling!" Kirk punched his index finger in Thorne's chest and grinned. "I happen to like red hair—might be one reason I married Katie."

"I know this kid. Brandon and him both think they're better'n anybody else. They're always hangin' out together. They think they are the teacher's pets. She gives them both straight As. I think they are copying from somebody else."

"Well, first off, Brandon had permission to spend the night with this kid. And secondly, Brandon has a sprained ankle, so he had permission to go to study hall instead of PE." Kirk continued to stare at Thorne. "You know, it sounds to me like you're jealous of them."

"Haw!" Thorne squawked. "I sure ain't jealous."

"What are you then—just angry? Huh?"

"Yeah, the redheaded dude's been tellin' everyone in the whole school I ain't nuthin' but white trash. I think Brandon told him I come from a druggy neighborhood in the city."

"Oh man! That's just wrong. I'll talk to Brandon about that."

"Well, you do just that…'cause I ain't taking that from him or no one else. My family don't take—"

"Thorne! Don't even go there. You've gotta drop the ghetto slang! You talk like that, and they've got a reason to call you white trash."

Thorne tightened his lips and looked away. Then with his teeth clenched, he tried to talk ventriloquist style, with his lips closed. "I am who I am—!" And he ended with a curse word.

Kirk turned the ignition off and took his foot off the brake. "Look, pal, you have the ability to be who you want to be. A person's future is not determined by the neighborhood he happens to live in. It's not even determined by his family or the genes he has inherited from them. I think we already had a discussion about that. God gave each one of us the ability to make the most of our life. You can decide to be who you want to be. No one else has the key to that door—just you.

"I think I already told you what kind of dad I had and what happened to me. You—and only you—are the one in charge of your life."

Thorne's face was still turned toward the passenger window. There was a slight sniffle.

Kirk's right fist gently touched Thorne's shoulder. "Do you believe that?"

"No." His hand shot up to his eye. "No, I don't believe that." He rolled his window down and hung his head out. "Let's just go."

Thorne picked at his food and was quiet. Katie had been clued in by Kirk. After supper, Kirk went to the barn to do the milking chores, and she went to Thorne's room, where she found him lying facedown on his bed. She sat down beside him and put her hand on his back. "Hey, guy, you wanna talk?"

He remained facedown and shook his head no.

"Well, let me guess. I think you're missing your mom."

There was a sniffle and then a faint whisper. "Yeah, and my brothers—especially Johnny."

"Johnny's your oldest brother, right?"

There was only a slight shake of the head to indicate that was right.

"How old is Johnny, do you know?"

"I don't know. He's my big brother."

"Was Johnny good to you?"

Thorne turned his face toward Katie. "Johnny would hide me out when Dad came in drunk 'cause he knew Dad would pull off his belt and beat me if I had done anything wrong—or even if I hadn't."

"So where was your mother when your dad would beat you?"

"She was afraid of him too—we all were." Thorne turned over and sat up cross-legged on the bed. "One time, he got in a fight with Johnny. He punched Johnny in the nose, and that just made Johnny madder. They fought and tore up half the furniture in the living room. Johnny threw a chair at Dad and knocked him out cold! We all got in the car and left."

"Where did you go?"

"We went to my grandma's."

"Really?" *Could there be another family member DFS doesn't know about?* "So where does your grandma live?"

"Oh, she died. Mom thinks Dad killed her to get her life insurance money."

Katie gasped.

"But then Dad found out she didn't have any life insurance."

Katie hugged the frail boy sitting there on the bed. "Honey, I think you've had a pretty rough life. I'm hoping all that can change now."

Thorne shrugged his shoulders. "Yeah maybe for some people—just not me."

"Why would you say that, Thorne?"

"'Cause my dad ain't no good, my mom is a whore."

"Who told you that?"

"Everybody says that. Johnny and Josh both call her a whore."

"I don't think you should ever call your mother that. You don't know all the facts, and besides, she is your mother. You are to show respect. Johnny and Josh should show respect for her—even if she might not deserve it."

"Josh was so bad they couldn't even find a foster home for him. He was doin' drugs every day—and Mom knew it! And my big brother, Johnny…Johnny's in prison!"

"Oh, honey—"

Thorne bawled, "So that's where I'm headed too!"

"No, Thorne, you're not headed to prison—not if I have anything to do with it. I don't know who's been feeding you those lies. You can decide to be your own man. You don't have to follow in the footsteps of your family. Kirk didn't."

"Yeah, he told me about that."

"Well, look at him now. Isn't he living a good life now? He didn't follow the path his dad did. And you don't have to either."

"I wanna see my brother, Johnny. Do you think they'll let me?"

Katie closed her eyes for a second. *How do I get through to him? His outlook on life is still tainted with past evil—maybe permanently.* "Honey, I don't know. We'll just have to wait and see."

12

John Barrow Jr. stepped through the cell door at the Oklahoma State Penitentiary. *Freedom! Yeah, freedom!* A whole year in this cage was enough to make anyone go nuts.

"Okay, Barrow, looks like this is your lucky day."

Johnny glared at the guard. "Luck has nothing to do with it. I served my time."

The guard opened the electronic door. "We're headed to the out-processing unit where your paperwork will be checked. Then they'll check it again."

Forty-five minutes later, the main gate closed behind him. Johnny turned back around, stretched both arms high in the air, and flipped his middle fingers upward, shouting obscenities at the guards back in his cell block. Those bean heads could use a course in common courtesy.

His stomach growled. A good Mexican restaurant on the way home would be perfect. The prison food had been appalling—corn cereal, corn bread, corn mush, corn on the cob. It was amazing how so many dishes could be made from the nasty yellow kernel. And the disgusting food was shoved through food slots by shifts of baboons with no personality whatsoever. These slop vendors pushed the tray through the slot without the slightest concern for the men they served.

The green T-Top Firebird was parked toward the front of the lot. A pencil-thin bleach blonde crawled out of the car and raced toward Johnny. With his thumbs hooked into his jeans pockets, he drifted ever so slowly in her direction with his usual you-owe-me arrogance. The reedy blonde reached for him. He grabbed her waist with both hands and lifted her a full two feet off the ground.

"Johnny, you made it!" Dana squealed. "I thought this day would never come."

He set her back on her feet and examined her from head to toe. "Babe, you are lookin' mighty good!"

She giggled, punched him playfully in the stomach, and then formed her mouth into a big O. "That's some rock-hard abs you've acquired while you were in there."

"Yeah, well, I've had a while to work on 'em." He took her hand and started toward the car. "I hope you've got some smokes with you. I've been bummin' for the last three weeks. Some cute little blonde hasn't been puttin' any money in my prison account lately."

She opened the driver's door and grabbed a pack of Marlboros from the dashboard. "There's a reason for that. They laid me off at the GM plant. So I've had no money to send—even got evicted."

"Evicted! So where're we gonna live?"

She shook the pack, a cigarette popped out, and she pointed it toward him. "We're back at my folks 'til one of us can get a job."

"You gotta be kiddin'!" He climbed in the passenger side and ran his fingers through his thick greasy black hair. He swore. "You know I don't get along with your old man!"

"Well, unless you can come up with a better plan, you'll just have to make it work."

"What about Dad's old place? Why don't we move in there?"

"That's been boarded up since right after your mom left, and there's a No Trespassing sign on the door. I think the city's condemned it."

The conversation came to a halt. He reclined his seat and closed his eyes. Forty minutes later, he woke up as she steered onto the westbound on-ramp of I-40. He stuck his right foot up on the dash. "So where's my two little brothers now?"

"Last I heard, Josh was still in the group home, but that's been a good while. He's probably out on his own now. Isn't he eighteen now?"

"What about Thorne?"

"I called down to DFS, and all they would tell me was he is in foster care."

"Where?"

"I said that's all they would tell me."

He stuck his other foot up on the dash and reclined some more, lit another cigarette, took a drag, and blew the blue cloud of smoke in her direction. "I asked you to find out what's goin' on with my brothers. A year ago, I asked you to do that! I would think you—"

"Look, Johnny, I can't just waltz into the DFS office and demand to know where they are. They're not gonna give me the time of day. We're not even married, so I'm sure they know I have no right to that kind of information."

"Well, it seems to me you would *find* a way to get hold of that info. That's the one—and only—thing I asked you to do. I assumed you'd done that!" He pitched the half-smoked cigarette out the side window. "Josh and Thorne is all the family I got left. I gotta find them!"

"What about your dad? Wasn't he right there in the same cell block with you?"

"Yeah, but they moved him out of state last month. I'll never see the old geezer again—and that suits me just fine! He snitched on another inmate that was about to get parole, and they were afraid for his safety, so they transferred him to some federal prison in Florida—don't know which one. That's all I knew before they took him away." He fidgeted. "Besides, I don't consider my old man to be family anymore."

"What about your mom?"

He laughed. "You mean Lana Lou, the Lewd Lady of the Night?"

"Johnny!"

"Well, what else would you call her? She sure ain't no June Cleaver!"

Johnny reached for the pack of Marlboros and grabbed the last one. Dana shot an evil eye toward him. "You're takin' the last one?"

"What? This was all you brought?" He stuck the cigarette in his mouth, crushed the empty pack, and tossed it out the side window. "Pull over at the next c-store and buy a couple of packs."

"I don't have any cash—zilch. There's not even any loose coins anywhere in this car!"

"Then how'd you have money to get gas for this trip?"

"Dad filled up my tank. I'm tellin' you, we are flat broke!"

"Well, ain't that just a kick in the pants! Nice welcome home I get!"

"Look, buddy, your year-long holiday is over!" She threw both hands off the wheel and up in exasperation. "You might just have to get off your lazy butt and find work." That earned her an attempted slap in the face, but her right arm arrested the attempt.

He looked down at his trembling hands. This was his last smoke 'til he could bum off her dad. "Yeah, well, I can do that. I'll find work. And another thing, I will find my brothers—something you couldn't do! Or wouldn't!"

13

Carol and Lynn Reynolds drove up to the ranch gate, and Carol called her daughter's cell. "Katie, we're here at the gate, and neither one of us can remember the code."

"It's 742. Come on in when you get here, the front door is open."

The blue Mustang pulled up on the gravel drive. Brandon bolted out the front door and ran into Carol's arms as she was walking through the gate of the picket fence. "Brandon!" Carol said. "You are shooting up like a weed. You're going to be as tall as your dad."

Lynn was pulling a couple of boxes out of the trunk of the car, and Brandon ran on over to him. "Grandpa! What do you have in those boxes?"

Lynn hugged Brandon with his one free hand. "Well, you'll just have to wait and see, won't you?" He put his hand on top of Brandon's head. "Man, someone needs to put a rock on your head. You're just getting way too tall. In fact…stand back behind me." Lynn crouched down a couple of inches behind Brandon. "Now tell us, Carol, who's the tallest?"

Carol waved her hand. "No question, Brandon is!"

As they walked into the big room, Carol tipped her head up a bit and sniffed. "Wow! What smells so good, Kate?"

"Mom, what you smell is one of Alton Brown's recipes. He calls it Dry-Aged Standing Rib Roast with Sage Jus. I've got twice-baked potatoes, your favorite green bean casserole, deviled eggs, and a fresh garden salad. Oh, and I've got a blackberry cobbler bubbling up in the oven. I think it's about ready to come out."

Lynn was sitting on the big leather sofa with both boys, one on each side of him. "Okay, you guys wanna see what I brought you?"

A simultaneous "Yeah" came from them. He handed one box to Brandon and the other to Thorne.

Thorne ripped open his box and pulled out a 1:18-scale die-cast '56 T-Bird, the model with the portholes behind the side windows.

"Wow! This is cool."

Brandon opened his box, and a big grin came over his face. He pulled out his die-cast 1965 model candy apple–red Mustang convertible. "Now I have a red one to go with the blue one you gave me a long time ago."

"I know how much you love Ford Mustangs," Lynn said, "so I wanted you to have the red one. You know, that candy apple–red was the most popular color of all time for the Mustangs."

"You mean, even more popular than the midnight blue like yours?"

"Yes, that's what Ford says. I like it too, but I like my midnight blue better."

Katie pulled the blackberry cobbler out of the oven and set it on the butcher-block table in the middle of the kitchen to cool. "Mom, do you want to set the table? We're using my good wedding china today."

"Oh my!" Carol said. "Are you sure? I thought you always save that for company. By the way, where is Kirk?"

"He and Ronnie are up at the barn. We've got twin calves they have to bottle-feed. Their mama didn't make it through the birthing. He'll be rolling in here in a few minutes. I called him as soon as you called me from up at the front gate."

Brandon had his red Mustang in his hand. "You want me to call him again and see how much longer he's gonna be?"

"No, I think I hear him now."

The back door slammed. Kirk walked in and kicked off his boots. "Hey, guys, I'll be with you in just a second. I need to wash up first."

The roast beef, green bean casserole, and the huge bowl of garden salad were all placed on the big oaken table in the center of the room, family style. Katie pulled a loaf of homemade bread from the oven and brought it to the table, covered by a kitchen towel to keep it warm. Thorne had plopped down in the chair at the end of the table while everyone was still standing, waiting to be seated. "Mr. Thorne," Katie said, "it's not polite to sit down ahead of everyone else. Wait until Dad gets in here, and we'll all sit down at the same time. Also, I'd like for you to sit over here. The seat at the head of the table is always reserved for special guests."

Thorne got up, shoved the big captain's chair back with a bang. "Well, that's just stupid! I got here first. Everyone else was just standin' around yakking."

Kirk was walking into the big room. "Young man, that's enough out of you! You had better show a little respect."

Thorne stepped back and crossed his arms in front of him. "Well, I'm hungry, and it looks like no one else is."

Lynn was standing next to Kirk. "Got your hands full, don't you," he whispered.

"Okay, everyone," Katie announced, "I think I've got it all on the table now. Dad, I'd like for you to sit at the end down there, and Mom can be seated next to him on this side. Boys, you may be seated on the far side of the table."

Kirk took the chair at the other end of the table, and Katie sat down next to him on the side closest to the kitchen. Kirk tapped Katie's leg under the table and whispered, "Watch this." He looked straight at Thorne. "Hey, buddy, would you like to ask the blessing?"

Thorne turned bright red. "Uh, I guess…no. Why don't you ask Brandon?"

"Come on, buddy, we'd really like to hear it from you."

Thorne bowed his head and started. "God…Jesus, we are thankful for this food… uh…amen!"

"Thank you, Thorne," Katie said.

"Oh, I forgot…" He bowed his head again. "Help me find my mom, and wherever she is, keep her safe."

14

SHE WAS SITTING on the curb in front of the Greyhound station. Her chopped beaver-brown-and-gray mat of hair framed her ruddy face beneath the colorful knit cap. He walked up and faced her. "Hey, lady, it's gonna get really cold tonight. Maybe you should think about a place to move inside."

She double wrapped the oversized orange-and-green blanket coat around her emaciated frame, looked at the officer, and ducked her left ear inside the collar of the coat, away from the cold.

The officer looked up at the sky as the fat flakes flitted downward. "They're callin' for freezing rain on top of this white stuff. You really should find a place to park inside for the night."

"And where would I find a place like that?" Her voice was raspy.

"The shelters around here are all full. That's what they're sayin'."

"You tried the Salvation Army?"

"Uh-huh."

"Red Cross?"

"Full."

"What about the Rescue Mission over on Sheridan?"

Her cough fogged the air in front of her face. It was more like a bark, a prolonged coarse scouring of the vocal chords. "It's like I said, officer, they're all full. I'll be okay. It won't be the first night I've spent out in freezing drizzle in this danged town."

"Lady, you spend the night out in this—with that cough you got already—you'll be lucky if you make it into next week."

"I'll make it."

She continued to sit there after the officer left. There were more shelters in Oklahoma City, but they were miles from downtown where she sat. An hour passed, and the purple sky darkened. A Ford F-150 pulled up and stopped at the curb beside her. A sixty-something cowboy rolled the passenger window down. "Hon, you needin' a ride somewhere?"

"Depends on where you're headed."

"I'm headin' outta town, down home to Pauls Valley."

"You think it'll be any warmer down there?"

"Well, it's south o' here, so maybe. Come on, looks like you could use a change of scenery. Snow's about to cover that pretty pink cap you got on."

She stood up and walked over to his truck. "You got a wife waitin' for you down there in Pauls Valley?"

"Naw, she ain't in Pauls Valley, and she didn't wait for me—divorced me when I was down on my luck a few years back." He reached across and opened the door.

She stepped up on the rusty running board and ground out a half laugh, half cough. "You ain't no ax murderer or somethin', are you?"

"You ever seen an old cowboy with his two front teeth missin' who was an ax murderer?" He grinned. "Come on, hop in. I think we'll run outta this nasty weather before we get to Pauls Valley. I know where a warmin' shelter is there in the town."

She climbed in the old truck.

He shifted into first gear. "I'll take you right to it if you want." The grin appeared again. "Or you can just come on home with me if you want to. I've got an extra bed, and I've got heat in the house. Might even scare up somethin' for breakfast tomorrow mornin'."

Soon they were heading toward I-35, and she looked over at the stranger. His oil-stained Stetson, older than the truck he was driving, sat cocked to one side. There was a bullet-size hole in the right sleeve of his faded Levi's jacket. "Looks like you've managed to make an enemy somewhere."

"An enemy?"

"Yeah, that hole in your jacket says you've taken a bullet in the arm sometime or 'nuther."

"Oh, that? Naw, it was there when I got this jacket. But you're right. It does look like someone got a piece of lead in 'em."

She stared at his face, chiseled cowboy-thin, with a day-old beard, and dark-brown eyebrows sheltering a pair of shadowy, deep-set eyes. "You know, you ain't half bad lookin' for an old toothless cowhand."

He glanced her way. "Well, hon, you ain't half bad lookin' for a gal with a funny pink hat coverin' that pretty head of yours."

They had been on I-35, headed south for half an hour. Those super-sized snowflakes had diminished, and then turned into tiny ice pellets. With the heavy traffic, the roadway was staying pretty clear.

She turned her head and looked out the passenger-side window. "I hate to ask, but I need a potty break."

"No problem, you hollered just in time. There's a rest area just up ahead. I think there's a McDonald's there too, if you're hungry."

"No, I don't have to have any food, but I'll run in to the restroom if you don't mind."

He pulled into a spot next to the ladies' room. She opened the door and started to get out. "I'll hurry."

"Take your time. I ain't in no hurry."

When she came back out, he was waiting outside the pickup with two cups of black coffee. He handed her a cup and opened the door for her. She stepped inside, sat down, and looked at the man. "Now that's a gentleman. I don't see many men with them kind of manners these days."

He smiled, closed her door, walked around to the driver's side, and climbed in. As he turned the key to start the truck, he turned her way. "Feel better now?"

She looked into those deep gunmetal-blue eyes. "Yes, much better." She tipped the cup upward. "Oh, and thanks for the coffee."

She sat there sipping the steaming brew. This might not have been a very smart thing to do, jumpin' in a truck with a total stranger. He seemed like a nice man—maybe too nice. Could she trust his intentions? "You know, I never even asked. Here I am headin' to a town I never heard of with a man I don't even know his name."

He grinned, tipped the greasy old Stetson. "Tom Greer." He reached over and touched her wrinkled sun-browned hand. "And you are…"

"Lana Lou Barrow."

15

"I'm home," Kirk hollered as he stepped inside the back door and kicked off his manure-caked Wellingtons he'd been wearing to muck out the barn.

Katie met him halfway into the big room. "You finished for the day already?"

"Naw, just thought I'd take a break." He wrapped his arms around his farm wife. "I've been thinkin' about some things."

"Should I be worried?" She kissed him and led him into the kitchen.

"No, it's just that I feel like I'm not getting anywhere with Thorne. He seems to listen to me—and I think he respects me—but I'm not seein' much change in his behavior. He still thinks he has to be defined by his genes, not by his own choices."

Katie poured them both a glass of cold milk. "I know the feeling. But give him time."

"But we've had him for a year now. How much time do you think he needs?"

"He's not going to change as quickly as we would like. He's still missing his brothers—and to tell you the truth, I think he misses his mom."

"Well, he sure doesn't have anything good to say about her."

"Maybe to you, but I'm getting a little different story out of him."

"Really?"

"Yes, I've seen a tear creep out from his eye when we're talking about her." She grabbed a couple of bagels from the bread box and set them on the table. "Honey, I don't think we can expect to see a huge change in his attitude until he's had time to grieve over the loss of his own family. He'll probably never see his dad again. His brothers are scattered—and really shouldn't be a part of his life now anyway. And his mom is absent without leave."

Kirk leaned back and tilted his chair backward on its two back legs. "Surely he can see he's got a better life here with us. He knows we care about him. I spend a lot of time talkin'—just me and him."

"Yes, but you're forgetting one thing."

"What?"

"He's lost his entire family. It doesn't matter some would consider them lowlifes or even white trash. They were all he had, and he loved them in spite of their faults."

Kirk downed the rest of the milk, swiped his mouth with the back of his hand, and rubbed his hand on his jeans. "I suppose you're right. I just had hoped to see some improvement. You know, when I talked to him last time up at the stables, I was pretty sure I had convinced him to ask Jesus to come into his life and—as Brandon called it—be his friend, but all he said was, 'I'll think about it.'"

"And he will. Give him time—you've planted the seed."

The phone rang. "Yeah, Childers ranch. Kirk here." He quickly handed the phone to Katie. "I think you probably should handle this."

"Katie, this is Betty. I've got a situation I thought I should run by you. Thorne's brother has contacted me and wants to have a visit with him."

"Which one?"

"It's Johnny, the oldest brother."

"I thought he was in prison," Katie said as she glanced at Kirk and frowned.

"He says he's been released—served his time."

"Oh, I…I don't know. That might not be a very good idea. We're trying to reform the guy and get him on the right track. I'm thinking that would really be a setback for him. I just don't think he needs that right now."

"I thought those would be your feelings. I'll try to hold him off for a while. I tend to agree with you. It's just that I'm not sure I can legally keep him from a visitation forever."

"How old is this brother now?"

"He says he's about to turn twenty-one."

Katie was quiet for a few seconds before she spoke. "I...I just think we need more time to work with Thorne before he's exposed to the old way of life he was rescued from."

"I agree. But with this guy turning twenty-one, I'll be fighting an uphill battle to keep him from seeing Thorne. He's already told me he wants his little brother to come live with him."

"You have got to be kidding! Straight out of prison, and he thinks he can be a good example for a kid?"

"I'm afraid that's right. He served his time. That's the way the law sees it. I can probably hold off the situation until he does turn twenty-one, but after that, I'm guessing he'll have to be placed with his just-released-from-prison brother—if Johnny insists and we can find no reason to not allow it. I don't think there are any other relatives."

"Oh dear God! That is just nuts!"

"Okay, hon, I'll do what I can to prolong this visit, but you should be aware it's probably going to happen."

"Maybe." Katie picked up a pencil and doodled on a paper napkin. "Unless he goes back to prison for something else."

Betty laughed. "You've got a point there, Miss Katie. Okay, I'll keep you posted."

Katie placed the phone back into its cradle and stared at Kirk. "Can you believe that?"

"So this kid wants to have a visit with his little brother?"

"Yes, and get this—he said he wants Thorne to come live with him!"

"Live with him!" Kirk slammed his fist down on the table. "The guy's just out of prison and still a punk kid himself!"

"She said he's about to turn twenty-one."

Kirk folded his arms on the tabletop and dropped his forehead onto them. His shirt muffled his voice. "Then we will have lost the battle."

"Honey, we just have to keep on doing what we've been doing until that happens. We're bound to make a difference in his life."

"I'm not so sure of that. It's been a whole year already." Kirk raised his head. "How much time is it gonna take to make a difference?"

"I don't know. You tell me. How long did it take for you to overcome the situation with your dad and get on the right track?"

"Oh, that may take a lot more time." He ducked his head again.

Katie took the glasses and Kirk's half-eaten bagel from the table. "Come on, it's about time for the bus. Do you want to go after them or should I?"

"No, I'll go."

Kirk walked out and got into the truck, slammed his palms down on the steering wheel, and stared ahead before turning the key to start the truck. He pressed the accelerator. Gravel flew. The distance up to the main gate blurred. He stopped just short of hitting the metal gate, staring out into an immense blue sky. The gate remained closed.

The guys climbed over the fence and hopped in the backseat of the truck. They started jabbering on the way back to the house. Kirk was quiet, and Brandon must have noticed. "Something's up," he whispered to Thorne. Kirk didn't respond.

16

The temperature was dropping, and snow devils were twirling and leaving a powdery fleece of the January elements. Kirk had just finished with morning milking when his helper, Ronnie, walked into the barn. "Kirk, I'm gonna need some help with one of our young heifers. She's having a hard time birthing. I'm afraid we may lose the calf—and maybe her too."

"Where'd you find her?"

"She's clear over in the south forty, just at the edge of the tree line."

"Let's go!"

Ronnie pointed toward the edge of the trees. Kirk stopped, grabbed his buckskin gloves from the dashboard, and pulled out a rope from the backseat. The heifer was lying on the ground with one hind foot of the calf visible. Kirk looked at Ronnie and shook his head. "This ain't good—another breech!"

The wind picked up and the blast of icy pellets bit at the men's faces. "You think we can reach in and turn the calf, Ron?"

"No, I don't think so. I already tried that."

"Okay, but pulling the little guy may not work either." Kirk quickly tied the rope around the calf's extruded foot. Ronnie spread his legs for traction and grabbed the rope just below Kirk's hold. Both men pulled, but made little progress. Only the lower half of the calf's leg came out. The little black heifer bawled.

After several minutes of pulling, the other hind leg came out but was bent forward at an awkward angle. "Oh man, that's not good!" Kirk said.

The snow pellets had turned to flakes, but were coming down so heavily and with such force by the driving wind, visibility was down to about zero. Exhaustion was settling in for both men. "Kirk, you think we oughta call the vet?"

"What good could he do? This is just gonna take our muscles to rescue this little guy."

After a little more progress, Ronnie said, "Yeah, you said it right when you said *guy*, 'cause it's a bull calf." Another hard pull by the men, and the calf surged toward them, slamming both guys to the ground, with Kirk landing on top of Ronnie.

Kirk laughed. "Well, that's one way to do it." He pulled himself up and looked at the baby Angus bull. "He's not breathing." After pressing on the calf's abdomen several times and getting no response, Kirk looked at his helper in defeat. "We lost him."

"Yeah, and the mother ain't lookin' so good herself. I don't think she's gonna be gettin' up on her own any ways soon."

"You're right," Kirk said. "We gotta get this girl in the pickup bed. I've gotta get her up to the barn, or she'll just lie here and freeze to death."

"Yeah, but that might be more difficult than pullin' the calf."

"Well we gotta do it somehow. Jump in the pickup and back it down here to her. I'm still hoping I can get the calf to breathe, so I'm gonna work on him while you're backing down the truck."

When Ronnie stopped the truck, the rear end was positioned in a low spot. He took out the two-ton Come-Along winch from the side toolbox. With the tail end of the truck lower and with the use of the Come-Along, the men managed to load the heifer. Something would have to be done with the body of the bull calf later.

Kirk steered the pickup over the clumpy pasture back toward the barn. Would DFS actually take Thorne out of a good home and place him back with his good-for-nothing brother? He relayed Katie's conversation with the caseworker to Ronnie. "I can't believe DFS would even consider allowing that brother—just out of prison—to get custody of him."

"Didn't you say he's Thorne's older brother?" Ronnie took hold of the grab bar just as the truck bounced over another clump of grass. "And didn't you say Thorne's old man's serving a life sentence for murder?"

"So what's your point?"

"Mom's vanished, right?"

"Yep."

"Kirk, don't you see? This brother's all the family the kid's got."

"Some family!" Kirk growled.

"So? Family is family, man! No one should be kept from their own family."

"Ron, I'm tryin' to make a difference in the kid's life. I don't want him falling back into the ghetto lifestyle he was in."

"You can't do that. He deserves to be with his family—and if this brother is all the family he's got left, then he should be with him."

Kirk slammed his palm hard onto the steering wheel. "Man! You don't know what the stinkin' heck you're talkin' about. He don't need to be swept right back into the pigsty he came from, tarring his lungs up with weed, and winding up in jail before he can even finish high school. No! Thorne deserves better."

"Okay, boss, but you know you ain't his family. You're just a temporary babysitter."

Kirk gritted his teeth. *Babysitter!* He rolled his side window down to get a breath of fresh air. The blowing snow swirled into the cab of the truck, and he quickly rolled the window back up. "Okay, Ron, I see we're not gonna agree on this, so let's just drop it. Now I've gotta figure out where to drop our poor, sick heifer. We gotta get her inside the barn. I'll call the vet if she doesn't get up on her feet in an hour or so."

17

Eighty miles south, Pauls Valley was also being blasted with the winter storm. The temperature plunged to the single digits. Lana Lou Barrow sat wrapped in her orange-and-green blanket coat at Tom's kitchen table, warming her hands around a steaming cup of black coffee.

Tom Greer walked into the kitchen in a pair of unbuttoned, faded, and threadbare Levi's. No shirt and barefoot. His thinning hair electrified by the night on his pillow. "You got any coffee left over there for an old secondhand cowboy?" His missing two front teeth spotlighted an otherwise natural grin.

"Sure, I set your favorite mug down by the coffeepot." Two minutes passed, and her undisturbed line of vision lasered through the partially frosted-over window and into the white infinity.

"Whatcha thinkin' 'bout, hon?"

"What? Oh, I guess I was thinking about my boys. Wondering where they are. It's been well over a year—almost two—since I've seen any of them. I guess Johnny's still in McAlester, along with his brutal old dad. At least they've got each other." She shook her head. "I've got no one."

"Didn't you say you have three sons?"

"My three sons…"

Tom grinned. "Just like on TV."

"No, not just like on TV. Times ain't like that anymore." She fidgeted in her chair and ran her fingers through her choppy dull brown hair. "I don't know where Josh and Thorne are. I hope they're okay. I should have never left them alone there in the house. It's just that I couldn't stand the sight of that house after

John did what he did. And I knew I could never support my boys. I had no money and no way of getting money. You know, life gets complicated."

"You wanna find 'em?"

Lana Lou looked at him like he had just asked if she'd like to find a jackrabbit to sit down and sing a lullaby to. "Tom, I think the real question is do *they* want me to find me."

"Aw, come on, girl. You know they do."

"No, I don't think so. I was a terrible mother, and I abandoned them right when they needed me the most. I don't know what I was thinking—don't know how I can ever forgive myself."

"If it's meant to be, you'll find 'em." He got up and refilled her coffee. "Hey, maybe I could help you find them boys."

She walked over to the window she'd been staring out of. "No, you've already done way too much for me. As soon as this storm lets up, I'll be movin' on."

"What? You can't—"

"No, I've made up my mind. You don't need my kind of baggage. You barely make it on your own."

"Where will you go?"

Lana Lou double wrapped her ever-present blanket/coat around her frail body. "Oh, I guess I'll head back up to the city. It's home, even though 'home' is a mighty strange place. Never thought I'd wind up livin' under a tarp next to a smelly old Dumpster." She ran a bony finger around the rim of the coffee mug. "Tom, did you ever have hopes and dreams—dreams that just never worked out?"

"Sure have. My life's full of 'em."

"When I was a girl, I dreamed of marryin' a handsome man— one who loved me and cared for me. Havin' babies with him." She twirled the loose-fitting and wire-thin wedding band on her finger. "I thought I'd probably bring up them babies right—thought they'd someday make me proud. But look at me. I married a big barrel-chested murdering beast, had his babies, lost 'em all. And now I'm livin' under the big-city lights." She laughed. "Big city lights, just outside the Greyhound station."

"Aw, Lany Lou, you know you're better'n that."

She hooked her finger in the handle of the mug, gently moving the mug from side to side and sloshing some coffee over the top. "No, Tom, I'm no good. If there ever was a God, He took my dreams and gave them to someone else—someone who wouldn't disappoint Him."

A coughing spell overtook the frail woman. She beat her chest, and after the coughing and hacking finally quit, she put both elbows on the table, ran her fingers through her choppy hair, and looked up at Tom. "No, I've made my bed. Now I've gotta lie in it. I heard that somewhere—maybe it was my mama said it." She shook her head. "So that old sidewalk is where I belong."

"Dang, Lany Lou, you can't go back and live on the street like you were doin'. It's still winter out there. You just need to plant your scraggy little body right here in this house with me." He leaned backward in his chair. "I mean, I've got two bedrooms..." The toothless grin appeared again. "...if you think we need two."

Lana Lou held her coffee mug to her lips and was quiet, finally setting it back down. She looked out the partially frosted window again.

Tom sat there with a blank stare as she tapped the table with her chipped and jagged nails. "You've got some heat here to warm them skinny brown fingers of yours. We've got food in the house." He grinned. "And you've got me."

She let out a long held-in breath. "No. I've already made one big mistake. I don't need to make another one. Thanks, but I'm movin' on soon as this storm lets up."

18

Johnny Barrow and his friend Dana walked into the DFS offices at 9:05 a.m. "I'm Johnny Barrow, and I'd like to speak to the caseworker about my brother, Thorne Barrow. I think she said her name is Betty."

"Do you have an appointment with Mrs. Sawyer?"

"No, I don't, but this shouldn't take long."

After Betty was informed about her visitor, she came to the outer office, greeted Johnny, and introduced herself to the girlfriend. "Hello, I'm Betty Sawyer."

"Glad to meet you, Mrs. Sawyer. I'm Dana Torgeson."

Betty turned to Johnny. "I believe we spoke last week on the phone about your brother."

"Yes, we did. I'm here to pick him up and take him home with me."

"Not so fast." Betty looked out over her cheap reader glasses. "But we do need to talk, so come on back to my office. Your friend may accompany you if you like."

Johnny again explained he was Thorne's oldest brother and their father was serving a life sentence for murder. "Our mother is out of the picture. I understand she walked away and left Thorne and my other brother, Josh, in the house alone with no food or anything."

"And just how do you know that, Johnny?"

"I've got my informants, Mrs. Sawyer."

"Yes, I guess you do. Well, that's when I came to the house and found the boys alone. You're right. There was little or no food in the house. Trash was piled up and infested with roaches."

"So when can we go get my little brother?"

Betty explained a visitation might be possible at a later date. "At this point, it's not an issue of custody of the child. He will remain in the care of the department until decisions can be made as to his living arrangements and eventual custody."

"That's crap!"

"Johnny, allow me to explain how the system works. When a child enters the foster care system because his or her home is no longer safe, a judge will usually appoint a volunteer. That person is known as a court appointed special advocate or simply CASA."

Johnny jumped out of his chair. "You mean a total stranger—a volunteer—is making decisions about my little brother?"

"CASA volunteers are screened and highly trained. They are appointed by judges to represent and advocate for a child's best interests while in the foster care system. We work very closely with the CASA volunteer to find a safe, permanent home for the child as soon as possible."

"Look, Mrs. Sawyer, I am Thorne's brother. My home is where he should be."

"Johnny, there are several possibilities. For starters, I'd like to locate his mother and have a visit with her."

Johnny jumped up again. "Our mother abandoned him! Why would you wanna find her?"

"Just listen to the lady," Dana said.

Johnny sat back down.

"Mr. Barrow, your mother is certainly first in line to care for her son, assuming she can be found and seen as a responsible parent."

"Look, lady, that's crap!" His fists were balled at his sides.

"Well, I'm sorry you feel that way, but I must follow protocol here. I've already confirmed the fact his father is serving a life sentence in prison. So, if I can locate her, his mother will be my first attempt at returning parental custody. Thorne's CASA volunteer is working with me to try to find her."

Johnny rocketed out of his chair, both fists balled. "Look, you stupid woman, I told you she abandoned him! She ain't here. I am!" He placed his fists on the front of her desk and screamed, "I want my little brother—and I want him now!"

Betty stood and stared into Johnny's reddened face. "First of all, your anger is alerting me to the possibility you may not even be capable of any kind of civil visitation with your brother, much less any custodial care. You certainly are not helping your situation by this outburst of wrath."

He leaned over the desk toward Betty, pointed his finger at her, and started to shout. Dana reached over, hooked her finger in the belt loop of his jeans, and pulled on it. "Cool it, Johnny!"

Johnny retracted the finger into a fist and turned to Dana. "Come on, I'm gettin' nowhere with this woman!"

19

"I'M NOT LIKE Brandon! Why can't you understand that?" Thorne threw the book on the floor. "All of these books are too hard for me! Brandon can read these. I can't! None of my family could read very good—my dad couldn't even write his name!"

Sitting on the bed beside Thorne, Katie put her arm around him and gave a gentle squeeze. "Hon, that doesn't mean you can't learn to read well. It just takes time and practice. That's why you've got me. See, I'm a schoolteacher, and I happen to know you are smart enough to conquer this. It won't happen overnight, and I'm not pushing you. We will work at it at your own pace. You're already getting most of the words. You just have trouble with a few of the harder ones. Don't give up. You're making progress."

Thorne ducked his head downward and ran his fingers through his crusty, spiked hair. A tiny tear dropped from his eye. This really wasn't about his reading ability. His frustration originated somewhere deep in his past.

"Sweetie, I know something else is bothering you. It's not just the reading. Let's talk about that."

One small barely audible sob filtered out from beneath his bowed head. "It wouldn't do any good to talk about it."

"You're wrong. It may not solve the problem, but it will get it off your chest—make you feel better."

He turned his head toward her just a bit.

"You see, Thorne, when we bottle up our feelings inside and refuse to talk about them, they gnaw at us. Pretty soon, if we don't open up and talk to someone, they make us sick."

The dam broke, and tears flooded his face and dripped on to his jeans. He raised his head and looked into Katie's eyes. "Where is my mom?" The exasperation was physically evident in his desperate voice and posture.

"Oh, honey, I wish we knew."

"Why did she leave me?"

"Oh gosh, I don't know the answer to that either." Katie knelt down on the floor in front of him. "Even though we don't understand why she left, we probably can assume she felt she had no other choice—she may have felt trapped."

"Why?"

"Let's just think about it a minute. As I understand it, your father had just been taken back to jail. Didn't you tell us she didn't have a job?"

"Yeah."

"Well, how was she supposed to stay there and care for you boys if she didn't have money to buy food, pay the utilities, or buy you clothes?" Katie patted his knee. "Don't you see—she felt like she was trapped. Let's do some guessing here. Do you think it's possible she's been out there trying to get a job so she can have money to support her family? Maybe she knows where you are, and she is waiting 'til she can have the money to provide for you. Do you suppose she knows you are being cared for right here? Do you suppose she is counting the days 'til she can bring you home with her?"

Thorne wiped his eyes with the back of his hand. "Maybe."

Katie handed him a tissue. "I'll bet she thinks about you every day. I'm sure she has cried, just like you are doing now."

He took the tissue and made a quick swipe at his eyes. "Do you think I'll ever see her again?"

"Oh, Thorne! I have no doubt about that. Yes, that will happen someday. We don't know when, but it will happen. Until then, I know she would like nothing better than for you to keep on reading and working hard to excel in school. Hey, that is exactly why I've been working with you all this time. I want her to be proud of the good grades you make in school when she sees you. I want you to surprise her by reading one of these books to her." She patted his knee again. "Your mom will probably cry happy tears then."

"Okay, I'll think about it. Can I go out and play with Noah now?"

20

"Mr. Barrow, the property was condemned for several structural reasons. Those issues will have to be resolved and repairs made before you are allowed to reside there."

"Okay, so give me a list of what's gotta be done, and I'll do it."

"I'll need some proof of ownership—a deed, tax receipt, copy of a mortgage—just so we can have some proof. You'll also need to bring me a copy of your birth certificate or something showing you are the son of the owner."

"I can have that to you this afternoon."

The city official handed Johnny the list of needed repairs. "You do understand no utilities can be turned on until these repairs have been completed and a city inspector has approved and signed off on them."

Dana's father pulled his pickup truck into the driveway just behind Johnny. Dana got out and ran back to the old green Firebird. The T-Top had been removed the day before. In one of his angry fits, Johnny had pounded one side of the Plexiglas top with a twenty-four-inch monkey wrench while arguing with a neighbor. The top had shattered in the twenty-degree weather.

Dana leaned down through the open top and kissed Johnny on his forehead.

He pulled her face toward his. "So did they hire you?"

"Yeah! I start tomorrow at the Sonic over on Santa Fe. So how'd your visit with the city go?"

Johnny handed her the list of repairs needed for the old Barrow house. "Some of these are gonna take some cash. You think your dad could loan us some money to get started 'til you get your first paycheck?"

"Wait, I'll ask him. He's probably anxious to get us out of the house. You know, you two have had your share of arguments."

Dan Torgeson was not only willing to fork over cash to buy materials, he also told Johnny he'd help him work on the house. A couple of windowpanes had to be replaced, results of angry fits by big John Barrow. The front porch had two boards missing on the floor, and the rotten wooden steps had been tossed to the side. After removing the half sheet of plywood from the back door, it was plain to see someone had busted in. The splintered door was beyond repair. Trash had to be hauled away—from inside the house, outside the house, and out of the old ramshackle garage at the back of the property.

Supplies were delivered, and the first day of work went well. Johnny asked the neighbor, Mrs. Knutson, if he could run an electrical cord from her house so they could use the power tools Dana's dad had brought over. The two men seemed to work well together, respecting each other with every task—until the second day. Then tempers flared, and several times the cold February air was fogged over by a string of curse words, mostly hurled from the mouth of the twenty-one-year old.

The two were working on replacing the missing boards on the floor of the front porch. After several miscalculated cuts and two ruined boards, the older man tried to show the younger one how to read a tape measure to prevent that from happening again.

Johnny's anger exploded. "I know how to use a stinkin' tape measure! What do you take me for, some kind of imbecile?" He hurled the Skill saw he was using to the floor. The blade guard broke off, and the saw bounced over and crashed into the door, knocking a hole in the thin lower panel.

"Yeah, Johnny, you just made that pretty clear to me. Now the door's gotta be repaired." Dan Torgeson picked up his remaining tools, loaded them in his pickup, and drove home—alone.

Three weeks later, a city inspector stood on the front porch of the old house and handed Johnny a list of unsatisfactory repairs. Again, the young buck revealed his limited vocabulary with sparks of anger arrowed toward the inspector. "All you office jerks wanna do is dictate to us what we can and can't do. I do the repairs you asked me to do to this old house, and you don't think it's good enough. I'm tellin' you, not everybody's got deep pockets like you office workers. We ain't got the money for fancy granite countertops and terrazzo floors. We make do with what we've got."

"No one is telling you you have to install granite countertops or terrazzo flooring. We are simply insuring the house is brought up to a safe condition. Now if you can't agree to that, you will never get city approval for habitation of the premises."

"This is what I think of your list." Johnny dropped it in front of him, put his foot on it, and ground it into the dusty ground. He glared at the inspector. "And I'll be movin' into my house tonight, whether I've got your permission or not!"

"Mr. Barrow, I only gave you permission to enter the house so you could make the necessary repairs. Under no circumstances are you allowed to occupy the premises as your place of residence until you've complied with my list of mandatory repairs—and to my satisfaction!"

Emma Knutson was sitting on her front porch and heard the vulgar tirade that erupted from the young Barrow offspring as the inspector was walking away. She went inside her house, pulled a pair of pliers out of a kitchen drawer, and walked out to her electrical outlet where Johnny's extension cord was plugged in. She pulled it out from the wall, took the pliers, locked on to one of the polarized plugs, and twisted it off. She put the pliers in her apron pocket and walked back in her house.

Six weeks later, Dan Torgeson finished up the repairs by himself and called for the city inspector to return.

21

He dropped a five dollar bill in her Folgers coffee can, the only bill among the few spare coins. She looked up, astonished. He was walking away. She hadn't even seen his face, but the greasy old Stetson perched atop the rangy old cowboy gave him away. She managed to stand up and started to run after him. She shouted his name as he turned the corner. "Tom! Hey, don't leave. Tom!"

She was running past another woman who was sitting on the sidewalk with a gallon jar in her outstretched hand. The woman stuck her foot out. She splatted face down on the concrete. A few of her loose coins scattered out over the sidewalk. She pulled herself up, turned, and thundered a few hateful words at the old panhandler. Then she realized Tom Greer might be getting away. Clutching her Folgers can, she ran around the corner in search of him. Blood oozed from her nose as she hobbled into the shop next door.

An old gentleman with a waxed handlebar mustache hollered at her. "Lady, we don't allow panhandlers in here. You need to move on."

She ran back outside. Her old blanket-coat, flying in the breeze, invited a biting blast of blustery winter weather in next to her skeletal frame. She wrapped the oversized coat around herself and headed for the coffee shop down the street, thinking he might be looking for a good cup of hot coffee to break the chill. But he was not there either. She'd lost him.

"You know that old cuss, do ya?" The woman held on to her gallon jar. "I knew you couldn't catch him."

She belted out her three favorite words, telling the old woman where she could go. Then she walked back to her self-appointed station twenty feet to the right of the door to the Greyhound terminal. One of her panhandling friends saw what had happened and came to her.

"Lana Lou, I saw that old bitty trip you."

"Yeah, just after my friend Tom dropped a five in my can. I tried to catch him, but he was gone."

"Is he the old toothless cowboy you went to Pauls Valley with?"

"Yeah, I should have stayed with him. He asked me to, but I didn't wanna be a burden to him. He's a nice man. I can't say much for his kisses, you know, with them two front teeth missin'."

"Give him time to get home. Then give him a call. You said he ain't married."

"Nope, his wife divorced him. He's got a cute little house there in Pauls Valley. Keeps it clean as a whistle. I ain't never seen a man do housework like he does. And he can cook too. Makes spaghetti better'n any I-talian. One night, he cooked us up some corn bread and beans—put a good old ham hock in them. Girl, I'm telling you, that was some good eatin'. I'm thinkin' that old cowboy must have been the chuck wagon cook in his earlier days. Anyhow, we ate real good while I was down there with him."

"You were crazy for leavin' him. You shoulda rode range with him. Any man who cooks and cleans house is a gold find. I'm tellin' you, you need to give him a ring-a-ding. Don't let that kind of man get away!"

"Well, I'd probably do that, but I don't think he's got a phone."

"Then write him a letter."

"I don't even remember what his address was. I saw some house numbers by his front door, but I couldn't recall them if my life depended on it."

"Maybe it does," her friend said. "You can't take another winter out here on the street. Look at you. Your bones are showin' through that paper-thin skin—used to be all wrinkled—now it's just stretched tight over them stubborn old bones. And you ain't got enough blood tricklin' through them veins to keep a bird alive. Nope, you ain't a gonna make it another winter out here on the street."

Lana Lou pulled the five dollar bill out of her can and held it up. "Oh girl, I'm fine. I've got some dough now. Let's me and you go grab a sandwich down at the corner cafe."

22

It was Saturday morning, and Brandon had asked several times to go see Katie's parents in the city. Lynn Reynolds had taken Brandon under his wing and latched on to him just like a storybook grandfather.

With Katie and Brandon away for the day, Kirk decided he and Thorne should cut some firewood. The timbered area of the ranch was over a mile from the house, and Katie had taken the pickup. "Come on, Thorne. Let's go hook up the stock trailer to the old Case."

"Why don't we just take the four-wheeler?"

"We could, but this way we'll have the stock trailer to haul the firewood back here to the house."

After some tinkering with the old tractor, Kirk got it started. He backed up to the stock trailer, loaded it, and they were bouncing across the pasture—chainsaw, gas oil, chain oil, wedges, a large flat-head screw driver, and extra pairs of gloves stashed in an old wooden crate and placed back in the stock trailer. Thorne was standing behind Kirk on the tractor with his arms securely wrapped around the driver. "This is fun," he yelled into Kirk's ear.

"Yeah, but don't turn loose. I hit a bump, and you might just bounce right off here and into one of those cow patties you seem to always navigate to."

"What'd you say?"

"Never mind. Just hold on."

A possum sauntered out from behind a clump of grass. Kirk slowed down. "Look at that, would you! Right out in broad daylight! Let's hope it's not rabid."

Thorne shoved Kirk's shoulder. "A rabbit! You just said it was a possum. Make up your mind—don't look like no rabbit to me."

Kirk laughed. "I didn't say *rabbit*. I said *rabid*."

"What's the difference? Sounds the same to me."

Kirk stopped the tractor and turned around to face Thorne, laughing. "I said let's hope it's not rabid—that's what you say when an animal might have rabies."

"Well, why didn't you just say so instead of saying rabbit?"

Kirk shook his head and grinned. "Come on, let's go cut some firewood."

Thorne's voice jumped to a falsetto. "Maybe we'll see another one of your 'rabbits' along the way." Then he giggled.

"Hey, pal, your voice already changing?"

Thorne punched Kirk again. "No, you're the one who keeps changin'. First you call a possum a rabbit. Then all of a sudden, that rabbit's a possum again."

They hadn't gone but maybe a hundred yards, and a big jackrabbit hopped across their path. Thorne shouted above the engine noise, "Okay, whatcha gonna call that? Is it a rabbit or a possum?"

Kirk laughed. "Too bad I don't have my gun."

Thorne bellowed, "Why? You wouldn't know if you shot a rabbit or a possum."

The rest of the morning was more of the same—teasing, give-and-take razzing each other, and a roll in the frosty bed of leaves under the trees.

Kirk reached out his hand for Thorne and helped pull him up off the ground. "Hey, pal, we're not gettin' much woodcutting done like this. You know, you should really try to stay on your feet." They both laughed. Then Thorne came up from behind Kirk and threw a pile of frost-covered leaves on Kirk's head.

Finally, they got down to the serious business of cutting firewood. Thorne wanted to use the chainsaw, but Kirk told him he couldn't allow him to do that. "What I need you to do is carry these logs over to the trailer and stack 'em in nice and neat-like."

Thorne groaned, and Kirk said, "I think you're askin' for another roll in those icy leaves."

"They ain't icy anymore. It's already melted off."

They had cut and loaded almost a cord of wood before the chain became so dull it just wouldn't cut any more. "Man, I shoulda brought a chain sharpener." Kirk looked at Thorne. "You didn't bring one, did you?"

"What's a chain sharpener?"

Kirk laughed. "Well, if you don't know what one is, then you probably didn't bring one." He loaded the chainsaw and supplies back in the trailer. "A chain sharpener is just a file with just the right slant on it to sharpen the teeth on the chain."

Thorne looked confused. "Teeth?"

"Yeah, kid, you got a lot to learn. Come on. Let's head back to the house."

They unloaded the firewood, stacked it up by the rest of the winter's stockpile. After taking the trailer back to the barn and unhooking from the tractor, the guys walked back to the house.

Kirk went to the kitchen and opened the refrigerator. "You hungry yet?"

"Maybe. What we got?"

"Looks like it's leftover meatloaf or maybe liverwurst for sandwiches. Which will it be?"

"Are you pullin' my leg again? What's this about a bad liver?"

Kirk laughed. "Oh man! You are one crazy kid." He pulled out the makings for sandwiches and pitched a jar of mayo to Thorne. "For your information, liverwurst is a type of sandwich meat. Now fix yourself a sandwich."

"Is it made out of liver?"

"Well, maybe. I don't know."

Thorne pushed the package of deli meat away. "So why would they use the worst kind of liver?"

Kirk ran his hand over Thorne's spiked hair. "Now you're pullin' my leg. Get to eating. We've got more work to do today."

Thorne pretended to be choking on his liverwurst sandwich, ate his potato chips, downed his glass of milk, and ran out the door to play with Noah.

The plan was to have a talk with the boy about his mom and brothers while it was just the two of them. *Naw.* All that back-chat might be more of what Thorne needed. There hadn't been much laughter coming from the little guy until today.

It was four thirty when Katie drove up. She and Brandon got out.

"Hey, you're back. How were your folks?" Kirk said.

"Oh, they're fine. I barely saw Dad. He and Brandon were stuck together like two strands of duct tape most of the day. He took Brandon to Chuck E. Cheese while Mom and I made ourselves salads at home. So how'd your day go with Thorne?"

"It was a good day for both of us. We managed to get some firewood cut and hauled in after a lot of foolin' around earlier. Thorne is a pretty funny guy. You should ask him to tell you the story about the possum and the rabbit." Kirk opened the gate to let the dairy cows march in to their allotted spots. "We also had a crazy conversation about liverwurst."

"I can imagine," Katie said. "So you guys didn't eat that stuff, did you?"

"Yeah, why?"

"You know it's been in the fridge for a week now."

Kirk gulped. "Oh man! Thorne may be right."

"What about?"

"He was calling it bad liver—you know, as in liver *worst*."

"You guys! Okay, I'm going on up to the house and see what the little prankster is up to. You and Brandon come on up as soon as you finish. I'll have supper ready—and it won't be liver!"

23

Johnny Barrow strolled into the DFS office with a Bible in his hand. "I'm Johnny Barrow. I have an appointment with Mrs. Sawyer." He was wearing a pair of black dress pants, a wrinkled canary-yellow button-down Oxford shirt with a four-inch-wide melon-colored tie—twenty years out of fashion. He led his girlfriend by her hand into Betty's office.

Betty suppressed a laugh, shook his hand, and said hello to Dana. "Johnny, you certainly have a different persona from the last time you were here. How's life been treating you?"

"Life is good, Mrs. Sawyer. Dana has a new job, and I start work tomorrow with my uncle, doing roofing."

"That's good. Dana, what type of work do you do?"

"I'm carhoppin' at a Sonic over on Santa Fe." She glanced over at Johnny. "I lost my good job with the big layoff at the GM plant."

"Oh, I read about that layoff—over four hundred people, wasn't it?"

"Yes, since I was one of the newest employees, I knew I'd be one of the first to go."

Johnny laid the Bible conspicuously on the desk in front of him. "I'm happy to say I've got my own place now. Dana and I have moved into my dad's old house. It was in need of a lot of repair, and I've been working on it for the last couple of months. But I finally finished, and we're all moved in. There's even an extra bedroom for Thorne."

Betty glanced at his Bible on the desk. "What about your other brother Josh? Have you made plans for him as well?"

"Oh, Josh—he may be a hopeless case. The kid was strung out on drugs before I left for my 'vacation' in McAlester." He glanced over at Dana. "My parents couldn't do anything with him, so he may be where he's supposed to be for now."

Betty lowered her glasses and looked over at Johnny. "No child is a hopeless case. I'm surprised you would feel that way. Josh deserves to be treated the same as his younger brother."

Dana elbowed Johnny slightly.

"Uh…I'd like to give Thorne some time to get settled in first and then see about bringing Josh home too. You know, families need to be together, not separated."

"According to my records here, Josh is about to turn eighteen. He will be free at that point to live wherever he chooses."

"Well, Josh will choose to live with us. That's what the Barrows family is all about. We stick together, no matter what. It's like I said, families need to be together, not separated."

"I agree with that—in most cases." Betty looked down at the case file before her. "Johnny, have you had any contact with your mother since your release from McAlester?"

"No, and I hope I never do."

Dana's elbow was on duty again.

"Uh…I mean, she abandoned my little brothers. Walked out on them when Dad blew away her lover. I have nothing to say to the woman."

Betty laid her glasses down on the desk in front of her. "She is still your mother. That part will never change. Now, I agree with you—walking out on the boys and not coming back is irresponsible. However, we don't know her situation. Is she out there somewhere, or has she somehow met with foul play?" Betty hesitated. "Do you know?"

"Look, Lana Lou Barrow made her decision when she walked out. She was fed up with the kids. You should have seen that house when I went back there to start work on it. It was filthy—trash all over the place, dirty dishes on every square inch of the kitchen countertop. Took me forever to clean up the mess. She wasn't a good mother. She only cared about herself. She was unfaithful to my dad. He walks in and finds her in bed—"

"Yes, Johnny, I know the story." Betty paused and then pushed Johnny's Bible toward him a bit. "So tell me, Johnny, are you a religious person?"

He reached up, took the Bible, and placed it in his lap. "Yes, ma'am, I am."

"So you consider yourself to be of the Christian faith?"

"Yes, ma'am!"

"Johnny, my Bible teaches us to forgive. It also says to honor your father and mother—even if they don't sometimes deserve honor."

Johnny gripped the Bible and said nothing.

"Look, it's not my job to be preaching, but I hope you'll address the anger you have for your mother. Let's wait and see if we can find her and get her side of the story. You know, she didn't have an easy life. Your dad had been in and out of jail, she had no way to make a living for you kids. I'm not defending her actions, I'm just saying let's not be quick to judge when we haven't lived in her skin."

Johnny ran his fingers through his greased-down dark hair, the comb tracks running around the sides of his head like furrows in a recently plowed field. "Okay, I see what you're saying. So when can I take my little brother home with me?"

Betty crossed her hands on top of the Barrow file. "We will not be rushing into any type of permanent custodial situation for Thorne. As I explained to you the last time you were here, I am working with the CASA volunteer to try to find your mother. If we don't find her, I will be taking a look at the possibility of Thorne coming home to you or another family member eventually. But—and please understand this—I will have to approve of the home you would provide for him. You will have to show me you can keep a job for a minimum of six months. I'll need to know you will have adequate finances to support your little brother. And, more importantly, I'll need to see that you have a genuine interest in him—without anger."

"Hey, Thorne is my brother. Of course I've got a genuine interest in him. I just told you, us Barrows stick together."

Betty ignored that comment and continued, "If I should find out that Mrs. Barrow has met with foul play and is now deceased—"

Johnny stood up with the Bible in his hand. "So you're tellin' me I can't get Thorne back unless Lana Lou is dead!"

"No, not exactly. I'm saying I want to cover all bases first. I hope to find her alive and have a visit with her. If that is just not possible, then I will look to another family member—possibly you—to see if a custodial arrangement would be possible."

"Okay, so when do I get to see him?"

"I can't give you a definitive answer to that. It depends on you. And when I feel that is a possibility, the visits will have to be supervised at first. That means here in my office."

"Look, lady! You can't keep my brother from me! He's my brother. I should be able to see him."

"Johnny, I just told you, I may be able to agree to a supervised visit here in my office at some future date, but I can assure you that you will not be granted custody of the child until I am convinced you are the best source of capable and proper care of Thorne."

Johnny flung the Bible to the floor, grabbed Dana's wrist, pulling her up out of her chair, and led her toward the door. A string of profanities trailed behind him as he walked out. The glass in the upper part of the door rattled as it was slammed shut.

Betty walked over and picked up the Bible he had left behind. She waited a minute to make sure he wasn't coming back for it. Then she opened it to the presentation page at the front. It read *Lana Lou Barrow.*

24

Brandon sat at his desk. He had just finished his homework, and Thorne was lying on the floor a few feet away, playing with Noah. "You got that math paper done?"

"Nope. It's too hard."

"You can't just give up on it. You gotta finish it and turn it in. You told me it was due tomorrow. Go get it, and I'll help you with it."

"Nope. I already trashed it, and I ain't diggin' it out. She can give me a big fat F. I don't care!"

"You're being really stupid! You can't just decide to be okay with an F. Go dig the paper out of the trash, or I'm tellin' Mom."

Thorne retrieved the paper and tossed it in front of Brandon. "Stupid math! Who would ever use that anyway? That's why they got calculators now."

Brandon spent the next hour working with Thorne on his math problems. Thorne kept trying to get Noah's attention instead. Katie peeked in the door and called Noah to come with her. Brandon patiently kept going over the same thing. "You should look at your math book. It's right there for you—plain as day."

"No, Brandon," he drawled in a mocking stretch of syllables, "it ain't plain as day!" He shoved the book away. "You just like to make everyone believe all this homework is easy. I think you and your redheaded buddy just cheat your way through."

"Okay. Just go ahead and get your stinkin' F in math. I tried to help you. You've got an attitude that's really gettin' under my skin! Why don't you just go on back to your own room now?"

Thorne stayed put, looked back at the door, and ran his hands through his prickly hair. "I'm sorry. Math is just really hard for me."

Brandon leaned back in his chair and stuck his foot up on his desk. "Well you aren't makin' it easy for me to help you. You should ditch the nasty attitude, and you might learn something!" He tossed the unfinished math paper to Thorne. "I think that's what the preacher was saying last Sunday. Don't you ever listen?"

Thorne bristled. "You can keep your stinkin' religion, Brandon! Religion's just for all you good little Sunday school boys. It ain't for guys like me."

"It's guys like you who need it the most!"

"Shut your piehole!" Thorne stomped out of the room, trying to unbutton the new shirt Katie had bought him as he walked out. He became frustrated with the stubborn buttons and yanked hard, snapping buttons off. "I hate shirts with stupid buttons. I'm goin' to bed!"

Kirk's baritone voice resonated from out in the hall. "Hey, guys, it's time to hit the sack—time for prayers. Brandon, I'll be in there in a minute."

When he walked into Thorne's room, there was a sniffle coming from the jack-and-jill bathroom between the boy's rooms. When he knocked, Thorne walked out. Tears were streaming down his face. Kirk wrapped his arm around him. "Hey, pal, what's that all about?"

Thorne swiped at his eyes and face. "I'm sorry."

"Sorry for what?"

He looked up at Kirk, and the tears broke loose again. "It treat others really bad. I just got through telling Brandon to shut his piehole—and he didn't deserve that! I called his friend a red-headed bozo—and he's really a nice kid. What's wrong with me?"

"Come on over here and have a seat." Kirk sat down on Thorne's bed and patted the area next to him. "Hey, pal, the only thing that might be wrong with you is you need to learn to love others. Christ teaches that, says to love one another. The Bible says three things will last forever—faith, hope, and love. He says the greatest is love." Kirk looked around the room. "Where's your Bible we gave you? I wanna show you something."

Thorne walked over to his dresser and pulled it out of the bottom drawer and handed it to Kirk.

Kirk flipped through the pages. "I think I know where it is—okay, yeah, here in First Peter, four and eight (1 Peter 4:8), '**Above all, love each other deeply, because love covers over a multitude of sins.**' God *is* love, and He gave us the ability to love."

"I'd like to do that—love others more—but you should just take a look at where I come from. My whole family—"

"Thorne, Thorne! I've told you many times, you can be who you want to be. You are not imprisoned by the genes you inherited."

"Well, how do I break loose from that? I've heard Mom tell us all, 'We are who we are.' I can't change that!"

"No, pal, *you* probably can't—but Jesus can. All you have to do is have a little talk with Jesus—just like we've been doing every night. You always ask Him to help you find your mom. Well, you can ask Him one other thing."

"What?"

"Ask Jesus to forgive you of all your sins. Tell Him you are very sorry for being mean, rude, and hateful. Ask Him to give you a love in your heart for others."

"That's all there is to it?"

"Yep, but you should determine that you will try your very best to do what is right from here on."

"I don't know how to say it. Would you help me?"

"Yeah, pal, I would be glad to help you say it."

After they prayed together, Thorne reached up with both arms and bear-hugged Kirk. Kirk pretended to be hurt by the powerful hug. "Wow! That's a pretty big squeeze you got there. I think you must be growin' some nice biceps on them arms."

With his arms still wrapped around Kirk's shoulders, he gave a gentle tap with his fist to Kirk's back. "I love you, Kirk."

"Yeah, pal, I love you too. You feel better?"

Thorne suddenly turned loose and started out of the room. "I gotta go tell Brandon I just made Jesus my friend."

Kirk grinned, walked out of the room, and bumped into Katie, who was standing on the other side of the door and to the right, listening. "That was awesome!" she said. "I knew it would happen sometime."

Kirk planted a kiss on her cheek. "Yeah, but it had to be in his time, not ours."

"You tilled the ground, planted the seed, and kept watering it. You did your part. God said it was time, and Thorne responded."

25

THE PHONE RANG. It was Betty Sawyer. Katie exhaled heavily. *God, don't let her be taking Thorne from us now.* "What's up, Betty?"

"Katie, do you remember our trail ride out there on the ranch a few years back?"

Good! So it wasn't about Thorne. "Sure, Betty, are you ready for another ride?"

"Oh, thank you, I was hoping you'd ask. Remember, we said we'd have to do that from time to time. Well, time has gotten away from me. They keep me running so much I don't even have time to spend with my husband like I'd like to. I hardly even cook anymore. We just run down the street and grab the latest special of the day at our favorite restaurant. I'm worn out. I need a break."

"So when do you want to come out?"

"It's gotta be some weekend. They keep me buzzing from court dates to office meetings, and I've got a caseload that keeps me roaming this city from one side to the other and in between. You know, this job used to take me to troubled homes in the inner city, but now I'm removing kids from middle—even upper—class neighborhoods. I blame it all on one huge evil. Drugs! Okay, see I am really tired. I just keep rattling on. So what do you have on your agenda for this Saturday? Would that work for you?"

"Sure, that will work for me. Come on out early morning like you did the other time. I'll have us a good old farm breakfast ready."

"Hon, can I bring anything?"

"Just your boots and a pair of old not-too-tight jeans."

It was Betty's familiar knock on the door—five knocks, a pause, then two more. She opened the big eight-foot alder arch top door. "Hey, girl! I'd recognize the shave-and-a-haircut, six-bits knock anytime. Come on in. I see you remembered your boots."

"Yes, I dug them out of the back of my closet. I haven't had them on since you and I went riding, what, one, two years ago?"

"Actually, I think it's been more like three years. Come on over and pour yourself a cup of coffee. I need to get these biscuits out of the oven."

Katie set the big fluffy golden-brown biscuits on the butcher block table.

Betty sniffed the air. "My gosh! Look at the size of those things! How do you get them to fluff up so tall? I've tried to bake my own biscuits a couple of times, and they always look more like pancakes than biscuits."

"Don't roll out the dough so thin. Keep it at least an inch thick—more if you can. Would you like to scramble some eggs for us? The skillet's right there on the burner, and I've already seasoned and whipped up the eggs in that bowl. Just heat up the skillet and dump them in."

"Where are Kirk and the boys?"

"Kirk took the guys down to the pond to fish. He bought a johnboat so they could get out on the big pond. He's already got our horses mounted up and ready to go, but he and the boys took the truck, so we'll have to ride the four-wheeler down to the stables."

Betty dumped the egg mixture in the skillet and started stirring. "We could just take my Buick, but I'd rather ride on the four-wheeler. Just don't tell anyone I rode without a helmet."

"Oh you can wear mine. Brandon's will fit me."

After the scrambled eggs, hash browns, thick-sliced bacon, and those giant buttermilk biscuits with homemade blackberry jam, Betty started clearing the dishes. Katie carried a few to the sink. "I'll just give these a quick douse with the spray hose. We'll leave them here and I'll do them later."

"You sure?"

"Yes, but if I know Kirk, he'll come in, see them in the sink, and work them up himself."

"You're kidding. Kirk does dishes?"

"Sure. We all do. This ain't no one-hen chicken coop. We all live here—even my three roosters—we all jump in and do the chores, whether it's chores in the barn or in the house."

"Amazing. You trained him like that?"

"No, that's just my Kirk. He's always been like that." She grinned. "He knows he'd better because he knows he'll need my help with the cattle at times."

"So you help out with the cattle too?"

"See, on a farm or a ranch, it takes all hands. Are you ready to head on down to the stable?"

Betty crawled on behind Katie on the ATV. Katie turned the key, revved the engine a bit, and popped it in gear. When she let out on the clutch, the old Honda Rancher leaped forward. She looked back. Betty had one hand on the grab bar. The other was plastered to the top of her helmet. Katie squeezed the throttle with her thumb, and the Honda bolted forward. At the stables, she braked to a sudden stop and jumped off. With a cloud of red dust surrounding them, she held out her hand for Betty.

"Katie!" Betty screamed. "You about scared the pants off me! I didn't know this was a NASCAR track!"

"Sorry, I'm just used to getting to where I'm going in a hurry. We'll take it easier going back."

Dandy and Lilly were waiting, saddled up and ready. Katie helped Betty to get one foot in the stirrup, gave her a shove, and Betty belly-rolled over the back of the horse. When she finally managed to pull her right leg over and sit up in the saddle, she burst out laughing. "Well, now we both know I'm not a cowgirl!"

Katie laughed. "Yeah, and the horse knows it too."

Lilly walked unguided through the stable door and waited outside. Betty took the reins that were wrapped loosely around the saddle horn. "Are we going to take the horses up to the water trough before we head out?"

"Yes, you remembered. They need a good drink first." Katie stepped into Dandy's stirrup and slung the other leg over the saddle. "I'm right behind you. Let's go."

It was a warm, sunny day with a virgin sky—not one cloud to interrupt the cornflower-blue pallet hovering over them. The two women rode northward for about a half mile, watched as a flight of geese flew overhead, and saw a red fox dart around a grove of redbud trees, just beginning to sprout buds of flamingo-pink.

The conversation centered on the beauty they were soaking in, but eventually it turned to all things female—shopping in particular. Katie talked about how the boys were sprouting out of their jeans. "I feel badly. Thorne's been wearing high-waters for a good while now. I can't keep him in jeans. He not only outgrows them, but he is the roughest kid I've ever seen on clothes. I've already used up his clothing allowance—that doesn't last long with prices the way they are—and I keep back most of Brandon's clothes he outgrows for Thorne, but Thorne tears them up or stains them so badly I can't get them clean."

Dandy and Lilly were strolling on down through the big bluestem grass on their own. Both women had dropped the reins over the saddle horns. "Katie, I know where you can buy kids' clothes dirt cheap. I've sent several of my foster moms there to buy clothes for the kiddos. They're secondhand, of course, but they're all clean and in very good shape—most are like new. It's a little out of the way, but it might be worth the drive over."

"Sure. Sounds good to me," Katie said. "Where is this place?"

"It's over on Sheridan. You know where the Greyhound terminal is?"

"Oh gosh, that is a ways over there, but I've got to buy him some clothes or he's going to be made fun of at school."

"Give it a try. It's called Klassy Kidz Downtown, and it's in the next block north of the Greyhound terminal. I shop there for my grandkids, and my picky daughter-in-law never knows."

"Hey, girl, let's ride back over to the old cabin where I ran those boys out last time you were here."

"Yes, I remember. That was a sight I'll never forget. You had those hooligans scared out of their wits, and all you had to do was reach behind you for that invisible pistol. Then you chased after them like Annie Oakley."

"Well, hey, they had no business cutting class—and they sure had no business tarring up their lungs with those nasty cigarettes."

"Hon, all I can say is, if I ever need a bodyguard, I'm gonna call on you. You even had me scared! I just knew you were going to pull out a pistol from behind and start shooting at them."

This time, the cabin was vacant, except for a huge rat that ran between Betty's legs when she ventured inside. "Okay, that does it! Let's get outta here!" Betty did her belly-roll act again, mounting the horse. "This old gray lady ain't what she used to be—and I'm not talking about the horse."

"Let's go see what the guys have caught. Maybe we'll have fresh bass for supper."

When they got down to the big pond, Kirk reached over the side of the johnboat and held up a stringer of fish. "Okay, girls," he hollered, "we've got seafood for supper tonight."

"Seafood? Now really!" Katie said.

Brandon stood up in the boat and hollered out, "Well, you *see* it, don't ya—and it's gonna be *food*—seafood!"

"Okay, okay. I get it." She looked over at Betty perched on top of the small horse. "You do like bass, don't you?"

"Oh yeah, but I wasn't planning on staying for supper."

"Kirk, we're going to head on back to the stable. Will you take care of Dandy and Lilly for us? I'll make us a good slaw, fry some potatoes, and bake some hush puppies to go with the bass. Brandon, you and Thorne clean the fish, while Dad's putting the horses up."

When they got back to the stable, Betty crawled off her horse and handed the reins to Katie. "Now let's see if old Bowlegged Betty can waddle back to the house."

"You forget. We don't have to walk. We've got the four-wheeler."

Betty stared at Katie. "I sure hope my life insurance is paid up."

26

"You blew it, Johnny! There is no way DFS will ever allow you to get custody of your little brother."

"Look, Dana, that old biddy just needed to see I am serious about getting Thorne back. He's got no one else. I'm the only family he has left. They have to. What's more, I'm countin' on DFS furnishing some support. They're havin' to pay out monthly for foster care for him now, so there's no reason why they wouldn't be willin' to do the same for a family member."

"You're nuts, Johnny! It's all about money, isn't it? You don't care about Thorne. You only want a monthly check!"

Before she could move out of his way, he had hurled the heavy set of keys in his hand at her, clipping the edge of her right ear. Obscenities spilled out of him as he turned and punched at the wall, leaving a hole in the same spot Dana's dad had repaired earlier. He turned back around to face her, and his balled fist was oozing red as he stooped over and sat in midair. He leaned back and slid down the wall and on the floor. "Baby, I'm sorry. I didn't mean to—"

"I thought you actually cared about Thorne. And now I see all you are after is a stinking monthly check from the state."

"Baby, I do care about Thorne. I just figured they could help us out with his support. It's not about the money. I just want him back with me. He looks up to me, thinks I hung the moon."

"No, you just hung yourself with that caseworker!"

"Shut up, woman! You don't know nuthin' about handling people. You gotta hold your ground. I couldn't walk in there with my tail tucked between my legs, beggin' for them to let me see my brother."

"Look, you don't get your way by pushing people around and throwing things. Why don't you try a little kindness?" She touched her ear and brought her hand back to see if it had been bleeding. "I was embarrassed the way you acted. You've been doing the same thing with Dad. He's not gonna take it anymore. He's about fed up with you, and that caseworker probably is too!"

Johnny looked up toward Dana. "Your dad's a jerk! Thinks he knows more than anyone else. Treats me like I'm a danged two-year-old. Truth is, I'm fed up with him!"

Dana pitched the heavy key ring to him just as Johnny looked away. The keys struck a blow between his legs. He bent over in pain, and Dana's hands went to her mouth, "Oh, dang! Johnny, I'm sorry."

"You little…"

"Johnny, I'm sorry. I thought you'd catch them."

She moved toward him in a show of sympathy. He raised his leg and thrust his foot full force into her stomach. "Now, how does that feel?" She fell to the floor.

"You ain't sorry. You hit your target." As he was walking out of the room, he muttered, just loud enough for her to hear, "You know, you get this way every time I say anything derogatory about your do-no-wrong dad."

Dana lay on the floor, clutching her stomach. Two, maybe three minutes passed. Johnny walked back in, sat down on the floor beside her, and touched her shoulder. "Baby, I'm sorry. I didn't mean to…"

She was quiet for a bit, and then looked up at him with rage blazing from her eyes. "Johnny Barrow, you said it exactly right. You are sorry!"

He reached for her hand. "Come on, babe, let's get up and forget about this. I just lost my temper, that's all. I thought you—"

"That's the trouble with you, Johnny. You don't think, period!" He tried to take her hand and she slapped it away. She grabbed the big wad of keys in front of her, got up, and started toward the door.

"Where're you goin' with them keys?"

Dana turned back toward Johnny, seething. "We are through! I'm not takin' your abuse anymore!" He tried to block the door. "Get outta my way, Johnny!" She pushed her way through. "I'll have my dad come over and get my stuff."

"Dana! Wait! We can work this out."

27

It was Saturday. Brandon had no desire to go with Katie and Thorne to shop for school clothes, so she dropped him off at her folks' house. Brandon was pumped. "This time, I'm gonna beat the socks off Grandpa."

"So it's going to be chess for you guys again today?"

"Yep, Grandpa's gonna eat my dust today! I've been stratergining."

"Don't you mean strategizing?"

"Yeah, that." Brandon grinned. "Dad bought me a book on how to win at chess. I've learned some very cool moves. Grandpa's gonna be shocked!"

"Well, I don't know. My dad's the chess expert. I can't ever beat him at his game. He's pretty clever. You'll have to stay more than a couple of steps ahead of him to outwit the old slyboots."

"Naw, he won't know my new tricks. After I've beat the britches off him, he'll be sittin' there with his finger up to his face, deep in thought, and saying, 'How'd he do that?'"

"Okay." Katie smiled. "You go beat the britches off him. I don't think I've ever seen that. Now, Thorne and I need to get rolling. I'll see you later. You'll probably have time for several games."

Thorne's high-waters and two-sizes-too-short Converse High Tops were the reason for the shopping trip to Klassy Kidz Downtown. Thorne crawled in the front seat beside Katie and buckled up. Katie glanced over at the shirt he had on. "Thorne, your shirt is a mess! I'll never get that clean. How did you get it so stained?"

"I slid into first base at recess. I guess that's grass stains with some dirt mixed in."

"And look, it's even ripped. I should always pick out your clothes for you. You can't wear stuff like that!"

"Well, you said we were gonna be shopping for me some clothes, so I didn't think it would matter. I'll be getting new ones now."

"Just the same, you let me see what you're going to wear before you go out in public. People are going to think I'm a terrible mother!"

The drive downtown was several miles through heavy traffic. Katie had to park about five blocks away from the area where she had passed the clothing store. There were no parking garages or nice, paved parking lots, just on-street parallel parking. The big extended cab Ford wouldn't fit in just any spot. She circled the block after she saw in her rearview mirror another pickup pull out.

As she tried to maneuver into the vacated spot, Thorne said, "You think you can actually get this big tank in there?"

"Watch me." She slipped the big truck squarely between the two parked cars.

"Nice job," Thorne said.

"Thanks. Now if these two cars will just stay here, I'll be able to get out easily enough, but if someone else pulls in too close and blocks me in, we'll be stuck."

Thorne had unbuckled his seat belt and was reaching for the passenger door. "I thought you saw that store way back there. So are we gonna walk all the way back from here?"

"That's okay, we'll get our exercise in today."

A few boarded-up storefronts lined the way toward the thrift store. They passed a seedy-looking tattoo parlor, a New Age shop, and an embarrassingly graphic signage on the front of an adult bookstore. She held Thorne's hand. "I'm not sure this was such a good idea. Stay right with me." She grinned. "I might need you to protect me."

"You'll be safe with me." Thorne's cocky arrogance emerged. "I'm used to these kinds of places. Just don't go wanderin' off on your own."

The Greyhound terminal was just ahead. There was a wrinkled old brown-skinned gentleman leaning against the wall of a store adjoining the Greyhound building, thin as a sanded-down toothpick, smoking what looked like a cigarette he had rolled himself. With one hand stuffed deep into his well-worn and faded Levi's pocket, he raised the other tobacco-stained hand in a friendly greeting and grinned. His eyes slowly laddered up and down Katie. *Creepy.* She gripped Thorne's hand tighter and picked up the pace.

Thorne caught her drift, and his changing voice cracked out loudly. "Don't worry, I could take him. He's just a used-up old geezer who still thinks he's the real tomcat."

Katie felt the blood rush to her face. "Come on," she whispered.

A teen with a thick mane of dark-brown hair hanging past his shoulders darted around the corner, his pants inching closer to the ground with each step he took. Another teen clone chased after him, refusing to move out of the way of Katie and bumping into Thorne. "Hey, move over, punk!" Thorne shouted.

"Stop it! You're going to land us in a heap of trouble," Katie said. "Come on, let's hurry. I don't like this place one bit. I wish we'd never come."

Just as they turned the corner, a big gallon jar with a few coins in the bottom was being shoved toward her. The spotted old hand holding the jar was shaking. The old woman's face—a very sad-looking one, maybe even angry—stared at her. Katie started to reach for her purse to find a few coins to drop in the jar.

Suddenly, Thorne broke loose and bolted ahead.

"Thorne! Thorne, wait! Stay with me—"

"Mom?" Thorne was now in front of a shriveled little lady with cracked brown skin and gray-streaked, greasy, beaver-brown hair, sitting on the sidewalk with her legs and feet pulled up close to her, holding a Folgers coffee can. "Mom! Mom, is that you?"

28

Katie raced forward. Thorne was only a couple of steps ahead now. "Mom! It's me—Thorne!"

Katie stood stock-still. *Could this really be?*

Surprise cloaked the lady's wrinkled face. She quickly turned away. Then she looked back; her whole body shook. A couple of coins were evicted from her coffee can, spilling onto the sidewalk in front of her. She ducked her head inside her big wraparound coat. "Go away, baby." The voice was somewhat muffled inside the oversized blanket of fleece. "Please, sugar. You don't wanna see me like this."

Thorne was touching her now. "Mom, what's wrong? Where have you been?" Then he reached around, took her face in his hands, and pulled it toward him.

Simultaneous sets of tears emptied from the faces of both mother and son. He knelt down on the sidewalk beside her and reached both arms around the frazzled lady.

Katie stood back with her hand covering her mouth. She watched as tears continued to pour from the faces of both mother and son.

Lana Lou was shaking so violently now, she dropped the can. Her remaining precious pennies, nickels, and dimes scattered out, and some rolled down through the nearby gutter grid.

Thorne's arms were still draped around her as he beat his fist softly into her back. "Mom, why did you leave us?" Their tears commingled between their touching faces.

The anger Thorne seemed to once have toward his mother had vanished now. Deep sobs continued as he gently pounded her back and held his face to hers.

Katie waited, her fingers touching her chin. *Dear God, this just has to be your work. I don't know what is right.*

After the sobbing had subsided a bit, Katie knelt down beside them. Lana Lou turned toward Katie. "Who are you?"

Katie started to answer, but Thorne broke in. "This is my foster mom."

Katie took the woman's hand. "I'm Katie Childers, and I think I can guess you are Lana Lou Barrow." The skeletal hand pulled back. "You know, Thorne has told me a lot about you. He has really missed you."

"I...I'm sorry he has to see me like this."

"Oh, sweetie," Katie said. "Don't worry about that. I believe this has been God bringing you two together again."

Lana Lou took Katie's hand and held on this time. "Mrs. Childers, I am such a failure. I think God has forgotten about me."

Katie felt her own tears forming. "First of all, please call me Katie. And secondly, God has not forgotten you. He loves you and cares about you."

Thorne held on to his mother, still crying. "Mom, I love you too," he said between the sobs. "Miss Katie told me someday I would find you—and she was right."

Lana Lou leaned her head against Thorne's. Her long hair, tangled and stringy, fell against Thorne's face. "Thorne, baby, I am so sorry. I never thought I'd wind up down here, panhandling for enough coins to buy something to eat. Honey, I'm a mess. You don't deserve to see me like this. I'm an embarrassment to my family."

"No, you're not!" Thorne shouted, loud enough that it brought stares from a couple walking toward the door to the terminal. "You're my mom, and I love you." He rested his head just under her chin.

"Hey, guys, I hate to break this up, but why don't we find a place to get something to eat. I'm starving."

Lana Lou stared at Katie with suspicion written on her face. "I can read right through that. You don't look hungry to me, so you don't need to do that for me. I make it. It's tough out here on the streets, but I make it."

"Well, I could use a sandwich and a good cup of coffee anyway. We could sit down and visit. I think Thorne needs that."

"Ka…Katie, there's a sandwich shop just around the corner. I guess we could go there."

Katie stood up and tapped Thorne's shoulder. "Come on. Let's help your mom get up."

Katie ordered three turkey club sandwiches with potato chips for them, coffee for the two adults, and a Sprite for Thorne.

Lana Lou felt in her pockets. "Katie, I lost all of the money I had back there on the sidewalk. I can't pay for my sandwich and coffee."

"Hon, you don't need to. I'm buying."

Their number was called. Katie picked up the food, brought it back to their table, and sat down.

Lana Lou took a sip of the black coffee. "This hits the spot. Thank you." She picked up her sandwich and smiled. Thorne quickly downed his Sprite, but he wrapped his sandwich neatly in a napkin and laid it aside.

"Lana Lou, do you have a place to stay, or have you been out here on the streets all winter long?"

"It's just me and the street. I make it okay. I spent a few days in Pauls Valley during that last ice storm, but other than that, I've been right here. I've got no other place to go."

"You could come home," Thorne said.

Lana Lou touched his hand. "Son, I couldn't make it like that. I can't get a job. I don't have an education…I…I couldn't even pay to turn on the electric or water."

"I'd help you, Mom. I could get a job."

"That's sweet of you, but it wouldn't work. To tell you the truth, I don't think I could ever stand to go back to that old house. The whole thing was my fault. John killed a man—that was my fault. My boys are scattered—that's my fault. So now I just exist out here on the streets. That's what I deserve."

"No, you don't! You don't deserve that," Thorne burst out. "I want you to come home—"

Katie broke in. "He is right. You don't deserve to live like that. You are God's child, and He wants something better for you."

"Katie, I told you, God don't know me. He gave up on me two years ago. I made some really bad decisions. God might work with good people, but He don't work with people like me."

"That's not true, Mom! I was bad—really bad—and I decided to make Jesus my friend." Another tear popped out of the corner of his eye. "You can do the same thing."

Lana Lou put her hand over Thorne's. "Baby, I'm happy for you, but I have to tell you something. Maybe God can forgive me, but I will never be able to forgive myself."

She took the first tiny bite off her sandwich. "You probably already know why your dad shot that man. I was wrong—so wrong! John was my husband—still is, I guess—so I was wrong to do what I did. Yes, I was lonely and broke. I couldn't even buy food for you boys. I foolishly thought that man would be our meal ticket." She set her sandwich down and pounded the table with her fist. "I wish I could take it all back!"

Katie reached across the table and took her hand. "Please don't keep beating yourself up over something that happened in the past. What's done is done. God is eager to forgive you and see you move on. Can you do that?"

Lana Lou picked up her sandwich again and then laid it back down. Her brown eyes looked right through Katie. "I'll think about it."

Katie wasn't sure how she should respond to that. She waited and then picked up her own sandwich and finished her coffee.

Her thoughts were interrupted when Thorne startled her. "Can Mom come and live with us?"

Katie's heart sank. "Oh gosh, I wish we could do that. I would take her home with us in a heartbeat…but…"

"But what?"

"But I don't think DFS would allow that."

"You could ask them."

Lana Lou reached over to Thorne. "Honey, I think she's probably right. They wouldn't let me do that. I'll be all right. You don't need to worry about me."

"When will I get to see you again?"

"I don't know… Baby, I don't know."

Katie felt a tear about to surface from her own eye again. "Lana Lou, would we be able to find you here at the same place if we came back to visit?"

"I'm never more than four or five blocks away. Most nights I stay about a block over. I've got a little hideout back there with a tarp. I come here and use their restroom, and if I've got any money, I'll grab a doughnut—and I gotta have my coffee."

"Would they let you use their phone sometime?"

"I don't know. I've never had any reason to ask. Why?"

Katie pulled out one of Kirk's business cards from her purse and circled the number. On the back, she wrote, *Call me anytime!* and signed it, *Katie*. She handed it to the frail woman. "Come on, Thorne, we've gotta get you down to the thrift store and get you some clothes."

Thorne clutched his mom's hand. This separation was going to be difficult, so Katie added a lighthearted ending.

"This kid is growing like a weed. I can't keep him in jeans."

The woman's chin trembled, and her eyes were damp. "I can't either."

29

A late March snowstorm started in Western Oklahoma and slowly made its way to the central parts of Oklahoma, dumping eight inches of blindingly white frosting on the Childers Ranch. The Angus cattle all wore blankets of snow fleece. The air was calm. Cold. Lazy plumes of gray-blue smoke spiraled from the top of the two ranch house chimneys. Brandon had kept the coals glowing in the big fireplace, and Katie had a crock of homemade chicken soup steaming on top of the old wood cook stove. School had been called off.

Kirk watched as Thorne waffled from one activity to the next, never settling down with any one book, TV, or his Game Boy. He pushed Noah away twice. "What's wrong, pal?"

"Nuthin'."

"Well, nuthin's got you in a restless state of mind. I haven't seen you like this in a long time. Hey, you wanna come with me? I need to go break some ice in the water tank up by the barn."

With no visible enthusiasm, Thorne said, "Yeah, sure."

"Well, grab your big coat. It's colder than a witch's—"

"Kirk!" Katie screamed.

"What?" He flashed his famous single-side-of-the-mouth grin at her. "I was just sayin' it's colder than a witch's broomstick in Alaska."

Katie's ruffled brow smoothed. "Kirk, what will I ever do with you?"

"Aw, just roll me in the snow out there and call me the Michelin Man."

"You two get outta here. Hurry back though. I've got hot cherry rolls coming out of the oven soon."

Kirk turned to Thorne and made a silent O with his mouth. "I think we could just wait 'til those gooey goodies come out of the oven, don't you, Thorne?"

***

Kirk pulled the hood of his parka over his head as he got out of the truck. "Hey, pal, grab that ax there beside you."

Katie had made sure Thorne had on his snow boots, his bright orange ski jacket with two layers of flannel shirts she'd bought for him at the thrift store, as well as a new pair of heavily insulated gloves. "Let me chop the ice," Thorne said.

"Okay, lift the ax up high and swing hard. That ice is pretty thick." Snowflakes the size of Pringles potato chips were thickening the sky and gently falling onto the thick mattress of snow already on the ground.

"Where are the horses?"

"They're probably cozied up in the stable. I left the gates open so they could get out and come up here to drink. You think we should go check on them?"

"Yeah," Thorne said. "I think they deserve a full bucket of oats on a day like this." He jumped in the front passenger seat and stared out his side window. A single Angus cow was approaching the water tank. A thick layer of snow covered her back. She bawled loudly and shook the snow from her head. "Why's she bawling like that?"

"Oh, Ronnie and I hauled off a load of calves two days ago, and she's still upset over losing her baby."

Kirk started the pickup and was backing. A tear oozed from Thorne's eye. "Hey, pal, I see that tear there. What's wrong?"

Thorne wiped at his cheek. "I'm just thinkin' about Mom out there in the cold with snow covering her, just like that cow." He stared out the window. "That cow's missin' her baby too." The dam broke loose, and a full flood of tears gushed out.

"Oh man! I'm sorry. I shouldn't have opened my mouth like that. I wasn't even thinking." Kirk put the truck back in park and placed his left foot on the center hump with his right leg doubled up on the seat between them. He placed his hand on Thorne's knee. "Hey, pal, I'm here to listen. Tell me exactly what you are feeling now. I know you're hurting."

The sobs continued. "My mom has no place to live. She's... She's got no money. I know she's got to be fr-freezing. She has no food. She is so... so skinny! She is all alone. I want her to come here. I'll give her my chair and put her right by the fireplace. I'll bring her something to eat. I'll even...I'll g-give her my bed, and I'll sleep on the floor. I..." He tucked his head between his knees and bawled loudly, echoing the cow on the other side of the fence.

Kirk reached over and wrapped his arms around the boy. "I don't know..." His own tears turned to outright sobs, and he joined Thorne in a groan of gut-deep sorrow, finally tapering off to a pulsating whimper. Several minutes passed in silence before Kirk released his hold on Thorne. "Buddy, I just don't have the answer. I wish I did."

Thorne's ski jacket was wet with tears. He grabbed Kirk's hand and squeezed. "I love you, Kirk."

"I love you too, buddy—big time!"

30

Kirk sat down with Katie at the breakfast table and told her about what had happened up by the water tank with the lone snow-covered cow missing her calf. "He asked why the cow was bawling, and before I even thought, I told him Ronnie and I had just hauled off a load of calves and that cow was just missing her baby."

"Oh, Kirk! That just made it worse."

"Yes, I feel so awful! I can't believe I said that. Wish I could take those words back. The guy was bent over with his hands covering his eyes, bawling loudly—just like the cow. I couldn't help myself—I joined in and we just sat there squalling uncontrollably for a good while. It was awful!"

Katie stood up, a distant look in her eyes. "How bad is the ice?"

"What?"

"How bad is the ice on the roads now?"

"Katie, what are you thinking of doing?"

"I'm going to go get Lana Lou!" Katie was already grabbing her coat.

"You are nuts! It was still snowing when we came in. There's ice under that snow. The roads will be a mess."

"Don't we have four-wheel drive in the truck?" She had slipped into her coat and was reaching in the pockets for her gloves.

"Look, I'm not gonna let you go out there in this weather! They probably haven't even cleared any of the roads yet."

"Kirk, I can't let his mother stay out there in this freezing weather—and besides, Thorne needs her!"

"No! You're not going—at least not today." He started to help her out of her coat. "Babe, I don't think DFS would even allow us to do that! You'd better think this thing through." His little one-sided grin appeared. "Think with that analytic brain of yours, not your bleeding heart."

She leaned into his arms. "Kirk, I'm seeing the frail woman now. Her cracked brown skin stretched tight over her brittle bones. She's shivering, hasn't eaten all day—maybe even two or three days—and she's wrapping that ugly big coat around her in a futile attempt to get some warmth."

"That's an awful picture you're painting."

Her balled fist tapped at Kirk's shoulder. "Yes, it's a picture Thorne and I both have etched into our memory. I will never forget it." Katie looked into Kirk's eyes. "So when can I get out to go get her?"

"Katie! Katie, we can't just go get her and bring her into our home here with Thorne. What's the name of the guy who is Betty Sawyer's boss at DFS?"

"Mr. Carrington, Carpenter, Carter, or something. I don't know—why?"

"This Carter-Carrington-Carpenter guy would go ballistic! Betty says he won't budge from the rules on anything. Remember, she told you that."

"Well, let him just go ballistic! It's not his mother shivering out there in this ten-degree weather! If it was, he would go get her and bring her home."

"Honey, we just can't do that. I'm sorry. I wish we could—for Thorne's sake."

Katie started toward the big room. "Where are you going?"

"It's time for the news and weather. I want to see what the weather looks like for tomorrow."

Kirk threw up his arms in exasperation. "Katie, sometimes it seems like I married Margaret Thatcher! When you set your mind to something, no military battalion on earth can change your mind."

She sat down in Kirk's La-Z-Boy, grabbed the remote, and clicked on the TV. "Kirk, you're probably right, DFS probably won't allow me to bring her here. But they can't stop me from taking her something to eat and some warm clothes."

Kirk plopped down on the sofa, leaned his head back, and breathed a sigh of relief. "Okay, now you're putting some brains into action to match that tender heart of yours."

The sun came out the following day and the roads had been cleared according to local reports. Kirk came back to the house after the morning milking, and Katie poured herself a steaming cup of hot chocolate. "You sure you don't want a cup?"

"No, but I'll have that last piece of coconut pie."

Katie put the pie on a dessert plate and handed him a fork. "Do you want to go with me, or should I go alone?"

"You're going in today?"

"Yes, I am. The sun's shining, the roads are cleared, and I've got a few things ready to take to her."

"Okay, I'll drive you over. Wouldn't you rather wait 'til Saturday so Thorne could go too?"

"No, I don't think he needs to see her there right away, maybe later."

"So what are you taking her?"

"I've got one of those reusable Walgreen's shopping bags full of canned food, the kind of cans with a pull ring that doesn't require a can opener. I've put in a package of plastic spoons and forks, two paperback novels, a comb, a toothbrush and sample-size toothpaste, a bar of soap, and a few paper towels."

"All that in one small green shopping bag?"

"Oh, and I'm taking her my sleeping bag. I will never use that thing again. Our last camping trip to Eufaula was my last!"

"Which closet is it in? I'll go get it."

"I've already set it out on our bed. Oh, and grab that big green army blanket of yours next to it. We've never used it."

"Yeah, it's wool. Should be nice and warm. Hey, I've got an idea. Don't we still have an extra school picture of Thorne?"

"Good idea! I'll get it."

Katie pointed out a parking spot not far from the bus station this time. She carried the bulging shopping bag while Kirk grabbed the sleeping bag and blanket. As they walked toward the terminal, Katie saw Lana Lou waving from a half block away. With her coffee can in hand, she stood up and started toward them.

Katie ran to her and took Lana Lou's cold shriveled hand. "Hon, how on earth did you make it through that snow and awful cold?"

Lana Lou's big grin spread across her brown face. "See, that snow was good. It covered my tarp and made for good insulation. I stayed in there most of the day and night. I just came out this morning to see if there's anyone feelin' generous."

Kirk had now reached the two women. Katie turned and took him by the hand. "Lana Lou, I'd like you to meet my husband, Kirk Childers." Kirk gently shook the woman's bony hand. "Kirk is really good to Thorne. You would be pleased."

The withered woman eyed Kirk for a few seconds. "I think I can see that. You've got a kind face. You are probably a lot better for Thorne than his own dad was. John didn't know how to be a good parent. He was way too rough on all the boys."

Katie held the bulging bag of goodies to Lana Lou. "We brought you some things to help out."

"For me? You brought this for me?"

"Yes." Katie dug inside the bag. "Hon, I've got some of those individual-size canned goods. You know, the kind with the pull ring. They don't require a can opener. Here are some plastic spoons and forks, a comb, toothbrush and toothpaste, and a bar of soap.

I put in a couple of paperback novels. I didn't know if you like to read mysteries or not. This one by Terri Blackstock is really good. I think you'll enjoy it. And this one's not a mystery, but almost anything by Lauraine Snelling makes for a good read."

The big sleeves of the blanket coat slid down as Lana Lou's tiny exposed arms reached up for Katie's neck. "You did this for me?"

"Yes, hon, it's for you. I wish I could have gotten up here before that awful cold front came barreling in, but—"

"Lana Lou," Kirk said, "this woman was gonna get in the truck and come up here yesterday with snow and ice still on the ground!"

Lana Lou swiped at her nose with her cracked brown hand. "I don't know what to say. No one does stuff like this for me." She took the overstuffed green bag in her hand. "Let's go find someplace to sit down. I guess my baby's in school today?"

"Yes, he is. Oh! I've got something else for you." She pulled out the picture from her purse. "I thought you might like to have this. It's his latest school picture."

Lana Lou quickly took the picture, looked at it, and held it to her breast. Then she looked at it again. "Oh, that's my boy! He is so handsome."

"Well, it's about lunchtime. Let's go show Kirk our café around the corner. He's agreed to buy lunch for us."

Lana Lou looked at the sleeping bag and blanket under Kirk's arm. "Looks like you guys are planning on camping out here with me tonight."

Kirk laughed. "No, these are for you."

"For me! You brought these for me?"

"Yep, they're for you. I'm planning on sleeping in my own bed tonight." He held up the old, green army blanket. "This thing is really warm. It did a good job of keeping me warm in the drafty old Army barracks many years ago."

"Why don't we take this to my hidey-hole and put it under my tarp. I'll show you where I shut my eyes at night."

Lana Lou had made a cozy den under a roof overhang behind a doughnut shop. There was an old folding chair someone had tossed out, a couple of candle ends, and a foam mattress with a once-white cover. The big, gray tarp above was propped up by a couple of two-by-four boards with some bent rusty nails remaining and some hefty limbs, probably broken off the tree by a recent ice storm. "You've made yourself a dandy, little den here," Kirk said.

The woman held on to the Walgreens bag and carried it in to the café with her. "I guess you're probably going to have to keep those goodies by your side," Katie said. "Someone might latch onto them, huh?"

Lana Lou tried to laugh, but a grinding cough overcame her. "Oh, I ain't about to leave these back at my place. They'd be gone by the time I got back."

"What about your sleeping bag and blanket? Will they be safe there?"

The woman shrugged her narrow shoulders. "We'll see. I sure hope so."

The café was almost empty. Lana Lou led her new friends to a booth near the restrooms. When Kirk asked her what she would like to order, her response was, "Oh, I'll just have coffee, thank you." Kirk easily read through those words and ordered chicken fried steak, mashed potatoes with white gravy, green beans, and hot buttered rolls for Lana Lou and him. Katie wanted a turkey club sandwich. When the food came, he could plainly see the woman hadn't eaten in a long time. All conversation came to a halt when she started to eat.

The subject of a mother-son visitation at the DFS offices came up. Lana Lou looked down. "Do you think they would allow me in their office, lookin' like I do?"

"Hon, you and I will walk in the office together with new duds." Katie tapped her index finger on the table. "I'll see to that!"

31

"Oh, Betty, that is just not right! Thorne needs to see his mother." How could the woman be so callous? The conversation had gotten off to a rough start and steadily declined.

Katie explained to the caseworker how Lana Lou was thrilled about the unexpected visit from her son. "You should have seen the look on her face. At first, she was ashamed for him to see her living there on the street, panhandling. But when Thorne called out to her and ran to her, she hugged her son, cried, and told him over and over how sorry she was to have left him and Josh alone.

"See, I knew for several months Thorne needed to see his mother. He had become depressed, his grades were going nowhere, and he continued to get into fights at school. He was the schoolyard bully. Kirk and I didn't know if that would ever change. He has since dropped his cocky attitude and replaced it with a more penitent outlook. He cries a lot for her. Betty, he needs to have communication with his mom! And she needs to see him."

"Katie, the Department rules are clear on this matter. Thorne has been removed from the home where his mother abandoned him and his brother. You said the woman is homeless and panhandling on the streets. There is no reason to allow a mother-son visitation under those circumstances. Until you disclosed her whereabouts to me, my hopes were for a future custodial arrangement—those were my hopes—but I was afraid she had met with foul play somehow. I expected to see her name in the news and a picture of a corpse being carried away. But now that I know the current situation, the backstory has become clear. We have a change of scene that in no way compliments my original hopes and prospects. I cannot see any form of a happy ending with a reunion of mother and child. It is my opinion visitation under these circumstances would be detrimental to this child."

"I understand the woman can't provide for him now, but that doesn't mean they should never see each other!" Katie's Margaret Thatcher tone was leaping across the phone line. "Come on! That's not even humane!"

"Katie, I cannot allow Thorne to visit his mother in those surroundings. It's not safe, and I'm sorry I even suggested the thrift store to you. Had I known Lana Lou would be so close by, panhandling—hooking—whatever, I would have never told you about that store."

"Betty! The woman is not a hooker! How dare you call her that when you know nothing about her!"

"Well, she was caught in bed with a stranger when her husband walked in on them and shot the man."

"That doesn't make her a hooker! It makes her a woman who made a serious mistake, not a hooker!" She held the phone out from her ear, stared at it a second, before bringing it back in place. "Where's the gentle, caring attitude I've seen in you for the last several years? It's like I don't even know the woman I'm standing here talking to."

"Okay, I probably shouldn't have jumped to conclusions—"

"No, you sure shouldn't have!" Katie paused and allowed that to fester in Betty's ear. "Okay, what if I bring Lana Lou here and let her stay with us?"

"If you do that, I'll be forced to remove Thorne from your home immediately. Katie, you need to get a grip on reality. With the life she is living, the woman is not a fit mother and should have no place in his life. I can't believe you would even consider doing such a stupid thing!"

"And I can't believe you can be so insolent and coldhearted!"

"All right, hon, this conversation is going nowhere. But I'm telling you, this foster child is to have no contact with the woman. Have I made myself clear?"

"All too well! Good-bye."

The temperature was dropping. There was no winter precipitation in the forecast, but the wind howled unrelentingly across Childers Ranch. Thorne had brought in firewood and Brandon was instructing him on the best way to get a fire started. "I always start with a layer of scrap kindling. Then I pile on some pine straw we keep in the big plastic can outside."

Thorne ran out and grabbed a handful, brought it back in, and layered it on top of the small pieces of scrap lumber. He looked up at Brandon. "What's next, bro?"

"Make sure you have some smaller pieces of wood chips or twigs ready. Now strike your match and let it blaze up a bit." Brandon looked at Thorne to make sure he was listening. "You gotta stay right here with it. Now slowly add a few pieces of the wood chips or twigs, letting them catch before you add more. If you throw on too much too soon, you'll smother the fire. Then you'd have to start all over."

"That's what I did wrong yesterday, and the fire just went out."

"Yeah, it will most every time. You gotta add it slowly. Let it breathe. Okay, now you're ready to lay a couple of very small logs, no bigger than a couple of inches in diameter. When those blaze up good, you can put on a bigger log."

"Why did we put the huge log behind to start with? It's not even split like the others."

"That's called the backlog. It helps to throw the heat toward the front and not so much up the chimney. It'll also hold your fire when the front stuff dies down. You gotta keep watch on your fire every now and then. If it gets down to coals only, you're gonna have to add some small pieces, let them catch, and then add a couple of your logs."

Kirk was sitting at the breakfast table with a steaming cup of coffee. "Brandon, you're a good teacher. I think that's your gift. Maybe, when you grow up, you should think about going into education like Katie did."

"Nope, I'm gonna work right here on the ranch with you," Brandon said proudly.

"Thorne, what are you gonna be when you grow up?"

Thorne thought for a moment. "I don't know, but I gotta get a good job so I can help my mom."

"Really?" Kirk said. "That's very admirable of you. That shows me you've got a good heart. A lot of kids would be too selfish to think about helping a parent."

"Yeah, but *my* mom is gonna need my help. It's really getting cold out there. Do you think Mom will be okay?"

"Yes, pal, I do. When Katie and I visited her and took the goodie bag and some bedding to her, she showed us her little den she had fixed up. She did a good job, and it looked like it would be pretty warm. I wouldn't mind hunkering down in a spot like that myself. You don't need to worry about her."

Thorne ducked his head and fidgeted with his fingers. "I do anyway."

32

Katie looked up and down the sidewalk in front of the Greyhound Station. Lana Lou was nowhere in sight. She wasn't inside the café either. *Oh!* Her sleeping den behind the greasy doughnut shop. That's where she'll be. Katie approached the familiar gray tarp. "Lana Lou, are you in there?"

A whisper of a voice penetrated the tarp. "Katie, is that you?"

Katie pulled back the tarp a bit. A raspy cough, more severe than she had heard the last time, bellowed from the frail woman—then another and another. Katie knelt down and crawled inside. She put her hand on Lana Lou's forehead. "Sweetie, you've got a fever, and that cough is not good. I should get you in to see a doctor."

"Oh, I'll—" More coughing erupted, coarse barking breaking loose from the bottom of her lungs, then grinding against her vocal chords. "I'll be all right. This cold night air does it to me." Another round of coughing erupted. "How's my boy?"

"Thorne is doing really well. You would be proud of him. His grades are good, and he's been learning to do the farm chores. You know, a farm or ranch is a wonderful learning experience for a child. Kirk has taken him under his wing, and he is gaining a wealth of knowledge about the cattle and other farm animals—but I don't believe the boy will ever want to be a rancher. He enjoys being with Kirk, but he thinks he can do without all the chores."

"It sounds like Kirk might be just what my boy needs."

"Yes, he is so good with the boys. When Brandon came to us—I think I told you we fostered him and later were able to adopt him—Brandon, of course, knew nothing about farm life. I say 'farm,' but it's really a big Angus cattle ranch. Anyway, Brandon has been helping Kirk with the cattle branding, the milking chores, and about everything else. It's not our ranch. Kirk just manages it."

The fragile little woman laid the back of her hand on her forehead. "I'm glad my baby's got a good place like that—and good people like you and Kirk to care for him. I could see he really likes you two." More coughing forced her to sit up from where she was lying on her tattered old foam mattress. She beat her chest with her fist. "Katie... You know, sometimes life just don't turn out the way you had hoped. I would've never thought I'd wind up like this."

"I know, sweetie, Kirk and I have learned to put our faith in God, and that helps. But, you are right, sometimes things happen which seem to be out of our control. I just have to believe God is the one who is in control, and I have to trust Him. I don't mean that to sound so over-simplified, but it has helped us cope with things we probably couldn't have if we didn't trust him."

The coughing continued, and Katie touched the woman's forehead. She pulled Katie's hand away. "Honey, don't worry about that. I've been worse than this. I'll be all right."

"I'm not sure. I still think we should get you in to see a doctor. Don't you have Medicaid that would pay for doctor's visits?"

Lana Lou tried to sit up. "No. See, you've gotta have an address to get Medicaid help."

"I've got a little money. I could pay for one office visit."

"No, you won't do that. I'll be fine. Spring's a comin' and this nasty cough will go the way this winter weather goes. You know, that blasted wind goes right to my old bones. So, yes, I'll be glad to see some warmer weather. I'd like to see some pretty flowers bloom out, but no flowers grow here around my hangout."

"I've got to be running along," Katie said. "But I brought you another goodie bag. I even put some cough drops in there because I remembered that nasty cough of yours."

"You are a sweetie, Katie. How can I ever thank you?"

"You already do. You love our Thorne. That's thanks enough for me."

Lana Lou lowered her head and said nothing.

Katie touched her hand. "Where's your coffee can?"

"No, Katie, you've done enough already."

Katie looked around but didn't see the can. She reached inside her purse and pulled out a ten dollar bill. She opened Lana Lou's bony hand, put the ten inside, and closed her fingers over it. "I'll be checking on you again soon."

33

Katie grabbed her helmet, climbed onto the old Honda Rancher, and rode up to the mailbox. Report cards would be out any day. She opened the door to the rickety metal mailbox and found two envelopes from Luther ISD.

The first one was Brandon's report card. She smiled as her eyes fell on the grades—all As and one B plus. The only comment at the bottom from Brandon's homeroom teacher was *Brandon is a delight to have in class. He is bright and never disruptive.*

Katie quickly ripped open the second envelope, holding her breath. She unfolded the computer printout—two Cs (one in math and the other in science), a D plus in geography, and a B in reading. "Yes!" she stood up on the ATV and held the paper high above her head. "Good job, buddy! You got a B in reading!" There was no one to hear her excitement. She tucked both printouts back in their envelopes and sat down on them to keep them from blowing away as she rode back to the house.

She stopped at the barn, where Kirk was bottle-feeding a new calf. "Hon, the boys' report cards came." She showed him Brandon's first.

"Way to go, Brandon! You're making me proud." When he looked at Thorne's, his reaction was different. "Well, this one ain't so good! I was hoping he'd do better than that."

"No!" Katie blurted out. "That is actually very good!"

"How do you figure? I mean Cs and a D doesn't sound like a brain child to me."

"Did you even notice the B in reading?"

"Oh yeah—well, that's better."

"Better?" Katie hollered out. "Getting a B in reading for him is a miracle! He wasn't even reading at second grade level, and here he is in third grade, about to go into fourth. Can't you see? This is a huge improvement for him. Now, if he can stay with us, by this time next year, he'll be up with the rest of his class, in every subject."

"I don't see any remarks about his attitude on there," Kirk said. "So what's Mrs. Dalton say about that?"

"I talked to her just last week. She didn't tell me what his grades were going to be, but she said I might be a bit disappointed in the six-week average, but he had made real progress in the last three weeks."

Kirk handed the printouts back to Katie. "Attitude, Kate, what's she saying about his attitude?" He grinned. "That's the part I've been working on. I want to see if I've made any progress with him in that area."

"Yes, there have been no more playground fights, and he's kept his mouth shut and not been disruptive in the classroom."

"Well now," Kirk shouted. "That's something I can get excited about! I think that calls for a celebration."

"What do you have in mind?"

"Water temperature is getting a tad bit warmer now with this past week's near-seventy-degree days. I think I'll take the guys fishin'. They've both been asking when they could get out their fishing gear."

Katie gave him a chilly look. "You can do that, but I was thinking more on the line of Maggie Moo's." She grinned. "And you better make sure to include me this time!"

Saturday afternoon fishing from the johnboat yielded not only a good supper of bass but also sunburns for all three guys. Sunday after church, a trip to Maggie Moo's topped off a nearly perfect weekend. But Monday after school was a different story. Thorne had been taking on the job of cleaning the separator equipment. Kirk came in to check on him.

"I have to tell you something, Kirk."

"What's that?"

"I lost my temper today at school again."

"What happened?"

"It was that redheaded dude again. He thinks he's better than everyone else—like, he told some of my friends I was nuthin' but a ghetto gamecock."

"What'd you do?"

"I started to punch his lights out, but instead I put my hands in my pockets like you told me to. But I still wanted to…well, you know."

"I'm glad you decided to avoid a fight."

"Something just comes over me. It's like my face gets all hot, and I can't help myself."

"But you did!"

"Yeah, this time, but I'm afraid I'll lose it next time."

Kirk reached for the drying towel hanging above the big farm sink. "Do you even know what a gamecock is?"

Thorne's eyes bugged. Then he grinned. "Uh…don't sound good to me."

"A gamecock is a rooster that is bred for fighting. See, you started off the school year with a reputation for fighting. So you kind of brought that label on yourself." Kirk started drying off the equipment Thorne washed up. "Now, since you walked away and didn't start a fight with the kid…that'll probably be the last time he calls you that. You're gradually going to get a better reputation. See if you can make this redheaded dude your friend."

"Yeah, I guess."

"Hey, isn't that Brandon's friend?"

"Yeah, why?"

"Maybe he can help to change the kid's attitude. Talk to Brandon about it. I'll bet he would be willing to put in a good word for you."

"Okay, we'll see."

"Thorne, remember, I said those gamecocks are bred for fighting. You were not! God made you exactly like He wanted—and that wasn't for fighting! There might be a time you have to fight to protect yourself, but that will be very rare—if ever—and you should never be the one who starts the fight."

"Kirk, I'm trying—I really am."

"I know you are. We can see that, and your classmates will start to see that too. Just remember, when you get that hot feeling come over you, put those hands in your pockets. You can never be accused of starting a fight with your hands in your pockets."

Thorne washed the last piece of equipment, and Kirk was drying it. "When will I get to go back and see my mom?"

Kirk laid the towel down and put his arm around Thorne. "I don't know, man. We're working on it. See, the thing is, the caseworker doesn't think you should go to the bus station where your mom stays. It's pretty dangerous down there. We're hoping we can let you meet her someplace else."

"That's pretty weird. She knows where I came from—not exactly the best part of town there."

"Well, I think the caseworker is just following the guidelines of her job."

Thorne ducked his head. "Someone needs to change those stupid guidelines."

"Maybe so, but we're not forgetting about it. We'll keep trying."

"Didn't Katie go down there last week?"

"Yep, Miss Katie's been going down there about twice a week, bringing your mom food and other things."

"I wish I could go too."

"I know, pal. I know."

34

Kirk came back to the house after his morning milking and found Katie sitting at the breakfast table, her finger circling the rim of the empty coffee mug. "Hey, why the gloom and doom?"

Katie looked up at him. "I'm just thinking about my last conversation with my friend Betty. I sort of lost my cool with her."

"You think?" He sat down beside her. "But from what you told me, she could have been a little more diplomatic herself."

"Probably, but two adults should be able to state their opinions without adding that nasty, overused spice of anger to the pot."

"Yeah, but sometimes sugar is overused too. And you know, it's gotta be the real thing when you use it, or it winds up like saccharin—leaves a bitter taste in the mouth."

Katie looked around the room. "Is that my phone or yours?"

"Gotta be yours. Mine's right here on my belt."

"Well, I've got to change my ringtone. I never know if it's mine that's ringing or yours." Katie spotted the flip phone lying on the table by the couch. By the time she got to it, the ringing had stopped. She picked it up and saw the familiar name on the front screen and laid it back down.

"So who was calling you?"

Katie walked back over to the kitchen, poured herself another cup of coffee, and sat down at her spot around the kitchen dinette. She brought the cup to her mouth and then set the phone back down without attempting to answer.

"Kate, you know that drives me nuts. Why do you have to take three detours before answering my question?"

She raised the cup back to her mouth, carefully took a sip of the hot coffee, and set it back down on the table before she looked over at him. "It was the person I was just talking about. Can you believe that!"

Kirk walked over, picked up her phone, and brought it to her. "So call her back."

"Kirk, I'm afraid I won't know what to say. I guess if I was truthful, I would have to say I'm still angry with her."

Kirk put the phone in her hand. "So get over it! Call your friend back. You don't ditch a friend over one heated phone call."

Katie sat there, staring at the phone.

"Kate, all you gotta do is tap the send button. It'll ring her right back."

"Kirk, I know how to use a cell phone. Now, if you'll make yourself scarce, I'll call her back."

Kirk started toward the back door, turned around, and grinned. "Be nice. But remember, saccharin leaves a bitter taste."

Katie stared at the flip phone. *The send button—wow!* That's a lot easier than redialing the number.

One tap of the send button, one ring, and Betty Sawyer answered. "Department of Family Services, this is Betty."

"Betty, this is Katie. I'm sorry. I couldn't get to the phone in time to catch your call. At first I thought it was Kirk's phone. I've got to change my ringtone."

"Well, that is a relief," Betty said. "I thought maybe you saw it was me calling, and you just decided not to answer."

"No, I finally saw the phone on the other side of the room. What's up, girl?"

There was a pause before Betty continued. "Katie, I just wanted to call and apologize to you for being so abrupt—no, rude—on our last phone call. I got to thinking about it, and I realized your compassionate heart was talking, and my legalistic ears were refusing to listen."

"Oh, Betty, I allowed my passion to turn into a bit of a blaze. I should have put a lid on it before it scorched our relationship."

"Honey, our relationship isn't scorched. I just failed to appreciate your Good Samaritan intentions. Please understand—I come in contact with adults every day who have no desire to do what's right for their children. Oh, they will all maintain they do, but the truth is they are too selfish to do that. So many people are just too lazy to get a job and support their offspring."

"And what if they are unable to work at a job? Thorne's mother is very sick. She couldn't hold down a job. She probably couldn't even get one. She doesn't have a high school diploma, and she's never worked outside the home."

"I guess my job has made me a bit calloused. People bring so much of this on themselves."

"I agree. Many times that is the case." Katie hesitated. "I think Lana Lou's case is a bit more complicated than that. The woman endured years of abuse from that awful man she was married to. I guess you could say she should have chosen her life mate better, but she was fourteen when she got pregnant with their first child. What fourteen-year-old knows how to pick a good mate?"

"Katie, you've met with Lana Lou. Do you think there is any reason to believe the woman can ever pull herself off the streets and give up her destructive lifestyle?"

"Yes, I do believe she can." Katie slapped at her right knee bouncing under the table. "Lana Lou Barrow is a good person. She loves all three of her children, but Thorne holds a very special place in her heart. She doesn't talk about the other two much."

"I can see why," Betty said. "That oldest one is gonna wind up back in prison—you just wait and see. I don't trust him one bit. He'd probably steal from her right there on the street! And the middle boy is a mess too."

Katie took a sip of her now-cold coffee and set it back down. "I believe those two older boys' attitudes and behaviors can be blamed on their father, not Lana Lou. And another thing—if Thorne's father hadn't been put away, the boy would have followed down the same path as his brothers. John Barrow is the monster in this family, not Lana Lou."

"Okay, so tell me, do you think there is any hope of Thorne's mother ever rejoining society as a respectable, wage-earning, and decent person capable of caring for Thorne?"

"Yes, I do." Katie instantly gave a thumbs-up, even though she was alone.

"How?"

"I don't know, but I've got some ideas. I will not give up until I've exhausted every one of them."

"Hon, you amaze me! I just can't understand how you can be so determined to rescue a stranger living on the streets and begging money for food, or booze, or whatever.

"She's not a boozer! And she's not into drugs." Katie felt her face flush with irritation. "She's met with some hard times. Life has not been good to Lana Lou Barrow."

"Okay, I'm sorry. I'm letting this job get to me. I've just seen too much, I guess. Drugs and alcohol seem to dominate most of my cases."

"Well, I know that's not the case with this woman."

"Katie, you have a heart like no one I know. I'm not sure I could be so benevolent, but if you think this woman is worth it, I'm willing to listen to you."

"Thorne needs to see his mother. He needs regular visits with her. I'm telling you, it will benefit him immensely. The CASA volunteer agrees with me."

There was a hesitation on the line. "Okay, here's the deal. I'm willing to set up an appointment for a parental visit, but it has to be here in my office. I still can't allow you to take Thorne down to see her. The thing is I don't know how the woman is going to get down here."

"I'll go get her!" Katie blurted out. "That's not a problem."

"Okay, but I don't want Thorne to be with you when you go pick her up. He doesn't need to see the scene down there."

"He already has!"

"Just the same, I don't want him back down there. If Lana Lou can manage to get down here for a visit here in the office, I'll allow that. Otherwise, this will not work."

"She'll be there."

"Okay, how about Wednesday at two?"

"Fine, we'll see you then." Katie closed her phone and blew a hefty breath of air upward into her cordovan-red bangs sagging over her eyes. How could she get her there without taking Thorne to pick her up? *I will find a way!*

35

EIGHTEEN-YEAR-OLD JOSH BARROW stepped onto the front porch of the old Barrow bungalow. The yearlong stay in the Caulfield Boys' Home had seemed like five. Coming back to this old house maybe wasn't such a good idea. Too many bad memories. Demeaning comments from Big John Barrow in front of the one friend he had fueled his hatred for the big man.

There was the ever-empty fridge, the shirts that never fit and always looked homemade—which they were. Lana Lou tried, she really did. Then there was old Mrs. Knutson with the spying eyes from next door. Why couldn't he have had neighbors with kids his age? This neighborhood was nothing but a broken-down city block for old folks.

He walked in the open door and found his older brother stretched out in his dad's old, brown recliner, asleep. He tiptoed over and poked him in the ribs.

Johnny jumped and sat up straight while spewing out a nasty three word phrase.

Josh laughed. "Gotcha!"

"Man, you scared the devil outta me. What are you doin' here?"

"I was about to ask you that. I thought you were still in McAlester. When d'you get out?"

"I spent my time in there. What's with you? You still in that boys' home?"

"I turned eighteen. They kick you outta the system when you turn eighteen."

"So what're you gonna do now?"

"What do you mean, what am I gonna do now? This is home. I've come back—same as you."

Johnny glared at him, but said nothing. Josh started asking him questions about the rest of the family. "So I guess Dad was still there with you in McAlester."

"Nope, they shipped his big butt to some federal pen in Florida after he snitched on a fellow inmate."

"And Mom? You ever find out what happened to her?"

"Nope, she probably found herself another man. She ain't showed her face around here." He walked over to his grandmother's old upright piano, picked up the one and only family picture, and turned it upside down with a crash. The glass cracked. "No, and I don't give a rip what happened to the old whore. This family don't exist anymore!"

Josh spotted Johnny's cigarettes there beside the picture. He pulled one out of the pack. "You got a light on you?"

"There's a lighter over there by my chair."

Josh lit the cigarette, took a drag, and coughed. "So you just decided you could move in here and take over, huh?"

"Look, bro, this old house had been condemned by the city. I got with the city officials and got permission to fix up the place. I spent two months over here makin' all the repairs the dude required—spent a fortune on it. So, yeah, I got a right to live here."

Josh asked his brother what bedroom he was in and then walked into the other one. He threw his bag on the old mattress on the floor. Johnny followed. "So you just waltz in here, throw your stuff on the bed, and make yourself right at home. Is that your plan, Josh?"

"Look, bro, I got as much right to live here as you do!"

"Yeah, well, you ain't gonna park your skinny butt here and not pay your way."

"I'll get a job. I can pay my half."

"Yeah, dude, you gotta pay me back for half the money I spent on this old house too. That's only fair."

"Whatever!" Josh blew a cloud of smoke in his brother's face.

"No, that won't work either." Johnny grabbed the pack of cigarettes out of Josh's hand and stuck it in his shirt pocket. "See, my girlfriend is stayin' here too. If you're hangin' out here, we got no privacy—understand?"

"Then kick her out!" Josh said. "I'm movin' in!"

Johnny stood up and got in his brother's face. "She's stayin', Josh! You can find yourself some other hole to crawl into."

They both took turns at shoving each other. Then an all-out fight broke out between the two, and Josh was left with a swollen left eye. After three days of constant verbal confrontation laced with obscenities and tossing shoes, a cast iron skillet, chairs, and even the TV, Josh decided he'd had enough. He picked up his gym bag and headed toward the door.

"Where you think you're goin'?" Johnny laughed. "I didn't think I could get rid of you that easy."

"You're not gettin' rid of me. I got as much right to this house as you do. But for now, I'm movin' out. I got a friend in Dallas that's asked me to come down there—said he could get me a job where he works."

Johnny went to his brother and wrapped his arms around him in a crushing bear hug. "Hey, bro, let me know when you find work down there in Dallas. Maybe I'll join you. There ain't nuthin' goin' on in this stinkin' town. I've been outta work for over a month now."

Josh slammed the door behind him and kicked at the recently patched-up section at the bottom. *Sorry, Johnny, you won't find me!*

36

"Okay," Kirk said. "What do you have on your mind? I can see those gears grinding up there under that gorgeous hair."

Katie threw back the covers and sat upright in bed. "She can't keep me from bringing Lana Lou to my folks' house, where Mr. Thorne will be waiting."

"Katie! You wouldn't!"

"Yes, I would!"

"Babe…"

"You should understand, Betty has to follow the rules set out by DFS. She's not allowed to tell me how to get around those rules, so I guess it's up to me to figure that out."

"Kate, you are the clever one—always have been. Just don't do something that would jeopardize Thorne's stay here with us. We can't afford to have the little fellow moved at this point. He's making too much progress right now."

"I know what I'm doing."

"When are you planning to execute your scheme?"

"I was thinking Sunday, but I need to call Mom and see if it will be okay with them. You want to go with me?"

With both boys dropped off at the Reynolds' house, Kirk and Katie made their way over to the Greyhound terminal. Katie had hoped to find the little homeless woman back out on the street, but she wasn't there. She took off at a fast pace toward the back of the doughnut shop where Lana Lou's hidey-hole would be. Kirk followed but lagged behind a bit. When she turned the corner at the back of the shop, the gray tarp was gone, and all remnants of Lana Lou's worldly possessions were gone. The area had been swept clean.

"Kirk!" Panic was beginning to set in. "Kirk, what could have happened here? You think she may have died?"

Kirk caught up and took her hand. "Let's ask around—see if anyone knows anything."

"Come on, follow me." Katie was running, heading back to the front of the doughnut shop. "I'm going inside to ask." She turned and saw Kirk several yards back. "Are you coming?"

Kirk's one-sided grin appeared, and he picked up the pace, catching up with her and opening the door for her. "You think they'll know anything?"

Katie spotted the owner behind the counter. The fat man was wearing his usual dirty white apron, with flour smudges here and there. "You know anything about my friend, Lana Lou? She was staying back behind your shop—"

"Yeah, I made her move out. She was scaring the delivery guys."

"Scaring them? That little woman wouldn't scare a chicken cornered in its own coop."

The man dusted some flour off the apron stretching over his basketball belly. "Just the same, lady, she was a nuisance to everyone. These bums are ruining my business. Good people are afraid to come in here. I've had it with the hobos. The city ought to be doing something—"

"Go check on your old lardy doughnuts! They've soaked in that nasty week-old hot oil long enough," Katie said, loud enough for the two customers in the shop to hear. "Come on, Kirk, let's get out of this grease pit!"

Kirk's one-sided grin reappeared. "That's my Kate!" They were turning to walk out. "So what's the plan now, Hillary?"

"Where are you getting this Hillary bit?"

Kirk laughed. "Well, you're quite the take-charge, give-um-heck kind of gal. All you need is the funky pantsuit."

Katie sneered at her wisecracking husband towering over her. "That old codger had no reason to kick her out of her home. She wasn't hurting anyone. In fact, she came in every morning and bought her doughnut. She was a paying customer!"

"Okay, I get it—sorta. Let's go check out that café where we had lunch with her."

Kirk followed, always about six paces behind. Katie hurried through the door of the café and spotted Lana Lou in the back booth where they'd had lunch with her before. As she was running back to her, she peeled off her windbreaker and threw it toward Kirk.

From two booths away, Katie's voice burst out. "Oh, thank God, you are okay!" She quickly sat down opposite Lana Lou. "When we saw your tarp was missing, I freaked out. Then that greasy old toad in the doughnut shop said he made you move away—said you were scaring the deliverymen! That's about the dumbest thing I've heard in a long time!"

Lana Lou started to laugh, then put her closed fist over her mouth, and the bark-like cough started. Finally she said, "That would have been old Richard. He's okay. None of these shop owners like us street people homesteading at their back door. We gotta move every week or so. I'll probably put up my tarp there again in time. He ain't as bad as he sounds."

Katie scooted over for Kirk to sit down. "Where are you staying now, hon?"

"I'm back behind—" The bark broke out again. Lana Lou beat her chest. "I'm back behind the old tattoo shop—Danny's the owner. He don't seem to mind me being there." She grinned. "He don't have any deliverymen for me to scare away."

Lana Lou looked at Kirk, then back to Katie. "Cat got his tongue?"

Kirk laughed. "Now, Lana Lou, how can I possibly get a word in when you two are yakking like schoolgirls?"

Katie slapped at his hand. "Lana Lou, I was hoping we could borrow you for a while today."

"What? Borrow me?"

"Yes, would you like to go to my parents' house with us and see your baby boy?"

"Oh my, yes! When can we go?"

Kirk held up his index finger, just like a school kid asking permission to speak. "Just as soon as we can get something to eat here."

"Now, Kirk," Lana Lou started. "I don't need—"

"Missy!" Kirk called as the waitress was walking toward them. "We're all ready for some breakfast now."

The waitress asked if they needed menus.

"No, just bring each of us a big, heaping plate of scrambled eggs, crispy bacon, hash browns, biscuits with butter and honey, coffee for me and my wife. And refill Miss Lana Lou's cup for her."

37

Carol Reynolds met them at the door. Katie introduced Lana Lou to Carol, and Thorne ran to meet his mother. She grabbed him with both arms and held on tight. A tear dripped on to his shoulder.

Carol stood back with one hand resting in the crook of the other arm and that hand covering her mouth. Katie wrapped both arms around her mother and then said, "Mom, we made it happen!"

"Yes, we did. This picture is priceless!"

Lynn Reynolds walked in from the back patio. "Hey, guys, I was out back pulling out the propane grill—thought I'd put on some tri-tips. You guys hungry?"

"Oh, Dad, not yet. We just finished a late breakfast. Kirk ordered us all plates heaped with scrambled eggs, bacon, hash browns—we're all stuffed. But that will sound pretty good later."

Thorne sat next to his mother on the colorful floral-patterned sofa. He clearly was excited to have this time with her. He talked nonstop, telling her about every event in his life over the past years, leaving out very little. He not only told her about the good things, but he went into detail about the twenty dollars he had stolen from his teacher, the stable talks between him and Kirk, and the fights he had gotten into at school.

He went on to tell her about the fish he'd caught there on the ranch and at the lake, but he never mentioned the incident in the camp restroom.

Lana Lou asked him about his grades and if he would bring her a copy of his report card. "Naw, you don't wanna see that. They're not very good. Brandon is the one that makes all As."

"Thorne," Katie cut in, "that last report card shows some of the best grades you've ever made. I think your mom would like to see it."

Thorne's repertoire of recalled memories evidently played out, and he joined Brandon, Lynn, and Kirk at a game of Uno.

Carol brought in three glasses of lemonade on a tray and set them down on the antique marble-topped coffee table. "Fresh squeezed, girls."

Lana Lou seemed a bit shy at first, but Carol and Katie got her to talking. She seemed anxious to tell about the family she once had. "My husband was very abusive to me and the boys. It wasn't a good marriage, but at least I had a home and three sons. Now I don't have a home, and I've lost my boys."

Carol reached over and touched her hand. "Hon, you've still got Thorne. Katie and Kirk are just babysitting for you—"

"I heard that!" Thorne shouted across the room.

"Oh, sorry, Thorne. My bad," Carol said.

"My bad?" Katie searched her mother's eyes. "Where did you come up with that term?"

"I think it was Brandon," Carol said. "Our language is changing fast. I've got to keep up."

Katie grinned and then looked back at Lana Lou. "So tell us how you and John met."

"Oh, that was a mistake for sure. I was fourteen, and all I could see was the big muscles and the full head of hair on this giant of a guy who was seven years older than me. I think it must have been on our first date when I got pregnant. I was such a fool!" She started to take a sip of her lemonade, and another coughing spell overtook her.

Carol jumped up and brought back a glass of ice water. "That lemonade may be too strong. Maybe this water will help."

"No, the lemonade is good." The frail woman beat her chest with her fist. "I just can't shake this hacking cough. Anyway, as I was saying, I got pregnant, and Johnny was born. I had just turned fifteen two days before."

"Fifteen?" Katie inhaled loudly. "You were just a child yourself."

"Yes, I was," Lana Lou ducked her head and picked at the dirt under her nails.

"So, what does that make you now? Thirty-six, maybe thirty-seven?"

"I've just turned thirty-six. I know I look like I'm seventy. Some even mistake me for eighty. I've had a pretty rough life."

Carol gasped, held her hand over her mouth. "Oh dear!" She then realized that wasn't a proper reaction and tried to cover her mistake. "Honey, we need to get you some medical care. That'll bring out your inner beauty."

"No, Mrs. Reynolds, any beauty I ever had has been stolen. I'll never get it back."

Carol patted the back of the bony and liver-spotted woman's hand. Lana Lou turned her hand over and grasped Carol's. "My dad was molesting me—you know—sexually. So I was glad to get out of that house. Little did I know I would be walking into another house with an abusive man. John never respected me, called me awful names, hit me, and threw me through the walls—several times. Those holes in the wall are still there. He never did fix them."

"Oh, hon, why didn't you take your baby and leave?" Carol asked.

"Where would I go? I couldn't go back home—no, that would have never worked." Lana Lou set her glass of lemonade down. She pulled at the top of her dirty T-shirt. "Carol, this is embarrassing. Would you mind if I take a bath here in your house? I haven't had one in a long time, and I know I'm stinking up your pretty home."

"Well, of course you may, but only if that's what you want. Come on back with me, and I'll show you where the towels and things are."

Carol also gave her a pair of her old faded Lee jeans, a clean T-shirt, and a sweater. "Honey, you can just keep those. I've got way too many clothes in my closet anyway."

While Lana Lou was in the bathroom, Carol went through her closet and found another change of clothes for the woman to take with her. "I hope these things fit, she's awfully small," she told Katie.

"Mom, while you're doing that, I'm going to start on lunch— or I guess it'll be supper. Dad said he was going to put a tri-tip on the grill. I'll get a nice big tossed salad started."

Lana Lou walked into the kitchen; the jeans hung loosely around her tiny hips, the T-shirt might have fit okay, but the frail little lady wrapped her arms with the big bulky sweater around herself, hiding the tee completely. "Well, the air in your house will smell a lot better now." She laughed, and then another coughing spell hit. Again, she beat her congested chest with her fist in an attempt to calm the rasping cough. Finally, she took another sip of water from the glass Katie handed her. "Thank you for the use of your shower."

Katie and Carol were busy preparing the food, and Carol asked Lana Lou if she would like to set the table. "Sure, I'll do that. But it's been so long since I've set a table, I'm not sure I'll do it right."

"Oh, you'll do it right," Carol said. "Any old way is good enough for us. You just do it however you want."

At the supper table, the conversation turned back to life in the Barrows house. Lana Lou picked at her food and told about times when her husband was so abusive, she would take the boys and run to a neighbor's house, sometimes in the middle of the night. There was never enough money for food, and clothing for her and the boys was what she could sew herself or was given to her by a benevolent neighbor.

After the boys had finished their meal, Katie whispered to Brandon to take Thorne out back where they had been playing with Bobber, the white-and-tan Holland Lop rabbit running loose in the yard.

Lana Lou continued to open up after the boys were outside. "John was put in jail three times—should have been more, but he just didn't always get caught. He was all the time bringing home stuff that didn't belong to him. I knew he was stealing, but I couldn't say anything, or I'd get more cigarette burns in the palms of my hands." She turned her palms up. "Just look at these hands!" Scarred, lumpy, discolored tissue covered both palms. The index finger on her right hand had obviously been broken, and it appeared there had been no medical attention. It crooked over awkwardly toward her thumb. Katie couldn't help but notice the badly bent out of shape gold band on her splotched left hand, no thicker than a paper clip, circling loosely around the thin ring finger.

Lana Lou told how she would try to discipline the boys, and John would burst in and take over. First it was a belt, and then when that didn't work, he would resort to smashing his fist into the boy's face. "Johnny was the worst at sassing his dad. John always left cuts and bruises on him. Johnny never learned. Then, when he had finished with whichever boy he was 'disciplining,' he would start in on me. I got to where I couldn't say anything to the man. I've had two broken arms, a broken collarbone, and a broken nose. And those burning cigarettes smashed into my hands. Oh, and this broken finger—he broke this with his bare hands one night after I threatened to leave."

"Could you not find someone to take you and the boys in?" Katie said. "There are women's shelters for battered women, you know."

"Katie, not back then. Those shelters didn't exist when I needed them. Things were different then. A woman had no rights. If I'd taken the boys and left, no one would have taken us in. Everyone would have said it was my fault."

Carol handed her a bottle of lotion from Bath & Body Works. "Here, rub some of this into your hands—and just take the bottle with you. I have several more."

Katie asked Kirk to bring Thorne back in from the backyard so he could visit more with his mother before they had to take her back. "Take her back?" Carol said. "Lana Lou, why don't you just spend the night here with us? We've got a lovely guest bedroom. I can find you some night clothes to wear. I've got a nice fleece robe that will warm your bones."

"Oh, I better get on back," she said. "My old street friends will be wondering what happened to me. I've got one friend down there who checks up on me. She's real nice like that. I might let her borrow some of this lotion. Her hands are chapped something awful."

Lana Lou hugged her son and said good-bye. Kirk opened the pickup door for her. She tried to step up onto the running board but was too weak, so he helped her on in. On the way to the bus terminal, Katie glanced in the rearview mirror and saw red eyes and a tear sliding down her brown cheek.

Lana Lou directed Kirk around to the alley behind the tattoo shop, where he helped her crawl out of the truck.

An hour later, Kirk and Katie picked up the boys at the Reynolds' house, and Kirk, Katie, Brandon, and Thorne were headed back twenty-six miles to the ranch—in silence.

38

He opened the door, peeked into the room, and quietly stepped into her office with a new image—clean blue jeans, a pair of Tony Lama full-quill ostrich boots, a straight-off-the-department-store-rack blue-and-white checkered shirt, and sooty-black hair slicked back, with a matching day-old neatly trimmed beard. He stuck out his right hand to greet her. "Good morning, Mrs. Sawyer, I won't take much of your time."

"Johnny, I see you've got a new look going on—looks nice. You've got that David Beckham swanky look. Have a seat. What brings you back here today?"

"First of all, I want to apologize for my previous behavior. I probably shouldn't even try to make excuses, but I was very stressed out back then. I've since been able to get a grip on life, and I am hoping you will allow me to visit my little brother, Thorne. It's been well over a year now, and I really do miss him. You see, Dad had always been very abusive to us kids, and I felt like it was my responsibility to try to protect Thorne—"

"What about Josh?" Betty said. "Did you also feel it your responsibility to protect him?"

"Yes, ma'am, I did, but Josh was quite a bit older and could protect himself better than Thorne. You see, Thorne has always been very small for his age. He was no match for our six-foot-four, two-hundred-fifty-pound gorilla dad."

Johnny told Betty about the times he would grab Thorne out of the angry grasp of John Barrow and run out the door with him. Many times he would hide his brother out until he was sure John was out of the house. "Thorne was always doing something that pi—uh—angered Dad." Johnny crossed his leg, exposing the Tony Lamas, without even a scuff on the leather sole. "Many times, I saw my dad grab hold of Thorne and shake him like a rag doll. That happened when Thorne was maybe two years old!"

"That's called," Betty said, "and could have inflicted permanent brain damage."

"Like I said, Mrs. Sawyer, I tried my best to protect my little brother from that monster. Maybe that's why Thorne and I have such a bond."

Betty leaned back in her office chair and crossed her arms. "Johnny, where were you when your dad was throwing your mother through the walls and beating her face to a pulp? I understand she also is a very small-framed person and probably was unable to defend herself."

"See, that's the thing, she could have taken us kids and left him. But she didn't. She stayed around for more abuse to herself and to us kids. I don't have a lot of sympathy for her. She could have gotten us out of there!"

"But, Johnny, this is your mother we're talking about here. During those last few years before you went to prison, you were old enough to help protect your mother." Betty clicked her ballpoint pen several times and laid it on the desk. "But let's talk about you now. What are you doing now?"

Johnny started telling Betty how he had completely renovated the old Barrow house, all the money and time he had spent doing so, and how the place was now a neighborhood showcase. "I've worked night and day on that house—spent a fortune on it."

"So have you also been working at a job?"

"Oh, for sure. I've been coming straight home from work and putting another eight to ten hours replacing Sheetrock, muddin' and tapin'. I've hauled off a ton of trash Dad had allowed to accumulate over the years. I've put new steps on the front porch, replaced some doors. It's been expensive, but it's been worth it. Our neighbors are commenting about how nice the place looks now."

"Really?" Betty's arms remained crossed. "So where do you work, Johnny? You must have a pretty good job to do all of that."

"I was in partnership with my uncle in the roofing business, until he walked out on me—left me with a dozen jobs and no help. I was also left with all the unpaid bills of the business. I finally folded, and now I've been offered a position with Sonic Drive-In."

"And what is that position?"

"I'll be their local customer service representative, probably floating from one location to the next."

Betty tried to hide the grin with her hand. "You mean a carhop?"

Johnny squirmed in his seat. "Well, you see, Mrs. Sawyer, uh… Sonic Drive-Ins has implemented a new division in their workforce. What you have called a carhop has now evolved into more of a client satisfaction representative."

"Bull! Johnny, can we drop all the crap and just be honest? A carhop is a carhop—no shame in that, it's a job—but to attempt to make it sound like an executive position is just laughable."

Johnny again squirmed in his seat and crossed the other leg. "Mrs. Sawyer, I'm just relating the job description that was given to me by company headquarters." He subconsciously reached for a nonexistent pack of cigarettes in his shirt pocket. "Okay, here's the deal. I spent everything I had trying to bail out my uncle's roofing business when he walked out on me, and I had already spent a lot renovating the old house. I had to have a job to pull me out of the hole I'd been pushed into."

Betty removed her blue rhinestone-clad eyeglasses. "Johnny, let's move past the position you now hold at Sonic Drive-Ins—oh, by the way, I'd like to drive by the house and see all you've done to it. I know it was in pretty bad shape the last time I saw it." She picked up her glasses and chewed on one earpiece. "If I were to allow an in-office visit with your brother, what might I expect from you?"

"What? I guess I don't know what you're asking, Mrs. Sawyer."

"To put it bluntly, Johnny, I do not want you giving false hopes to your brother that there might ever be a possibility he would be allowed to come live with you. This child has endured enough disappointments already. He doesn't need more coming from you."

"Well, Mrs. Sawyer, you know that has always been my hopes. Thorne needs to be with me, end of story." Johnny scooted his chair back a bit from Betty's desk, crossed his legs, and touched the Tony Lama boot, fingering the quills. "Uh, I know the state sometimes furnishes a stipend for the care and maintenance of a child under these circumstances, so with that, I would be able to give him the good stable environment he so deserves."

Betty stood up and pushed back her chair. "Johnny, if you're looking for a monthly check, go talk to your boss at Sonic Drive-In. The state will not be writing you a check! Have I made myself clear?"

Johnny glared at her, uncrossed his legs, and kicked the edge of the desk with his left boot. "Look, lady! All I want is to see my little brother. So get off your high horse and tell me when I can see him!" A string of obscene language spewed from his lips, and he kicked at the desk again.

Betty picked up the phone, pushed the button for in-office assistance, and waited. Bob Murphy, another caseworker, six foot three and an obvious weight lifter, opened the door, walked in, and stood there with his legs spread and his huge arms folded. Betty continued. "Mr. Barrow, your intentions regarding your brother are self-seeking. At this time, I do not believe a visit with your brother would be in the child's best interest, so I will not allow the visit you say you are requesting. I suggest you look elsewhere for a paycheck!"

Johnny stood, put one knee on the desk, and appeared to be climbing over to get at Betty. Both of his hands were raised, tightly fisted, and various expressions of vulgarity blistered the air. Before the other knee had topped the desk, Bob Murphy was behind Johnny, wrapping his big arms around him, and starting to usher him out the door.

In Bob's heavy grip, Johnny turned his head toward Betty and shouted, "I'll find my brother. Whether you like it or not!"

39

It was Wednesday, and Lana Lou's scheduled visit at the DFS offices was in less than an hour. Katie had already dropped Thorne off at her parents' house and was pulling into the only parking spot big enough for the big extended cab pickup. It would be close if she could grab Lana Lou, hurry back to pick up Thorne, and get down to the DFS offices by two o'clock.

She jumped out of the pickup and quickly slammed the door shut, forgetting to remove the keys. With her purse straps draped over her shoulder, she ran the three blocks toward the bus station. The frail woman was nowhere in sight. With her purse bobbing up and down at her side, she raced around the corner and up the side street toward the tattoo shop. She had seen a back door on the shop the last time. Rather than running to the next block to get to the back where her friend's tarp was, she plunged through the front door of the tattoo shop. A young man sat with his arm stretched out while the tattoo needle was at work. The shirtless tattoo-covered artist hollered at her. "Hey, lady! Where do you think you're going?"

"Sorry."

"You can't go back there, lady!"

She grabbed the heavy metal door, yanked, but it was locked. The skinny artist with the colorful collage of dragon characters covering his arms and chest was at her side. He grabbed her arm. "Hey, I said you can't come back here. This is not a customer area."

Katie pulled away from his grasp, saw the dead bolt lock on the door, flipped it around, and jerked the big door open. "So tattoo me!" she hollered as she sprinted out the door.

The familiar gray tarp was just to her right. "Lana Lou, are you in there?" She pulled the flap of the tarp back. There lay the old foam mattress and the sleeping bag she had brought her. The Folgers can was on the ground—empty. "Lana, sweetie, where are you!" Katie said, with no one to hear. "We've barely got time to get you and Thorne down to your appointment!" She then ducked out of the makeshift tent and jogged down the alley, turned the corner, and headed toward the doughnut shop, glancing from side to side. Lana Lou was nowhere in sight.

The sprint around the last block had left her winded. The brass bell hanging from the top of the door tinkled as she pulled the door open. One customer was trying to decide which greasy sugar-and-lard pastry to buy. Gasping for breath, she said, "Have you seen my friend, Lana Lou?"

The fat dirty-aproned shopkeeper gawked at her. "If you're lookin' for that bag of bones that camped out behind my shop here, I think she died."

"Died!" Katie gulped. "Who told you that?"

"Well, that's the scoop around here. Someone saw an ambulance loading her body in it a couple of days ago." His bulging belly extended over the counter, and he plopped down the gooey carbohydrate concoction the customer had chosen. "If you ask me, this area would be a lot better off with these vagrants all gone from here—probably smell a lot better too."

Katie ran back out the door. "No, your greasy frying vat is what smells around here! You should replace that week-old grease in there—maybe you'd attract a few more customers." She glanced back. The customer had laid the pastry back on the counter and was walking away.

The trek around to the café had again left her out of breath. She saw the cute girl who had waited their table the last time. She was taking an order from a couple in a front booth.

Katie grabbed her arm, interrupting, "Sweetie, have you seen my friend Lana Lou?"

The girl jumped. "Oh gosh, you scared me! No, I haven't seen her in a couple of days. I was wondering what happened to her. She always comes in for a cup of coffee. She's a sweet lady—always leaves me a tip, even though it might just be a few pennies. She hardly ever eats though."

"Thanks, hon." Katie stepped outside and pulled out her cell phone from the baggy purse at her side.

"Betty, this is Katie. I can't find Lana Lou. Our appointment is in five minutes, and she is nowhere in sight. I just can't imagine what has happened to her."

"Katie," Betty said, "I could have guessed that might happen. Honey, you are my friend, but I've gotta tell you, you are so naive. Those people can't keep a schedule. You should know that. She probably found some man to take her in for the night—"

"Betty! Here you go, assuming the worst. I'm gonna keep looking for her. I'll let you know when I find her."

Katie closed the phone and dropped it in her purse. *Oh, gosh! What if she did die? How could she ever tell her son?*

Still determined to locate her friend, Katie went back out on the street and into a couple more shops, asking about her. No one knew, or at least weren't saying they knew anything about her. She had made the rounds of all of the hangouts where she thought her friend would be, and even a few she was pretty sure she would never go in.

She wandered around to the front of the terminal where Lana Lou usually sat with her coffee can. A stout old woman in a threadbare cotton dress sat on the sidewalk with her legs sprawled out, holding a gallon jar with a few coins and a dollar bill showing through the glass. "Ma'am, have you seen my friend, Lana Lou?" Katie asked.

"Yeah, I seen her. She died. They's a-cartin' her skinny body off a couple a days ago." She held out the gallon pickle jar toward Katie. "You got a dollar or two for an old lady needin' a bite to eat?"

Katie stepped over the sprawled-out legs of the old woman on the sidewalk and walked inside the terminal.

She sat down on a bench, along with an older lady eating a sandwich. Katie laid her big, floppy purse on her lap and ducked her head downward. She was exhausted and incensed at the uncaring people she'd come across. Maybe a life just wasn't worth much around this place. She watched the woman working on her sandwich. The woman chewed slowly, and it became obvious she had no teeth. The lady struggled with each bite and seemed to choke before she could manage to swallow.

"Would you like for me to go buy you a soda or get some water to help wash that down?"

The lady acted surprised and put her hand on Katie's. "Would you? I love Dr. Pepper, but water would be okay too."

Katie walked over to the soda pop machine and bought a Dr. Pepper for her friend and a Sprite for herself. The lady was grateful, and a conversation between the two ensued. Finally, Katie asked her if she happened to know Lana Lou.

"Oh, yes, do you know her?" The lady crammed the last bite of the sandwich in her mouth.

"Yes, she is my friend, and I can't find her. I've looked everywhere."

The lady was trying to chew her last bite, held up her index finger, and started to chew faster. She swallowed and said, "Lana Lou took real sick. Someone found her back in her tent—I think it was Monday—they said she was unconscious." The lady tipped the Dr. Pepper can up and swallowed. "I'm tellin' you, that girl had been coughin' her fool head off—somethin' awful!"

"So what happened?"

The lady took another sip of her soda and slowly set it down on the bench next to her. "I'd been tellin' her she oughta get herself to see a doc, but you know, she wouldn't do it. She was stubborn like that."

"What happened to her?"

"You know, when that woman set her mind to something, there weren't no army could ever turn her around." The woman lowered her head and shook it slowly. "I'll say..." It was obvious she was deep in thought. "That poor woman..."

Katie glanced several times at the clock on the wall in front of her. "Hon, can you tell me what happened to her? Did she die?"

The woman raised her head and stared at Katie. "Well, I just don't rightly know. When they found her, she was unconscious. Someone musta called the ambulance, 'cause one come roarin' up here. I was standin' right out there in front of this bus station." She took another sip of the Dr. Pepper. "They's a askin' 'bout the woman someone had called in about. It was two good-lookin' guys—I mean they were real lookers! I couldn't take my eyes off them. Whew! One had an earring in each of his ears. I don't know why them young men do that nowadays."

Katie stood up, tilted her head to the ceiling, and let out a heavy sigh. "So was my friend alive when they picked her up?"

"Well...I s'pose she was. They didn't cover up her face, so I guess she weren't dead."

"What hospital did they take her to?"

"Well..." The lady hesitated. "I jist don't rightly know. They don't ever tell you that kind a thing, you know."

"What ambulance service picked her up?"

"It was red and white, had a snake-lookin' symbol on the back."

"Okay, thank you. I've got to be going now."

40

Katie walked the three blocks back to her pickup, reached into her purse for the keys, and wound up dumping everything out in the bed of the truck—checkbook, cell phone, wallet, a bag of Cheetos, and a Snickers bar she'd brought for Lana Lou—all scattered out on the bed of the truck, but no keys. She looked inside the driver's side window. The key ring, with Brandon's picture in the small plastic frame, was hanging from the steering column. *Oh great!* She gritted her teeth. This had been one disastrous day!

She gathered up all of the previous contents of her purse and stuffed it all back in the floppy bag, took her cell phone, and called Kirk.

"Babe," Kirk said, "I don't have a way to come to you, unless you think I should get on the old Case tractor. But I might get stopped out there on I-35."

"Kirk, I'm in no mood for jokes. I've had a bear of a day. Now what do I do?"

"You got your cell phone. Call a locksmith."

Well, duh!

An hour later, Katie gave her credit card information to the locksmith, opened the truck door, turned on the ignition, and sat there in a daze. A red-and-white ambulance with a snakelike logo on the back. Weren't all ambulances red and white with a serpent entwined around a staff logo?

After a call to Baptist Hospital and no patient by the name of Barrow, she called St. Anthony's Hospital. Lana Lou Barrow had been admitted on Monday and was listed in serious condition. *Why didn't I think of that hospital first?* St. Anthony's was the closest one to downtown.

The parking garage was full, and the few spots left on the lot were way too small to fit the big truck into, so she had to park two blocks away. She grabbed the wad of keys out of the ignition and threw them in the big purse on top of the now-melted and oozing-out-of-its-wrapper Snickers bar.

Just as she tried to catch the closest slot in the big revolving door, a young woman jumped in front of her, blocking her way. Then an elderly man with a walker saw his opportunity for the next open slot. On the third try, Katie got through and made her way inside and to the information desk.

"Third floor, elevator's to your right, but you can't use it now—they're working on it."

Katie stared at the woman. Then she walked around the corner to the right and found a nurse entering it. The Up arrow glowed green above the door, and Katie stepped inside.

"What floor?" the nurse said.

"Third, please."

"Can't do, deary. They've got that blocked off. You'll have to take the stairs or take a left down this hall, and then there's another elevator down the hall in the west wing. But to be honest, the stairs would be a lot quicker."

Katie's nerves were razor thin. "And this is a working hospital?"

"Sorry, hon, it's temporary, they say."

Three flights of stairs seemed like Mount Kilimanjaro. She was out of breath by the time she reached the room they had told her Lana Lou was in. She peeked inside. It was empty.

After tracking down an employee who was rushing back to her station, Katie learned Lana Lou had been moved up to the fifth floor. "Do I have to climb the stairs up to that floor too?"

"No, just hook a right here, and your lift will be on your left."

The oh-so-welcoming elevator door opened, and she rode on up. Room 538 was at the far end of the hall. The door was already open, and she saw the frail woman—shrunken cheeks, her head to one side, and her eyes staring at the ceiling. Katie walked over and took her hand. "Hey, sweetie!"

Lana Lou jumped. "Oh my gosh! Katie! How did you find me here?"

"Honey, you don't really want to hear about that. Let's just say I've been given the runaround all day long, but I'm glad I finally found you. How are you doing?"

Lana Lou took Katie's hand and squeezed lightly. A tear formed in her eye. "Katie, I was supposed to be with my son several hours ago. We had an appointment. I'm so upset!"

"Let's not worry about that right now. What are they doing for you? You still got that awful cough?"

"I do, but it's better. How's my baby boy?"

Katie relayed some of Thorne's more recent adventures—a spelling test he'd made a hundred on, a new friend at school, and a trail ride on Katie's mare, Lilly. "So when are they saying you can get out of here?"

Another cough sprang from deep in the sick woman's lungs. "Oh, they don't tell me nuthin' around here. I shouldn't complain though. It's a lot better than I had it out there on the street. And they bring me three meals a day! These nurses they've got around here are true angels. They're always comin' in and checkin' on me, fussin' over me. One lady even brought me a—what do you call it—a talking book."

"An audio book?" Katie said.

"Yes, the title of it, I think, is *Indebted*. It's about this doctor who finds out he was adopted when he's about to graduate from medical school. I've listened to the whole thing—couldn't stop, it was so good!"

"Well, you hurry and get well, friend, and I'll reschedule your visit at the DFS office. I'm gonna run now. I haven't been home since before noon. Our boys are probably famished."

Katie pulled through the ranch gate at seven fifteen. When she got to the house, Kirk had already been grilling, and Brandon and Thorne were cramming their mouths with thick, juicy Angus burgers, just the way each of them liked them. Katie tossed her big purse on the coffee table and stretched out on the seven-foot leather sofa.

"Want me to make you a burger, Kate?"

"No, I'm too tired to eat much. I'll just have one of those meat patties and a glass of milk later. I'm totally wiped out!"

"I'll stick a patty in the fridge for you. You can just nuke it when you're ready." Kirk walked over, stooped down, and kissed his wife on the forehead. "I know better than to ask how your day went, but did you ever find Lana Lou?"

"Yeah, two or three people there at the bus station told me she had died, but I found her on the fifth floor at St. Anthony's."

"Well, get yourself a snooze. Thorne's got some news for you when you are up and around."

41

Katie's easel sat by the east wall of the big room. When she woke up from her much-needed nap, her eyes focused on the empty easel, then over to Thorne watching TV. "Hey, buddy, what happened to your charcoal drawing we were displaying on the easel?"

"That's what I wanted to tell you about." The ten-year-old's eyes sparkled. "I may get to have it displayed in a museum in Oklahoma City!"

"No way!" Katie sat up. "You are kidding me! How's that going to happen?"

Thorne came over and sat down on the couch beside her. "Mrs. Stephens liked it so much, she entered it in the all-school Children's Art League. That was two days ago—didn't you miss seeing it then?"

"Honestly, Thorne, I've been so busy, I just never allowed my eyes to wander over in this direction."

"So today she told me I had won first place among *all* the grades at Luther. And—get this—it will now be entered in the district competition, and if I'm the winner, it will be displayed in the National Cowboy & Western Heritage Museum in Oklahoma City!"

"Oh, Thorne! I knew it was really good. I was pretty sure you would be the one to win in your fourth grade class, but I had no idea…"

"Mrs. Stephens told everyone it was a beautiful representation of country life in Oklahoma."

"Oh, man! I knew it was good. Remember, I told you that little paint horse—"

"Yeah, that was Puzzle!"

"Yes, Puzzle sticking her head over the gate in the stable, all of that was in the background. And you even drew *Childers Ranch* lettering up in the gable of the stable. And the fence, curving along the country lane in the foreground, was exactly like ours! Remember, I told you someday you are going to be quite an artist. Now do you believe me?"

"Yeah, Dad was—I mean Kirk, he was telling Ronnie about it. He wants to know when we'll get it back."

"You know what I'd do? I'd start on a new drawing. Put Kirk in it. Make him leaning over, branding one of the Angus heifers."

"Great idea!" Thorne went to his room and got his charcoals and sketching pad, put them on the big dining table in the center of the room, and sat down to pour out his creativity on the white pad. Katie watched in amazement for half an hour. He was sketching in the scene with Kirk leaning over with a branding iron in his hand next to a Black Angus. He had no picture to go by, just his memory. She leaned over closer. "My gosh, Thorne! That even looks like Kirk!"

"Well, you said to make it him, didn't you?"

"I did…but I had no idea you could capture his face like that! Sweetie, you have a talent you'd better not waste. You can make your living doing this someday!"

Thorne laid the charcoal down and ducked his head. "I wish my mom could see them."

"She will, buddy. I'll make sure she does. You can even make one for her to keep."

His eyes met Katie's. "Why didn't I get to visit my mom yesterday? You never told me. I asked Brandon, and he just stared at me, like, 'duh!'"

"Sweetheart, I thought I told you she is in the hospital, sick with pneumonia or something."

Thorne shot up out of his chair. "Then that does it! You can take me to visit her there! Forget the stupid DXS office and their dumb rules."

"It's *DFS*," Katie corrected. "And I agree with you, sometimes their rules do seem pretty dumb. I think yesterday I was saying that myself."

"Okay, well, let's go! Can I just leave my stuff here?"

"Thorne Barrow! You are definitely the impatient one. We can't go now, but I'll see what I can do. You had a pretty good idea."

"You let me know when you're gonna follow through with that, so I'll have time to do a drawing for Mom, like you said. Fourth grade is a lot harder than third was. We have a lot of homework. I wish I had more time to do what I like."

Katie sat back again and watched the boy work, shading in areas to bring the scene to life. He was sketching in the chute around the heifer in exact detail. He had Kirk's body stance down perfectly, and his face was so obviously Kirk's. Kirk had brought the charcoals and sketching pad home one day after a trip into the city, thinking it might help with the boy's boredom and his lack of interest in the ranch chores.

Katie had seen his first sketch of their dog, Noah. He had also sketched a jackrabbit and a possum. After Kirk had seen that one, Thorne had ragged him again about not knowing the difference between a rabbit and a possum. They were all very good, but nothing compared to what he was doing now. He finished the piece the next evening after supper.

Brandon was back in his room, helping Thorne with his homework. Kirk and Katie were alone in the big room. Kirk stood with his legs spread in front of the easel where the finished drawing was displayed. He stared at the amazing piece of art, his mouth open wide. "Wow!" Then he said, "I can see this kid has a real gift—a God-given gift!"

"Yes," Katie said, "he is talented beyond anything I've ever seen." The boy could never again be labeled as just another nameless kid from the inner city—having a father serving a life sentence, a mother living on the streets, and brothers who were considered failures in society. Katie looked back toward the bedroom wing. "God's got a plan for Thorne. I can't wait to see what He's got in mind."

Kirk took Katie's hand. "Yeah, and we have quite a responsibility. It's up to us to make sure those plans don't get derailed."

42

The front yard was much the same. What little grass that was left needed to see a mower blade in the worst way. The broken and uneven cement had been removed, but had never been replaced. There were several bags of garbage that had been tossed just outside the front door on to the porch. An animal had torn into them and scattered the contents. The front door was standing ajar, and it appeared the bottom panel had been replaced at one time, but subsequently, even that had been kicked in.

Betty knocked on the old door, causing it to swing wide open. "Hello, anyone home?" There was no answer. "Johnny! Are you home?" This might be a mistake. She probably should have just driven on by.

The windows were bare, allowing sunlight to spill into the small living room. With both feet still outside, she leaned inside and peeked at the room—empty beer cans were piled in a corner by the old, brown recliner, an ashtray on the spindly table next to it was overflowing with cigarette butts. Betty stepped inside, pulled out her cell phone, and started snapping pictures of the disheveled ten-by-ten cubicle. Then a noise in another room caused her heart to skip several beats. She hid the cell phone behind her back and waited, afraid to take a breath.

The source of the noise she'd heard suddenly flew overhead and, in a desperate attempt to escape, flew into the window and crashed just to the right of her. The blue jay lay on the dirty carpet inches from her feet.

Was the bird dead or just knocked out? Betty was startled but relieved. She stepped away from the blue-and-white motionless heap and began assessing the room again. A pair of seemingly new Wranglers were tossed in the corner, along with shirts, socks, and underwear. Those fancy Tony Lama ostrich boots were decorating the center of the floor. She noticed a huge hole in the wall, opposite from the hole she'd seen when she first visited the house. There had been an attempt at patching the original hole. New Sheetrock had been nailed in place, but the mud and tape job on it could have been done by a two-year-old. It was even more noticeable because it was unpainted. Maybe these pictures would prove her case for rejecting Johnny's demand for custody of his brother.

She returned the cell phone to her purse and stepped outside. Then she hooked one finger over the top of the doorknob and gave a gentle pull. The old door swung easily and latched, making a slight noise. Betty turned to go back to her Buick, looking down at the uneven and weathered porch boards, and carefully stepping around a bloated trash bag.

"What are you doing here!"

Johnny jumped up on the porch from the side and stood about six feet from her. An old pair of threadbare Levis were all he was wearing. The obscene tattoo on his chest announced his far-reaching anger. His right arm bore the names of three different women, each one overlaying a design of a nude female body part. Water dripped from Johnny's straight black hair.

"You stole my little brother. Now what else have you stolen from me today?"

Fear pounced on her like a cheetah from a treetop. "Johnny, you startled me!" She looked at the half-naked guy and wondered if there was a knife inside the pocket of those unbuttoned Levis. "I...I told you I thought I might drop by...drop by to see all the work you've done on your parents' old home place."

"So you think you can just waltz into someone's house, unannounced, huh?"

"No, I simply stepped just inside the door, hoping to find you." Betty felt her voice quiver a bit. "I knocked and called out to see if anyone was home."

"Don't give me that line of bull. I heard that door slam when you came out." It was amazing how many obscenities could be inserted inside a simple sentence.

Goose bumps on her arms were doing a tap dance, and she belted out, "I told you I barely stepped inside that filthy house." Her eyes shot irritation straight into the eyes of the young guttermouth. "Look, if you're worried about those fancy boots of yours, you'll find them occupying the center of the room, just like you left them."

"If you didn't go inside, how'd you know they were there?" He pointed his index finger at her sharply, and an ugly sardonic grin swathed his unshaven face. "Gotcha!"

The smirk disappeared, and he said, "You lyin'—" He paused and then ended by tacking on the age-old derogatory term for a female.

"Look, young man! You don't use that term to refer to any woman!" Her courage was back. "I can see why your mother walked away from you and the mess she was in here. Now, move out of my way so I can return to my car."

"You ain't goin' nowhere 'til you empty that ugly purse of yours out here on the porch." Johnny stepped closer to her. "I wanna see what you took from me."

"I'm not doing any such thing. Now get out of my way, before the real beast comes out in me!"

Johnny grabbed at her purse and, with the force of a bull angered by a matador's red cape, she kneed him at the point where those faded Levi's legs intersected at the button fly. He doubled over, and she ran to her car.

A stream of vulgarities cracked the air behind her. Betty opened the door and slid inside, quickly pushing the electronic lock button. She was digging in her purse to excavate the bulky wad of keys and looked up after catching a glimpse of movement.

A neighbor sitting on a porch swing next door had a telephone to her ear. The neighbor slowly got up and hobbled out toward

Betty's car, motioning for her to roll her window down. The old woman was still holding the phone close to her ear.

Betty finally found the keys and turned the ignition to the accessory area and rolled her window down a few inches.

"I saw that rascal bullying you." She laughed. "You sure knew how to jingle his jewels!"

Betty blushed. "Actually, I should have never stopped here. He had told me how he spent a fortune fixing up this old place and all the hours he'd spent in doing so. I just wanted to see for myself what he'd done—if anything." Betty glanced toward the house where Johnny had disappeared inside.

"I'm Emma Knutson," the woman said. "I've lived next door here to this clan of copperheads since that obnoxious Johnny you came into intimate contact with"—Mrs. Knutson grinned—"was just a snot-nosed toot, running around in my yard, stark naked. There's been a many a time I've wanted to kick him in the bejingles, just like you did! He followed right in his daddy's footsteps—ain't none of them Barrows brood worth two cents, 'cept maybe that sweet Lany Lou."

"You know her, do you?"

"Honey, let me tell you, that poor thing endured many a beatin' at the hands of that monster husband of hers. But I hear tell, he cain't touch her now. He's doin' life in the pen for murder—murder! Right here, next door to me! This was a pretty good neighborhood when I moved here. Them Barrows and a few other hooligans who moved in around here have flat ruined this community."

"Tell me more about Mrs. Barr—"

"Oh, mercy!" Emma said. "Looky here! I'm standin' here holding this phone, yakkin' at you, and I've still got the cops on the line." She placed the cordless phone back up to her ear. "Officer, I'm sorry to bother you, it looks like everything's okay now." She held the phone out as far as her arm would stretch, stared at it, and punched the end button with her index finger. "I guess he thinks I'm a loony tune."

"Mrs. Knutson, I was going to ask if you know what happened to Mrs. Barrow. She seems to have been missing for quite some time now." Emma had turned and was looking back at the Barrow front door, and Betty wondered if she had even heard her.

Emma laid the phone on the windshield of the Buick, resting it against the driver's side wiper blade. "Honey, we ain't seen her since the day John shot that biker friend of hers. She just up and disappeared."

Betty, of course, knew where Lana Lou was, but she was hoping to garner more information from the lady.

"If that woman was smart, she woulda found her another man to furnish her meal tickets—couldn't be any worse than what she had all them years with Big John. Honey, he was a gorilla! A big angry gorilla. I always looked forward to his next stint in the slammer."

Just then, a black Corvette pulled up beside Betty's Buick, waited a couple of seconds, and sped away. Emma shook her head. "There's a constant string of them fancy vehicles comin' and goin' from this house. No one stays but a few minutes." As she was telling this, a BMW slowly drove past. "I just don't know what's going on here. John and Lany Lou never had this much company when they lived here." She pursed her lips and shook her head. "And now I see Johnny's gone and bought himself one of them big boxes on wheels—what do they call 'em—hum bees, or somethin' like that."

"Okay, Mrs. Knutson, it was nice visiting with you. I've gotta run." Betty toggled the window back up, and Emma turned and started toward her house.

Betty opened the door and hollered at the lady. "Hon, you forgot your phone."

43

"One way to Dallas. That'll be fifty-six dollars. Cash or credit card?"

Josh Barrow pulled on the chain hanging at the side of his sagging jeans, grabbed the attached wallet, opened it, and paid the ticket agent with the three twenty dollar bills he had left.

"Your bus will be out there on the left of that door, but it's running late. You might have time to grab some lunch if you haven't eaten. You should check back here in about forty minutes."

Josh walked out the front door, looked down and searched his wallet to make sure all he had left was the four one dollar bills he'd been handed in change. Without looking up, he stepped around some woman holding out a Folgers coffee can. *Stinkin' panhandlers!* He walked on down a ways and encountered another moocher. This one, in a rag-thin dress with her legs spread out, extending over most of the narrow sidewalk.

"Son, you got a couple of dollars you could spare me so I can get somethin' to eat?" The few coins in the bottom of the big glass jar rattled as she held it up toward him and shook it.

He stopped and stared at her. "Move them ugly legs sticking out there. You're blocking the sidewalk, woman!" She didn't move, just shook her big jar at him again as he stepped over her.

A man with a briefcase was facing him and paused at the obstruction of legs stretching over the sidewalk. He cleared his throat, but the old woman never budged.

Josh looked at the man and said, "If these leprous outcasts would go get a job, they might not find themselves sitting out here on the street, homeless, with their hands stuck out, begging for a dollar." The man ignored him, stepped over the outstretched legs, and dropped a few coins in her jar.

Josh found a café just around the corner, walked in, and seated himself at a booth toward the rear. A cute waitress appeared, wearing tight jeans and a white T-shirt with a ketchup stain in front. He stared at the paper menu she handed him. The only item under four bucks was a toasted cheese sandwich. He pointed to it. "That come with chips?"

"Yep, and a pickle."

"Coke?"

"Yeah." She pointed at the menu. "Sodas are down at the bottom. They're a buck fifty."

He handed the menu back to her. "I guess I'll have water with the toasted cheese."

After washing down the greasy sandwich with water, he accepted the bill from the waitress, pulled out the four one dollar bills left in his wallet, slapped them down on the table, and stared at the interior of the wallet.

The waitress started to pick up the cash. Josh quickly laid his hand over the cash on the table and looked up into her ice-blue eyes. "No money left." His voice cracked. "No driver's license, no pictures of a girlfriend—I am one pathetic dude!" Josh laid open his empty wallet for her to see. "Don't suppose you could trash this meal ticket, huh?"

She took the cash and the dirty plate. "I'm sorry." And walked away.

He ambled back around the corner, stepped over the sprawled-out legs of the old panhandler, looked up toward the front door of the bus terminal, and froze!

44

Their eyes met. "Josh!" She made an effort to get up on her feet but was too weak. "Josh!" she cried again. "Come here, son!"

He walked closer and stopped, took three more steps, and stopped again. "Mama? Is that you?"

Lana Lou turned her frail body to one side, put one hand down on the sidewalk, and managed to pull herself up on one knee. "Josh, come on, give your mama a hand."

He walked closer to her. "No way! I'm not believing what I'm seeing!" He stood in front of her and stared into her eyes for a few seconds. Then he stuck out his hand toward her. She grabbed it and tried to get up, but fell back down.

Josh backed off, wiped his hand on his jeans, and continued to stare at her. "Mama, what are you doing here?"

"Oh, baby, I'm sorry you had to see me like this. It's a long story, son. Won't you sit down here with me so we can talk?"

He looked at her Folgers coffee can, then back up at her fragile sun-splotched body. "Mama, you're nothing but one of these stinkin' panhandlers! How could you?" He turned around as if to see who was watching. A four-letter word slithered from his lips. "This is embarrassing!"

Lana Lou patted the sidewalk next to her. "Josh, come on, sit down with me, and let's talk. You need to hear my side of the story."

Josh took a couple of steps back. "Mama, this is disgusting. Are you really living out here on the street like these other hoodlums?"

Her voice was weak. "I've got no place else, son."

"You mean you are homeless? No money. Out here begging for a few bucks?" He kicked at the sidewalk. "I don't know you!" He shook his head and walked into the building, started to sit down on a bench, and saw his bus pull up and park on the west side of the terminal. He turned and looked back toward the front door, and then quickly walked out to his bus marked for Dallas.

45

"Childers Ranch, this is Katie."

The raspy cough gave the caller away even before the first word. "Katie...is this Katie?"

"Yes, Lana Lou. Where are you?"

"Well, I'm out of the hospital, back here at the bus station. A nice man is letting me use his cell phone, so I can't talk long. I'm just so upset I missed my visit with my baby. Do you think they'd let me try again?"

"Yes, hon, I'll get it rescheduled for you. I see you've still got that awful cough. Couldn't they do anything for that?"

"Well, it's like this—I've got no inshorance, so they probably didn't want to keep me in there 'til this cough was gone."

"Lana Lou, if you're gonna be there tomorrow, I'm coming to see you. I can meet you there at the Greyhound terminal about two o'clock. Okay?"

"Oh, I'll be here all right." She laughed, and that started another coughing spell. "Hold on." Finally the coughing ended, and she inhaled heavily. "Yeah, I'll be right here. It ain't like I've booked myself on a cruise or got an appointment at some fancy spa." That brought on another belly laugh, which spawned more coughing.

Katie ended the call for her. "Hon, I'll see you tomorrow about two."

Clouds had moved in, and a fine mist saturated the city air. Katie parked and walked the three blocks to the terminal. Her friend was sitting in her usual spot, just under the roof overhang.

"Hon, you're looking some better. I brought you some flowers from my garden." Katie handed them to her, sat down next to her, and leaned back against the wall.

Lana Lou's brown eyes glowed through the afternoon mist as the breeze swirled under the overhanging eve. "Oh, these are beautiful! Irises—ice blue, and I love these plum-colored ones. I used to have some like these, but John kept mowing them down. I never could have anything pretty around the place—not with three rowdy boys and a man who tore up everything I tried to pretty up."

"Well one of your boys has sent you something I'm sure you will think is very pretty." She pulled out Thorne's eight-and-a-half-by-eleven charcoal drawing from the manila envelope and held it up for his mother to see. "Hon, your son drew this for you."

Lana Lou put her right hand to her chest and stared at the drawing. "My Thorn did that?" Clearly stunned, she said, "Oh my! I had no idea he could draw like that!"

"Yes, and look at the little dog peeking around the corner of the barn. That's our dog, Noah. And it looks exactly like him. He's a Border collie mix Kirk got at the animal shelter. Thorne loves that dog! I watch them chasing each other outside my kitchen window."

Lana Lou touched the picture of the dog and then looked up at Katie, her brown eyes a bit sad. "I got the boys a puppy once, brought it home, and it peed on the floor in front of John's recliner. We never saw the dog after that." She coughed. "Then there was the time Thorne brought home a pretty calico kitten. It was a sweet little thing. Thorne fed it, cleaned out its litter box, and he'd take that cat for rides up on his shoulder. He loved that beautiful black-yellow-and-white kitten. But me and him was the only ones that did. John even called Thorne a sissy for keepin' a cat—said cats was for girls.

"I was workin' next door for my neighbor—cleanin' her house to make extra grocery money—and all of a sudden, I heard this awful screaming over toward our house. I looked out the window and saw Johnny, my oldest boy, squeezin' the daylights outta the cat, and my Johnny—he was cussin' a blue streak. His dad thought it was funny. We never did get any more pets."

"Well that's sad because Thorne loves all the animals. He's not too crazy about our big Angus bull, but he loves the horses, and he loves that dog!"

Lana Lou was staring at the charcoal drawing. "Is that one of them four-wheelers I see there in front of the barn?"

"Yes, he even drew it just right. He made it look just like our Honda Rancher. The boy is a natural. Oh! And I forgot to tell you the best part!" Katie put her hand on Lana Lou's. "Thorne's teacher entered one of his drawings in a contest there at our school. I knew it was good and might be the best in the class—but get this—he won first place in the entire school! Then it was entered in a district competition for young artists. And he won! So now his piece is going to be displayed at the National Cowboy & Western Heritage Museum here in Oklahoma City!"

Lana Lou pulled her hand away from Katie's and wiped her teary eyes. "Oh, I wish I could see that."

"I'm coming and picking you up," Katie said, "and we're taking you with us to see it, just as soon as it is displayed there."

"Will my baby get to come too?"

"Yes, we'll all go together!"

"What about that caseworker you've been telling me about? Will she allow that?"

"Honey, it will happen just like I said," Katie's lips tightened. "Anyone tries to stop it, and this red hair of mine is gonna burst into flames right there! Thorne's mama's gonna get to be there with her son at such a special event." Katie's voice lowered a bit. "Just don't even mention it to the caseworker when you see her."

Lana Lou was grinning, looking directly at Katie's eyes. "Girl, you got some spunk! I like you."

Katie blushed. "Sorry. I don't usually get riled up so easily. But when it comes to kids, and what can keep them from having happy childhoods, I can become a racing fire engine with a deafening siren blasting out for anyone in a country mile to hear."

Lana Lou giggled.

"So, hon, tell me how you've been since you got back down here? Anyone been dropping enough coins in your can to buy you a good meal?"

"I've been gettin' by. Oh, did I tell you I saw my middle boy, Josh?"

"No! When?"

"It was just this morning." She ducked her head. "But he was embarrassed to see me. Wouldn't even hardly talk to me. I know he wasn't expectin' to see me out here on the street like this, but he just walked away from me."

"Oh, that's awful!"

"I had me a good cry after he was gone."

"Well, I'm sure! What was he doing down here? Did he get on a bus to somewhere?"

"I don't know. He just yanked up on them droopy pants he wears and disappeared inside. I don't know, maybe he was catchin' a bus. He wouldn't say."

The woman held the irises up to her nose one more time. "Mmm. This brings back memories of when I was a young girl out in my grandma's flower garden. She grew irises just like these."

Katie pulled herself up from the concrete. "Sweetie, I've gotta run now. Enjoy those flowers."

Lana Lou handed the drawing back to Katie. "Tell him I think he is a good artist."

"No, he wants you to keep this." She handed it back. "He made this just for you. I told him to make it pretty small so you could keep it better. He usually does his drawings on a big sketch pad, but I knew you wouldn't have a place for one that big."

The woman clutched the drawing. "I'll show this to everyone I see!"

Katie smiled. "Hon, I'll get us another appointment with DFS for a visit and come get you. We'll go shopping down here at the secondhand store, and I'll buy you a new outfit to go see your son. Oh! And when we find out when Thorne's art will be displayed in the museum, we'll come get you for that." She pulled out a ten-dollar bill she had prepared to give her, dropped it in the Folgers can, and walked away. She turned to wave good-bye and saw the shriveled brown hand wiping her eyes.

46

Brandon and Thorne had both asked to go see *Flicka*, and it was showing at the AMC Quail Springs Mall. As they walked inside the sprawling complex, Kirk looked at the various movie titles that were showing.

"I can see several movies I'd rather see," he whispered to Katie. "I think I bought that book for Brandon last year. Maybe we should see something else."

"Kirk, this is not about us. We're doing this for the boys! You go buy our tickets. I'll get them some popcorn to share."

The smell of the fresh buttered popcorn had drawn Brandon toward the concession stand. Thorne was wandering around the area, gawking at the movie posters.

Kirk waited in line behind a young man holding his scantily-clad girlfriend's waist with one hand, while trying to dig out his wallet with the other. "Two for *Horror in the Attic*." Finally, he retrieved a bulging leather wallet, laid it on the counter, pulled out a hundred dollar bill, and handed it to the clerk. The clerk held the bill up to examine it and then handed the guy his change. He quickly stuffed it inside the overstuffed wallet, turned, and bumped directly into Kirk.

"Hey," Kirk said, "watch it, man."

There was no apology from the guy, just a cold stare as he started to walk away. Kirk stepped back a bit, looked down, and noticed the heavily-starched Wranglers topping a pair of full-quill ostrich boots.

Just then, a teen with a purple-and-green Mohawk cut in line. Without saying a word to him, Kirk waited while the kid bought a ticket. After the kid moved on, Kirk stepped up to the counter. "Two adults and two children for *Flicka*."

Katie met him with a large bucket of popcorn. "Where's Thorne?"

Brandon reached into the big paper bucket. "He was right over there, looking at those movie posters."

"Yeah, he was…" Katie said. "But I don't see him now."

Brandon pulled out a handful of popcorn, spilling some on the floor. "Maybe he went in the men's room."

"Kirk, you better go check."

Brandon pointed. "Nope, I see him. Here he comes."

Two attendants were taking tickets. Kirk handed one guy theirs, accepted the stubs, and then led the way down the hallway. He looked back to wait for Katie and saw the guy in the starched jeans and fancy boots heading toward them from halfway down the hallway.

Brandon and Thorne were bouncing ahead. Katie caught up with Kirk, touched his arm, and whispered, "Kirk, I just heard someone behind me call Thorne's name! I turned and saw this guy starting toward us."

"You sure he said 'Thorne'?" He looked back.

The guy was plunging toward them. "Hey, Thorne!" he hollered.

"Babe, follow me," Kirk said.

He ran ahead and caught up with the boys, grabbing Thorne by the arm. "Guys, stay with me."

There was a hallway leading off to the right. Kirk pushed the boys inside the first theater door with Katie following close behind. Brandon protested. "This isn't the one, Dad!"

"It is for now." He shoved the boys into the back row in the darkened theater. Katie sat down with them.

"Dad! This is not the right movie. It's even rated R."

"Be quiet, Brandon!" Kirk said. "Don't say a word!"

Kirk had sat down in the outside seat next to the center aisle. A flash of light appeared as the door opened. Kirk looked down at the ostrich boots standing next to him. The guy was searching the darkened theater and then ran back out the door.

"What's going on, Kirk?" Katie whispered.

"That was the guy who was hollering at Thorne back there by the ticket attendant. And I'm pretty sure it's the same guy who bumped into me when I was waiting in line to buy our tickets."

"Well, how did he know Thorne?"

"I don't know. Let's just wait here for a few minutes. I thought maybe he was just ticked at me for tellin' him to watch it when he bumped into me at the ticket counter, but that doesn't explain how he would know Thorne's name. Something's not right about this."

Brandon reached around Katie. "Dad, what's the deal? Why are we sitting in here?"

"Yeah," Thorne laughed. "This sure ain't *Flicka*!"

"Guys! Just sit still for a few minutes. We'll go to the right one in a minute."

Katie handed the bucket of popcorn to Brandon and started to climb over Kirk's legs.

"Where you goin', babe?"

"I'm going to go look around and see if I can spot him—find out what he's up to."

"No!"

But she was already headed for the door. A minute later, she ducked back inside, climbed over Kirk's long legs again, and plopped down in her chair. "Kirk," she whispered, "that guy is looking inside every theater door! What's with him? This is spooking me!"

The previews were starting, and Brandon was complaining. "Dad, we're gonna miss our movie!"

The door opened. A flash of light burst in, and Mr. Fancy Boots appeared again. He walked down toward the front of the theater. Kirk saw his chance. He grabbed Katie's arm. "Get the boys. Let's get outta here now!"

Just outside the door, Kirk said, "Hurry up, follow me!" He bolted toward the *Flicka* door. "Get inside, guys! Quick!"

The back row was empty, and the theater was dark. "Okay, boys, sit down and don't say one word!"

The previews continued, and Katie looked over at Kirk. "I think we should report this!"

"What's there to report?"

"The guy is stalking us!"

"Nope, he's lookin' for Thorne. I have a feeling Thorne might even know who he is."

"Well, I don't like this!"

"He comes in here and tries anything, you can just stomp on them fancy boots he's wearing, and I'll take care of the rest."

47

Brandon was spending the night at his friend's house in town. Thorne jumped down from the bus and ran to the pickup. "Kirk, Mrs. Stephens says my charcoal drawing will be on display Saturday."

Kirk could see the kid's eyes were sparkling with enthusiasm. "This Saturday?"

"Yep."

"Well, we'll just have to go check out this new budding artist. Hop in, pal, let's go tell Miss Katie the good news."

Kirk eased up to the fence in front of the house. Thorne opened his door before the pickup came to a complete stop. "Whoa!" Kirk said. "Let me get stopped first."

Thorne raced into the kitchen where Katie sat at the breakfast table with a cup of vanilla chai tea and her latest Karen Kingsbury novel. He reached down and covered the book with his hand. "We gotta go to the museum Saturday. My drawing's gonna be there."

Kirk followed and sat down next to Katie. "I'll have to call my folks," she said, "and see if we can drop off Thorne while we go pick up his mother."

"Why don't we just let him go with us to pick her up? These DFS rules are pretty silly."

"Kirk, we have to abide by them."

"No, I'll stay in the truck with Thorne, while you go fetch Miss Lana Lou. That's not breaking the rules. He won't even get out of the truck."

Kirk convinced his follow-the-rules wife it would be okay, so Saturday morning they drove over to the Greyhound terminal.

Lana Lou was in her usual spot by the front door with her coffee can. Katie helped her up from the sidewalk and told her she was going to see her son's display in the museum. "But first, girl, I'm taking you down to the secondhand store and buying you a new outfit."

"Oh, honey, you don't need to do that."

"Look, Thorne's mother is going to have a new outfit to go to his premier art showing. Now don't argue with me. I've made up my mind!"

Forty-five minutes later, Kirk got out, opened the door, and helped Lana Lou climb into the backseat of the truck. "Well, look at you, Miss Lana Lou!"

"Yes." She pointed first at her slacks. "Katie bought me these new slacks. This blouse and these sandals—and the slacks—only cost Katie nine dollars. The lady let me wear them out of the store when Katie asked."

Kirk grinned. "I'd say Miss Katie got a bargain. You look nice."

Thorne sat in the middle of the backseat, reached over, and held his mother. She laid her head over on Thorne's shoulder and patted his leg.

Katie turned around and faced Lana Lou. "Hon, your son is starting to use oils. He's already finished one painting—I should have brought it to show you—anyway, he painted our big pond with a beautiful sunset mirrored over the perfectly still water, broken only by a mama duck and her three ducklings making their way across the pond. It is really beautiful."

"Oh, I'd love to see it."

"I just handed over my old set of oils and a canvas, and he sat right there at our dining table and created a gorgeous scene, the sky bursting with brilliant reds, oranges, yellows. And he did this all from inside our house. There wasn't even a sunset for him to look at! I'm telling you, your son is a natural!"

The woman squeezed her son and kissed his forehead.

The National Cowboy & Western Heritage Museum was brimming with visitors. Many license plates in the parking lot were from out of state. It was fairly obvious Lana Lou had never been to the museum. Her brown eyes were full of excitement as she walked hand in hand with her son toward the towering atrium entrance.

Once inside, Thorne pulled at his mom's hand. "Come on, I know just where to go. My teacher gave me good directions."

A dozen or more people were gathered around the student displays. Thorne's was at one end, and his rural scene charcoal was drawing some attention. One lady read the inscription under the piece to her friend. "Thorne Barrow, from Luther Elementary—fourth grade! Can you believe that?"

Her friend replied, "That is amazing! I hope we see more of this kid's artwork."

"I find it pretty hard to believe a fourth grader actually did that. Let's hope it's legit."

The comments were all very positive, except for one. A twenty-something guy, with a baby-blue sweater draped over his shoulders preppy style, said to his girlfriend, "I don't know why they want to display this kiddy junk in here. This is a museum of world-renowned Western art pieces—Remington, Russell, Crowley—not a show-and-tell display for grade school kids."

Katie pushed her way over to him and got in his face. "Look, you clearly don't know good art when you see it!" The guy was backing away from her. "And furthermore, what you see here may just be a foreshadowing of tomorrow's great artists."

He backed farther away, held both hands up and palms facing her. "Sorry, lady!"

She stayed on his trail, put her hands on her hips, and glared at him. "Young man, you don't go spouting off criticism in a place like this! Didn't your mother ever teach you any manners?"

Kirk grabbed Katie's arm and whispered, "Kate, cut the guy some slack."

She pulled away from Kirk's grasp, never taking her eyes off the young man, and pointed a stiff finger at Thorne's drawing. "You see this? You just may be looking at a piece that will fetch thousands someday! In case you don't know it, this, my friend, is very good art!"

Kirk was rolling his eyes, but an older lady in the crowd broke out in a handclap, and most of the others were grinning. Lana Lou stood quietly behind Thorne.

"Way to go, Mom, you tell him!" Brandon said.

Kirk put his hand over Brandon's mouth and whispered, "Quiet, son. Your mother is making a big-enough scene."

One well-dressed man stepped up to Katie. "So is this your son's piece?"

"No, this little lady standing back here is the mother of this artist," Katie said, pointing to Lana Lou.

The man turned toward Lana Lou and saw Thorne standing in front of her. "Are you Thorne Barrow?"

Thorne reached out and shook his hand. "Yes I am, sir!"

"And you are how old?"

"Ten," Thorne said.

"Young man, I am Landon Throckmorton. I have a gallery downtown, in the Skirvin Tower on Park Avenue. When your time is up to display your piece here, would you be interested in bringing it to my gallery?"

Thorne looked at Katie. Katie quickly answered for him. "Yes, I think he would, as long as it is okay with Mrs. Barrow."

Throckmorton looked toward Lana Lou. She smiled and tipped her head ever so slightly. "Mrs. Barrow, I believe this piece will bring quite a handsome sum in my gallery. We can talk about a percentage. Does he have more pieces?"

Katie stepped up. "He has a few more charcoals, but he also has a beautiful oil he just completed."

Throckmorton looked a bit confused. "Are you related to the boy?"

Katie got up next to his ear and whispered, "I'm just his foster mother."

Throckmorton paused, shook his head, and looked back over at Lana Lou, then back to Katie. "Wow! Astounding!" He mouthed the word *foster*. "I want all of the pieces this young man can deliver."

Lana Lou stood with her right hand on her chest, her eyes focused on the drawing. The crowd was now staring at her.

The young man Katie had scolded was nowhere in sight.

48

Emma Knutson was sitting in her favorite afternoon spot, her front porch swing. She was holding a tall glass of iced tea with a sprig of mint from her garden when Johnny Barrow walked out his front door. No shirt, just a pair of well-worn jeans. "Mornin', Mrs. Knutson."

"Johnny, them old jeans you're wearin' are more holes than denim. Appears to me you'd be gettin' plenty of air coming through there. Ain't you got anything more decent to wear?"

Johnny laughed. "Don't you know you're too old to be lookin' at the holes in my jeans?"

"Johnny, I've seen you runnin' around my front yard plenty of times with nothin' coverin' that skinny butt of yours. Your mama couldn't even keep your diaper on you. You ain't changed a bit."

"No, and you're still just a nosy old neighbor who can't keep her tongue in her mouth." He grinned. "You and old What's-her-name from across the street." He sauntered over to her porch and hung his thumb in the waistband of his worn-out jeans. "You two are just alike. Old gossip-bitties, that's what you two are!"

"Well, Johnny Boy, you give us plenty to gossip about."

He stepped up on her porch and sat down beside her. "I'm glad to furnish you with some much-needed entertainment, Mrs. Knutson." He grabbed her glass of iced tea and took a swig. "Otherwise, life would get pretty dull for you around here, huh?"

Emma grabbed her glass of tea back. "Ain't you got no manners? I know Lana Lou tried to teach you better'n that!"

"Nope, she didn't teach me a thing."

"Well, it wasn't because she didn't try! But then, what could she expect. You got your old daddy's genes!"

"Well, that's where you're wrong, Mrs. Knutson." Johnny laughed. "I don't wear my daddy's jeans. I buy my own."

Emma pointed her finger at the big hole in the knee of his jeans. "Yeah, and I think it's high time you went and bought yourself some new ones."

"Aw, come on. There's at least a couple of years wear left in these. Why would I wanna go and buy new ones? Besides, the young ladies dig 'em."

Emma picked up the fly swatter next to her and swatted at a fly on Johnny's leg. "I guess you saw in the paper where your brother had some kind of drawing or painting displayed out there in the Cowboy Hall of Fame. I guess they're a callin' it something else now. Anyway, you know what I mean—that big cowboy museum, sits high up on the hill out there, just off the interstate."

"Who you talkin' about? Thorne?"

"Yeah, it was Thorne Barrow. I seen it in the paper."

"You're kiddin'! Thorne? Is it still there?"

"Well, I guess it is. The paper said he and a bunch of other budding artists—is what they called 'em—was havin' their art displayed out there all this month."

"Well now, maybe I can find my little brother after all." He sat there for a second without saying a word. Then he looked at her. "I'll just have to go check it out. I'd sure like to find him. He could be a big help to me in my business."

"And just what business would that be?" Emma snapped. "You, Johnny Barrow, got a business? You ain't never held a job for more than two weeks in your life!"

"Yeah, I'm in the wholesale business."

Her dark eyes drilled deep into his face. "Wholesale…sure. Whose fool do you think I am, Johnny? I got eyes."

"Yeah, and you got a mouth too, woman! Could get you in big trouble."

Emma set her glass of tea on the floor opposite Johnny. "Tell me something, Johnny…what's with all this company you got showin' up here at all hours of the day and night? Whizzin' in—then whizzin' out. We ain't never had this many cars buzzin' through this neighborhood."

"Friends, Mrs. Knutson, just friends," he mumbled. "I better be getting back to what I was doin' before you were so kind as to offer me a glass of iced tea."

Emma slapped at the air in front of Johnny. "I never offered you no tea. We both know you always just take what you please. Lana Lou, bless her heart, she tried to teach you right, but it just never took with you. You've been a scoundrel from day one."

Johnny reached around Emma, grabbed her iced tea again, and started to get up to go. Emma grabbed his arm. "You ever hear anything 'bout your sweet mama?"

"Nope, and I hope I don't either. She's a no-good—"

"Johnny Barrow! Don't you even think about talkin' 'bout Lana Lou like that! She's the only one of you Barrows who had any manners. That pint-sized lady was a hard worker too. And that's more than you can say 'bout that thievin' husband of hers. Back when I was workin' down to the sewin' factory, I had her help me with my housework. I couldn't have never found any better help. That woman—"

Johnny's gaze was fixed on the silver Audi pulling to the curb in front of his house. "What? What were you sayin'?" He stood up.

Emma reached over and took her glass of iced tea from him, frowned, stood up halfway, and pitched the contents over the side of the porch. "Looks like you're gettin' more company," she hollered as he raced barefoot over toward his front door.

He scanned each of the twenty-three pieces of student art before the last one caught his eye. The inscription read, *Thorne Barrow, fourth grader at Luther Elementary, Luther, Oklahoma.* "Well, I'll be…" Johnny muttered aloud.

A thirty-something woman in a business suit stood next to him and looked at the charcoal drawing in front of them. "Nice."

"That's my little brother's piece. Pretty good, huh?"

"Is this the first time you've seen it?"

"Yeah, looks like I barely made it. The lady up front directed me back here but told me this is the last day for the display," Johnny said. "They're taking them down tomorrow."

The lady kept staring at the drawing. "I'd say your brother is quite talented!"

Johnny stuck his hands in his jeans pockets, started to walk away, and then he turned back toward her. "Where's Luther?"

49

GROUND FLOOR OF the Skirvin Tower was home to Throckmorton Gallery, specializing in Western art with works including Fred Fallows, Bill Anton, James Reynolds, and other well-known Western artists.

Kirk, Katie, and Thorne were greeted by Landon Throckmorton soon after they had walked in. Thorne stepped up and shook his hand heartily. Then he walked over to a sculpture showcased on a marble base and set on a large round table in the center of the room. Katie looked at the gallery owner and nodded toward Thorne. The boy's eyes were glued to the piece.

"Mr. Barrow, you're looking at a beautiful bronze casting by E. E. Heikka titled *Peigan Scout*. In my opinion, he ranks right up there with Remington and Russell."

Thorne held his finger close to the sculpture without touching it. "Wow! I want to do this someday."

Throckmorton smiled. "Thorne, this man had no formal training. By the time he was eighteen, this artist was sculpting pieces which today are considered masterpieces."

Thorne walked around the table, inspecting the sculpture from all angles. "Is this like a hard metal?"

"What you see here is a bronze casting of the artist's original clay model. An artist will always work with clay first. The bronze casting is made up of about 90 percent copper and 10 percent tin. The artist doesn't normally do the actual bronzing. That's done later by a company specializing in that form of metal work. Mr. Heikka sculpted the clay model for this in 1931, when the artist was only twenty-one years old. It is considered to be one of his finest sculptures."

Thorne continued to stare at the sculpture from up close. He stepped back a bit, with his eyes still fixated on the piece.

"Mr. Throckmorton," Katie said. "We brought that charcoal drawing you saw at the museum last Saturday. I also brought the oil I told you about. Would you like to see it?"

"Yes, I would. I believe my clientele would be very interested in this young man's work. Someone his age, with that kind of talent, will capture people's hearts—and wallets. I have one investor in particular who is eager to buy in to the early works of promising artists like Thorne."

Kirk headed toward the door to go retrieve Thorne's art. Throckmorton motioned for Katie to follow him to a desk on the opposite side of the room from Thorne. "Mrs... you know, I don't think I ever got your name."

"Childers. Katie Childers, and that's my husband, Kirk, you see going after Thorne's pieces."

"Mrs. Childers, did I understand you are Thorne's foster mother?"

"Yes," Katie said, "and the lady who was with us at the museum was his mother."

"So this young man has been removed from the home of his mother?"

"Yes, that's correct."

"Wow! That is amazing. Those kids are not what I would think of as having talent like this young man."

"Why would that surprise you, Mr. Throckmorton?"

"Uh, well...you see, I guess we would normally think of those kids as having little or no training in the arts. I guess you might say society would normally exclude them from any such special endowments."

"Look, Mr. Throckmorton! No child is of a lower class in God's eyes. Every child has a special brand, put there by the Almighty, and specific to that child alone. Many times we try to cover it up with our ridiculous ideas of social class or skin color. It is still down there somewhere. It is up to adults to expose it by getting rid of our prejudices that cover the incredible artwork of God."

The gallery owner stood perfectly still, his arms crossed in front of him and pressing inward. Finally, he ducked his head and spoke softly. "Mrs. Childers, you are so right. I see I have some soul searching of my own to do. Please forgive my condescending manner. Sometimes this business I'm in makes me forget where even I came from."

"Yes, I suppose that's true for many of us," Katie said. "Would you like to discuss financial arrangements for this young man's art? His mother has given me authority to work with you on his behalf."

"Yes, I'll show you my standard consignment contract."

Thorne had moved over to a beautiful painting titled *Compadres*. An old cowboy in a bright-blue jacket was standing next to a creek holding the reins of his horse with one hand and reaching down and petting a little dog with the other. The rust, brown, and green background colors in the rocks and brush showcased the cowboy's blue jacket. Thorne seemed mesmerized, studying the piece with silent intent. Katie walked over to him. "Thorne, that is absolutely stunning! You have an excellent eye for art. And the dog looks a lot like Noah."

Thorne took Katie by the hand and pulled her to another painting by Tim Cox titled *Waiting for Dad*. A young cowboy, about the age of Thorne, sat on the ground in a field by his horse, petting his dog, with a few Hereford cattle in the background. The price was posted at $29,500.

"You seem to be drawn to these paintings with a dog in them," Throckmorton said. "Do you have a dog?"

"We have a dog named Noah on the ranch where I live. I like to draw him with charcoal. But now, I think I'd like to paint him with the oil paints Katie gave me. I've got an idea for one with Noah in the back of Kirk's pickup, with his front feet up on the bed rail, about to jump over and chase a rabbit he sees."

"I think that is a great idea." Throckmorton said. "You paint that and bring it in to the gallery here. I think it might just be a hit!"

"Yeah, and I want to paint him barkin' his fool head off at one of the big, black bulls."

"Young man, I can see you have the imagination of a true artist. I'll be waiting to see those when you finish them." "

"I'm getting a lot of good ideas here," Thorne said, "but I need another canvas. Do you think—"

Throckmorton cut in. "Young man, how many would you like? And what size?" He grinned. "There's just one catch. You will have to fill each one I give you with vibrant colors—much like this one you're looking at, but straight out of your own head—and bring them back to me to showcase here in my gallery."

Thorne stuck his hand out to Throckmorton. "Deal!"

50

The backseat of the pickup held fourteen canvases, ranging in size from a small ten by ten to several twelve by sixteen. One large eighteen by twenty-four was leaning behind the rest. A hundred-dollar set of Williamsburg handmade oil colors, along with brushes, solvents, varnishes, and artist knives occupied a cardboard box on the floor. Thorne picked up one of the Grumbacher oils. Cadmium red. "Mr. Throckmorton sure was nice to me."

Katie turned around to look again at the stockpile of artist's supplies. "Just remember the bargain you made with him. You've got to fill them with your own special imagination and take them back to be displayed in the gallery."

"Can I take the easel in my bedroom so I can work in there? It's too noisy in the big room."

"Yes, you may. Maybe we should look around for some kind of cabinet to store all of your supplies in." She turned to Kirk. "Maybe Kirk will build you a cabinet if you agree to mow the lawn this summer."

Kirk looked in the rearview mirror. "Deal!"

The door to Thorne's room remained closed. He had made it clear to everyone he wanted it left that way. "I don't want you guys seeing what I'm painting 'til I've finished."

For three days, he hardly came out of his room. Katie had to call him to the table, and then he would scarf down his food, jump up, and run back to his room. A half-eaten hamburger was left on his plate at dinner. Kirk caught his arm as he jumped up to go. "Hey, pal, are we ever gonna get to see that painting you've been working on?"

"I'm almost finished." Thorne pulled loose and bounced back to his own private artist den. Two hours later, he came back in the big room, grinning from ear to ear. "Okay, you can come see now."

All three Childers marched behind Thorne to his room. Thorne threw open the door. Katie walked in first, followed by Kirk, then Brandon. The easel stood in the corner of the room with a twelve-by-sixteen blank canvas.

Katie stared at the white canvas. "What's this all about?"

Kirk laughed. "And it took you four days to do that?"

Brandon made an attempt at funny. "Looks like a giant white elephant in a snowstorm."

Thorne walked over to his closet, opened the door, and gently pulled out another canvas, still wet. He removed the blank one and placed one bursting with color on the easel. Katie gasped, Kirk stood speechless, and Brandon mouthed, "Wow!"

There was Noah, with his rear end up in a pouncing stance, and an obvious angry bark blasting forth from his open muzzle. The dog's back was bristled. A big Black Angus bull, pawing at the ground and staring at Noah, was the target of the dog's rage. In the background, a big cadmium-red barn and a chalk-white rail fence added to the scene without dominating it. The burnt ochre straw on the ground, with patches of Oklahoma red dirt exposed here and there, emphasized the blackness of the bull and the little black-and-white dog. The entire scene was shrouded in a cold madder-blue fog, eerily adding to the unnerving atmosphere of the upset canine. Thorne had signed his name in the lower right corner with Prussian blue.

"Thorne, that is absolutely marvelous!" Katie said. "Where did you learn to paint like that?"

A slight grin broke loose on Thorne's face. "I don't know."

"Hey, pal, that is just natural-born talent!" Kirk looked even closer, examining the way the fog was shrouding the scene. "I don't think that could ever be taught. You are amazing!"

"One time, I drew a picture of a dog. I used colored pencils. Mom put it on the refrigerator, but when Dad came home, he saw it and said it just cluttered up the place. He grabbed it off the fridge, tore it up, and threw it on the floor."

"Well, buddy, you won't find this one on the floor! We're going to get it framed."

Thorne studied Kirk for a second. "Could you make one for it?"

"A frame?" Kirk knelt down in front of the boy. "Yes, that's exactly what I'll do. I've even got an idea for the wood to use. There is an old weathered gate, lying on the ground back behind the barn. I've been meaning to get it out of there and burn it. It just might make a really cool frame for your painting. I'll pull it out, clean it up, and see if I can work some magic with my table saw and the new miter saw I got for my birthday. What do you think?"

"Cool! Stamp your name on the back of it, 'cause that will be art too—your art."

Over the next month, Thorne completed three more paintings. The old tree shanty on the back side of the ranch, used by some deer hunter in the past, was the subject of one. Thorne had put his own twist on the scene by turning it into a landscape with snow glistening in the winter sun. A closer look at the piece drew attention to the barrel of a rifle poking out between the weathered old boards. The colors he had used were not straight out of the tube. Instead, he had mixed them to come up with the rich presentation of pigments, giving the painting a most unusual effect.

The second painting was exactly as he had described with his idea to the gallery owner. There was Noah in Kirk's pickup bed, with his front feet on the bed rail, about to jump out and chase a jackrabbit a few yards away. The intensity of the dog's posture characterized the scene. "I've got a title for this one." Thorne's eyes were sparkling. "I call it *Sic 'Em!*"

When he brought out the third one, Katie grabbed at her chest. Her voice was soft. "Oh…oh, Thorne!" A tiny tear popped out of her eye.

Even though it was very abstract, it was obviously Lana Lou, sitting on a sidewalk holding out a Folgers coffee can. Katie wrapped her arms around the boy. "Sweetie, that one drills right through to my heart."

Thorne solemnly looked up at Katie, waited, and then said just two words. "Mine too."

51

Katie drove up to the barn where Kirk was bedding down a sick calf. She got out of the truck and walked inside. The Angus calf was frail and obviously premature, unable to stand.

"Hey, you come down to give me a hand?"

"Not really, but I can if you need me. Where's that little thing's mama?"

"She's out with the herd, doin' fine. Her calf was so tiny, she hardly knew she was giving birth."

Katie rested her arms on the rail of the ten-by-ten stall. "Is she going to be able to feed her baby?"

"Nope, since the calf came so soon, she doesn't have enough milk for it. We'll have to bottle-feed this little guy. Brandon thinks that's his job, so I'll have some help with it."

Kirk dropped the last of the straw in the stall, put the pitchfork down, and glanced up at Katie. "What? No baggy sweatshirt and old faded jeans? Where you headed?"

"I'm going back down to the Greyhound terminal today to take Lana Lou an outfit I bought for her at a garage sale in Luther. I've also made up another goodie bag for her with a few snack items and some toiletries."

"Why don't you stop by the gallery and see if he's got Thorne's drawing and painting up yet?"

"You read my mind. I was just thinking about doing that. I was even going to snap a picture of them hanging in that fancy gallery with my cell phone to show his mother."

"Tell her I said hi."

Throckmorton Gallery was eerily quiet. No one was there to greet her. She looked around the room, searching for Thorne's pieces. They weren't there. She walked back to the individual cubicles, each showcasing a featured artist. She was staring at a painting titled *The Blowup*, by Western artist, Tim Cox. It was oil on Masonite. Katie was intrigued by the colors, some of the same ones Thorne had used in his piece he was calling *Sic 'Em*. She was starting to feel like an intruder when a beautiful tall lady with a striking resemblance to Raquel Welch walked in, wearing a full-length black dress. With a hint of a foreign accent, she said, "Good afternoon, may I help you?"

"Oh, you startled me."

"You're looking at one of my favorites." The accent sounded Swedish. "Tim Cox is a wonderful artist, depicting the contemporary West with its rugged cowboys and hardworking ranchers. As you can see in this piece, he is famous for his glorious skies and wide open spaces."

Katie noticed the $45,000 price posted below the painting. "Yes, it's very nice. But, actually, I came here to see a specific artist."

"I apologize. My name is Rhena Throckmorton."

"Katie Childers. It's nice to meet you. I came in to see a couple of pieces you have here by a young artist by the name of Thorne Barrow."

"Oh, I'm sorry. Both pieces we were featuring have been sold."

"Sold!" Katie's eyes established her degree of astonishment. "Both of them?"

"Yes, a young man came in just yesterday. He said he was the artist's brother. I believe he said his name was John, or maybe Johnny. Barlow—no, I believe he would have said Barrow."

"You have got to be kidding! And you let him buy them?"

"Well, yes. He paid full price for both, so who were we to argue with that?"

"And what price did you have on them, if I may ask."

"Mrs. Childers, that is a question I would normally be hesitant to disclose, but several people had already seen them, so I guess it's okay if I disclose that. The drawing was priced at fifteen hundred dollars, and the painting was four thousand."

"Four thousand!" Katie's mouth fell open. "Oh my…I had no idea!"

"Do you know this artist?"

Stunned, Katie said, "Well, yes, I do." She swallowed. "I am his foster mother."

"Oh yes, Landon told me about you. We are still amazed at the talent this young man has. To tell you the truth, I think we priced those pieces too low. His brother got a bargain!"

"Mrs. Throckmorton, I'm curious. How did his brother know Thorne's pieces were here? He has no contact with Thorne whatsoever."

"I have no idea. He came in, specifically looking for a piece from this artist."

"And he just dropped down fifty-five hundred dollars for them?"

The lady smiled. "Yes, you said it right. It was in cash."

Katie told the lady she was in fact the one handling Thorne's financial arrangements with the gallery. "Will you be mailing a check, or how will Thorne get his money?"

After some checking with their bookkeeper, the lady told Katie the check was already in the mail. "You should have it in a couple of days, three at the most."

Katie thanked her and started to walk out, but then she remembered she had three more paintings of Thorne's in the truck. "Are you interested in having more of this boy's paintings?"

"Honey, we will take all he can deliver. My husband believes this child is well on his way to becoming a renowned Western artist. We haven't seen this kind of talent in a child—ever."

"Let me just run back out to the truck. I'll bring in the three he has just finished."

When she returned with the pieces and leaned them up against the wall, Rhena Throckmorton stood in awe. "Mrs. Childers! This young man is amazing!" Her eyes were stuck on the one Katie had placed in front of the others—the one with the dog barking at the bull. "That blue fog! How did he do that?"

"I'm not sure. He stayed in his room, wouldn't let us come in until he had finished. We walked in and saw all three pieces. But I agree with you, this one is astonishing. This kid has had no training. I gave him what few oil paints I was holding on to. He picked them up, and has amazed us with what he has done. Mr. Throckmorton thrilled him when he gave him all of those art supplies. These are three of those canvases he gave him, and I'm sure the oils he used are from the set of Williamsburg oils your husband gave him."

Rhena glanced back toward an office. "Good investment, Mr. Throckmorton!" Then she laughed. "You can tell this young man we will furnish him with any art supplies he needs, as long as he brings this kind of investment quality art to us."

Katie reached out to take Rhena's hand. "I will tell him." She then removed the painting with the fog Rhena had been talking about, and placed it behind the other two. When Rhena saw the abstract of Lana Lou holding out the Folgers can, she sucked in air, held it, and finally said, "Oh! Oh! I can't wait for Landon to see this!" She took Katie's hand again. "You know, this painting tells a story in itself."

"Oh, you have no idea!" Katie took a step closer to the lady. "Yes, this is Thorne's mother, in abstract of course. Isn't it wonderful?" Then she looked into Rhena Throckmorton's eyes. "You should know Mrs. Barrow is a homeless person, living on the city streets. She panhandles for the few coins she can get to buy a meal."

"Katie, Landon told me the boy had been removed from his family, and he had seen his mother at the National Cowboy and Western Heritage Museum. I would like to meet her sometime and tell her what an incredible artist her son is."

"I'm going there now. She lives behind the Greyhound terminal under a makeshift tent, propped up by a couple of blown-down tree limbs."

Rhena Throckmorton stood still as a statue. Finally she removed her eyeglasses, letting them drop with the chain around her neck. "Oh, that breaks my heart! Now I really must meet her."

"Katie, I am not going to put this out until Landon has had a chance to see it and price it. If I put it out for sale now, it will be gone before Landon returns." Rhena got down on her knees to have a closer look at the painting sitting on the floor and leaning against the wall. Then she stood, moved away several feet, and continued to stare at the piece. "This young man is amazing! What really is amazing is that he can do abstract just as well as real-life." She gently grabbed Katie's arm. "Oh, I don't think I can part with this one. I want it in my home!"

Katie looked confused. "Actually, I think it will need to be sold. We are hoping to save all of the profits from Thorne's art for his education. I'm thinking he should go to a prestigious art school."

"Oh, honey! I would agree totally. Let's have Landon price the piece without him knowing my intentions, and I will then purchase it at whatever price Landon places on it."

Katie could see room for some shady dealings, and her face must have exposed her thoughts. "I'll tell you what, Katie, maybe you should have this piece appraised by a few more art dealers. That might be fairer. Then I will pay the price you set, as long as Landon is in agreement with the appraisal."

Katie hesitated and then broke her silence. "I will agree to that as long as the artist has an option to purchase it back from you at some future date for the same price you pay for it."

"Oh, that can be arranged." Rhena looked back at the painting. "I've got to have the piece! We'll draw up a contract after you've had it appraised."

52

"Get in, Alexa!" Johnny jerked the Hummer into reverse. "Either you're with me or you're not."

She climbed into the passenger seat just as Johnny started to back out into the street. "Johnny, I just think this is crazy! You can't go barging into a school and pulling Thorne out of the classroom just like that!" She buckled her seat belt as Johnny slammed the big black boxy vehicle into drive and gassed it. "They'll have you back in the slammer before you can even get out of town!"

"Look, baby, I just wanna see my brother. They've been keepin' him from me for way too long. You just sit back, hold on, and shut up." He had programmed the GPS to take him to the town of Luther, and the female voice began navigating him through the Oklahoma City streets, heading northeast. He was sitting at a red light at Sooner Road and Northeast Thirty-Sixth Street. "Don't you understand? Thorne is all the family I've got now."

"Johnny Barrow, you don't care a hoot about him! I know what you're up to. You're thinkin' the kid can sell your goods to all his school friends."

"Shut up, Alex!" The light turned green, and Johnny chirped the tires. "You know you're in this too." Six blocks on down the street, the female voice on the GPS instructed the driver to turn at the next corner, but neither Johnny nor his friend heard it.

The female voice came back on. "Turn now!"

Johnny slammed on the brakes and cut the wheels sharply to the right. The vehicle behind him skidded to within inches of his back bumper as the Hummer careened around the corner. Alexa slapped her hands on the dash. "Johnny!"

"Aw, get over it, Alex! I made it, didn't I?"

"Johnny, I'm not liking this!"

"What? So I about missed my turn. So what?"

"Yeah, you about got us rear-ended, but no, I'm not talking about your driving skills. You're going to be putting me in a position that will get me in as much trouble with the law as it will you."

"What're you talkin' 'bout, woman?"

"Johnny, I know what you're up to. I'm not stupid. You find your brother and take him with you—that's called kidnapping! I'll be an accessory to that!"

"You don't know squat, Alex!"

"And if you do get your brother and have him selling, the cops would be all over me too."

"You're already an accessory. I haven't seen you refuse to take the cash from a sale yet. So just shut up about it, okay?"

Alexa Cavanaugh turned, looked out the dark-tinted side window, and said no more.

Several miles down the road, Johnny must have missed a turn. The GPS voice kept saying, "Recalculating, recalculating."

"Now this stupid woman don't know how to read a map. Alex, turn her off. I think I know where I'm headed." An hour and several wrong turns later, Johnny admitted he was even more lost. He punched the GPS back on. "Hogback Road? Where the heck is that?"

Alexa stared at the GPS screen. "I don't know, but this says we're heading south. I thought we should be going north."

Johnny's patience was running thin, and the yellow school bus in front of him didn't help matters. "Wait a minute," he said. "Wasn't that the turnpike we just crossed over?" Just then, the bus slowed and the stop arm came out. Johnny stopped and reached for the cigarettes on the dash. Just as he was lighting up, two boys exited the bus on the right, walked in front of the bus, and headed to the other side of the road. "Hot dang! That's my brother! That's Thorne!"

Johnny rolled down the dark-tinted window. "Thorne! Is that you?" The stop arm retracted, and the bus drove on.

Johnny bolted out of the Hummer. "Thorne! Hey, it's me, Johnny!"

Thorne started running toward him. The other kid was right behind him, yelling, "Thorne, what are you doing?"

"That's my brother—that's Johnny!"

Thorne ran into Johnny's arms. Johnny bear-hugged the boy. "Hey, buddy, I can't believe I found you!" He looked over at the kid behind Thorne. "Who's your friend?"

"That's Brandon. He's my foster brother."

Johnny stuck out his hand to Brandon. Brandon backed away.

Thorne was hanging on to Johnny. "But how'd you know I live here?"

"Guess I just got lucky," Johnny said. "Hey, hop in, kid, we can sit here and talk."

Thorne was eyeing the big shiny Hummer. "That yours?"

"Yep, it's all mine. You like it?"

Johnny opened the door and held it for Thorne. Brandon yelled at him, "Don't get in there, Thorne! You're not allowed—"

Thorne turned toward Brandon. "It's okay, it's my brother." He jumped up in the backseat of the big black boxy vehicle.

Brandon stood there screaming at him. "Thorne! Stop it! You get out of there now!"

Johnny slammed the door shut and climbed in behind the wheel, shut his door, put the Hummer in gear, and spun the tires in the gravel at the side of the road.

53

Brandon stood there watching as the vehicle sped away. After it was out of sight, he removed his backpack, took out paper and pencil, and wrote down the tag number he'd memorized.

He ran toward the ranch fence, yelling into the Oklahoma wind, "Where's Dad when I need him!" He vaulted over and put some speed to his size-9 Reeboks. This time the quarter-mile lane seemed like three miles. Before he even got close to the barn, he began yelling for Kirk. The ATV was nowhere in sight, and he knew Katie had taken the pickup to her parents' earlier.

The big barn was quiet. The tiny bull calf was sleeping on the straw bed Kirk had made for him. Brandon was breathing heavily but decided to run on to the house, hoping to find Kirk there, but when he came in sight of the house and saw no ATV, he turned and headed back to the barn.

His yelling was being drowned out by the nasty wind, so he put his two fingers in his mouth, like Katie had taught him, and produced an earsplitting whistle. He whistled again. And again. Panic was setting in, much like the time he'd climbed way up the sycamore tree and heard the branch crack under his feet.

Kirk was simply nowhere in sight. Brandon walked inside the tractor shed and saw the old Case. He jumped on, hoped for the best, cranked it, and the old tractor came to life with a puff of smoke from the exhaust pipe.

Now where do I search? He full-throttled the old farm tractor, barely keeping his balance as he bounded over the clumpy grass. Eighteen hundred acres takes a good while to cover, but he finally spotted the ATV next to a grove of blackjack trees on the far side of the ranch.

Kirk was working with a heifer struggling with birthing just inside the tree line. The old Case roared closer. Kirk turned around.

Brandon braked to within ten feet of Kirk. "Dad!" he screamed over the engine noise. "Dad, Thorne got in the car with his brother and he's gone!"

"What? Brandon, kill the engine. I can't hear you. What's this all about?"

Brandon turned the key off, still screaming with the sudden silence around the area. "I'm telling you, Dad, Thorne has been kidnapped!"

"What? Kidnapped?"

"As soon as we got off the bus, Thorne saw his brother, Johnny. I told him not to, but he got in the car with him anyway. It was a big, black Hummer. And it took off."

Kirk dropped the end of the rope he had been using to pull the calf and reached for his cell phone. "Oh man! I left it back in the barn. Come on. Get on the ATV with me. It'll be faster!"

Brandon crawled on. Kirk turned his head toward him and said, "Hold on, buddy!"

The Honda Rancher was in fact faster, but the ride was even bumpier than the tractor. Brandon's hands gripped the rear rack, and he still had trouble staying on.

Coming up to the barn, Kirk put on the brakes and skidded sideways, leaving a red dust cloud that quickly vanished in the angry wind. He jumped off and ran into the barn, picked up the phone and dialed 911. "This is Kirk Childers out here at Childers Ranch. We've just had a young boy kidnapped."

While Kirk was giving more details, Brandon came in and interrupted his dad. "I've got the tag number." He pulled the paper out of his back pocket. "Here it is."

Kirk grinned. "Way to go, buddy!" After giving the emergency operator that information, he plopped down on the bale of alfalfa nearby and motioned for Brandon to sit down also. "So, you guys got off the bus at three-thirty?" Kirk glanced at the watch on his wrist.

"Dad, I had to run from the gate to the barn. When I didn't find the ATV there, I ran to the house, didn't see it there, so I ran back up here. I jumped on the old tractor. It started right up, and I finally found you there on the other side of the ranch."

"So it's been over forty-five minutes? Dang! We've lost some precious time."

"There's a lot of land to cover here. I didn't know where to look."

Kirk picked up the cell phone and dialed Katie. "Babe, I've got bad news. You should head back home. Thorne's been kidnapped!"

54

The TV in the big room was tuned to KOKY. Kirk, Katie, and Brandon all sat glued to the screen.

"This just in. A ten-year-old boy has been kidnapped out on Hogback Road, just south of Luther. A black Hummer was stopped behind the Luther school bus. Two boys exited the bus. One of the boys, a foster child living nearby, reportedly got in the vehicle. It is unclear as to whether the boy knew the driver of the vehicle. An Amber Alert has been issued. The Oklahoma tag number is KRG9980. Authorities have set up road blocks in the area," the news anchor concluded the report.

"A lot of good that'll do." Kirk clicked the off button on the remote. "They were long gone before my nine-one-one call."

"Kirk, as soon as you called me, I got a call in to Betty." Katie's eyes reflected the fear they all felt. "I knew she had the former Barrows home address. I thought maybe that would be a possibility."

Two phone calls came in. The first was the sheriff, calling to pull out any more information he could that might aid in the direction the search should go.

The next call was from Carol Reynolds. "Katie, have you heard anything yet? Have they found him?"

"No, Mom. I guess you just heard the six o'clock news. An Amber Alert has been issued—Mom, I've got to go, another call is coming in." She punched the send button and then the speaker button.

"Katie, I just got word from the Oklahoma City Police." It was Betty. "They checked the Barrows house, where I told them

Johnny was living. No one was home. Does Brandon have any more clues that might be helpful? Did Johnny continue heading south, after Thorne got in?"

"Betty, we've given them all that information. Brandon is so upset. He feels like it is his fault. Feels like he could have done more to keep Thorne from getting in the car."

"Yes, and I feel a bit guilty also." Betty's voice cracked. "I remember Johnny telling me once he would find his little brother, whether I liked it or not. Katie, the guy is evil! I think he's a drug dealer. No one from that neighborhood comes out of prison and immediately buys a big fancy vehicle and wears eight-hundred-dollar boots—"

"Yeah, and I found out he paid fifty-five hundred dollars cash for a couple of Thorne's pieces which were on display downtown at Throckmorton Gallery."

"Katie, he's dealin'—"

"Betty, I've gotta go. Another call's coming in. Childers Ranch, this is Katie."

"Kirk Childers, please."

Katie handed the phone to Kirk. "I think it's the sheriff."

"Kirk Childers here." Kirk then said nothing, just listened. Then he clicked the end button and slammed the phone down on the end table and dropped his head.

"What! Kirk talk to me. What'd he say?"

"He said the Hummer had been spotted out west of Sweetwater, about to cross over into Texas. The informant had the license number and gave them the exact location, but by the time the law got there, the Hummer was already gone. They think he took some of the oilfield roads—and there are a lot of them out there."

The ten o'clock news didn't have any further developments in the story, other than to say law enforcement believed the vehicle might still be heading west, through the Texas Panhandle.

"How on earth could a big black Hummer like that evade the law?" Kirk looked at Katie. "Someone's gotta spot the big box out there. That kind of vehicle isn't that common."

55

For the fifth time, Thorne asked his brother, "Where are we going?" Each time Johnny ignored the question.

This time, Alexa spoke up. "Thorne, your brother is nuts! Even he doesn't know where this is headed."

"Well, I wanna go back!" Thorne leaned forward. When his brother didn't respond, he punched Johnny's shoulder. "I said I wanna go back, Johnny!"

"Shut up, Thorne! Just shut up!"

The two-lane road was deserted. Johnny had avoided the road block where Highway 6 took off at I-40. Suddenly, the sign announcing the Texas state line flashed by. Alexa Cavanaugh's glare penetrated the guy she had only known for three weeks. "Now look what you've done, Johnny Barrow!"

"What're you yappin' about now, woman?"

"Johnny, you've just crossed over into Texas. They're gonna get you for kidnapping and taking a minor across state lines. You've really blown it now!"

"Look, Alex, this is my brother—my brother! This ain't kidnappin'. This is family! I got a right to take my brother with me, wherever I choose."

"You are wrong, Johnny! DFS has custody of your brother. You can't just yank him away from the school bus like you did. They'll get you for kidnapping. You had no right to run off with him, and now you've taken him across state lines."

"Shut up, Alex!"

"No! I won't shut up, Johnny! I want no part of this. You're putting me in a place I don't want to be. You'd better turn this big monster around right now and take us back."

At seventy miles per hour, Johnny slammed on the brakes, throwing the Hummer into a tailspin, careening off the roadway, and sliding to a stop just before the vehicle would have plowed through a barbed wire fence. "Get out, Alex!"

"Come on, Thorne," Alexa said, "we're getting out here."

Johnny swore, his jaw clenched, and his fist tightened around the steering wheel. "The boy stays!"

Alexa opened the door and jumped down into the ditch below. Her ankle twisted, and she mouthed a curse word. She started to open the back door for Thorne. Johnny clicked the locks, and the big, black box leaped forward. Dirt, grass, and gravel blasted Alexa Cavanaugh's face. She stood there, miles from the nearest town. A dozen Hereford cows stared at her from across the fence.

Her cell phone was back in the center console of the Hummer. She sat down in the brown grass and leaned against a weathered fence post. The wind bit against her face and her eyes watered. Tumbleweeds rolled over the highway and joined the ones already piled against the fence. She turned and saw several of the Herefords curiously inching toward her. Picking up one of the big tumbleweeds, she tossed it toward the cows. It hung up on the top strand of barbed wire.

As she sat there, thinking about her predicament, she heard an all too familiar rattle. She turned to the side just in time to see a monstrous rattlesnake inching toward her. Ever so carefully, Alexa stood and then sprinted back toward the pavement. After walking down the highway for a quarter-mile, she sat down again. Her ankle was throbbing.

Twenty minutes later, a Dodge Ram slowed and came to a stop near her. The passenger window rolled down, and a fifty-something man tipped his greasy hat. "You look like you might be needin' a lift, girl."

Alexa was already on her feet. "Sir, you got a cell phone on ya?"

"Naw, wouldn't do no good no ways," he said. "They ain't no coverage out here." He reached over and opened the door. "Climb in, sweetheart, I can get you down the road a ways. Where you headed?"

"Mister, I don't even know where I am. My boyfriend's in a black Hummer, and he's kidnapped his brother. I've got to get to a phone."

"Next town is Wheeler, probably fifteen miles, and there ain't no cell coverage 'til we get there—even if either one of us had one of them blasted things. I hate 'em. Had one once. Couldn't get away from my wife. Finally pitched the danged thing in a farm pond and told her I lost it."

"You think we could stop at some house and use their phone?"

"Lady, you see any houses out here? There ain't nuthin' between us and Wheeler but bob wire fences, tumbleweeds, and a few scrawny cows tryin' to find 'em a few blades of grass over an inch tall."

***

The streets of Wheeler, Texas, were deserted at eight-thirty, except for the one convenience store. The Dodge one ton pulled up to the store, and Alexa got out. "Girl, I hate to leave you here, not knowin' nobody. You sure you'll be okay?"

"I'll manage," she said. "I just need to get to a phone. Thanks, Mister."

Less than a minute after she'd hung up the phone, an Oklahoma Highway Patrol car pulled up next to her in front of the store. "You the lady called in about the kidnapping?"

Alexa gave him the information. Fear was in her eyes. "I'm not gonna be in trouble over this, am I?"

"Honey, don't worry about that now," he said. "We just need to find your boyfriend and get the child back to where he belongs."

"I'm telling you, officer, I had no part in this. This was all my boyfriend's doing. I told him he was wrong to take the child. He wouldn't listen."

"Sounds like you might need to find yourself a better boyfriend. This one's gonna be in a heap o' trouble when we get hold o' him."

56

Johnny saw the lights up ahead. He braked suddenly and steered onto the one-lane dirt road to the left. The Hummer shot ahead, barely missing the A-frame side of a cattle guard. Then the vehicle took on a mind of its own and veered sharply to the right, through a fence. The barbs on the fence scraped across the hood, grinding like fingernails on a blackboard. Then the fence wires snapped when they hooked onto the roof rack. The car took a dive into a shallow arroyo with a thud, bounded back to the other side of the gulch, and came to a stop. The engine died. Johnny stared out the windshield at a two-thousand-pound Hereford bull directly in front of the Hummer.

He glanced in the rearview mirror at Thorne. "You okay, kid?"

Thorne unbuckled his seat belt, started to reach for the door handle, and hollered, "I'm outta here, Johnny!"

"Not so fast, kid!" The door locks clicked. Thorne tried to open the door, but Johnny had activated the child locks. "You just need to hang with me. I'm your brother, remember? Mom's gone, Dad's back in the pen. I'm in charge now."

"I don't care who you are! I'm not goin' with you! Let me out of here now!" Thorne beat on the side window and tried the locked door again.

Johnny turned the key in the ignition. The Hummer came to life again. The bull had moved on. Johnny put the Hummer in reverse and steered back out of the gully. Back on the narrow cow-trail-of-a-road, a farmhouse came into view a quarter of a mile down the way. The only light was an electrical service pole lamp. As he approached, he could see a new F-150 parked out front. Johnny stopped alongside the new pickup. He sat there a minute with the lights on bright. He tapped the horn. No one came to the door, so he jumped out and opened the pickup door. "Hallelujah!" he yelled. The keys were in the ignition. He pulled out his Leatherman multi-tool and removed the license plate, pitched it back in the pickup bed, and ran back over to the Hummer, removed the plates from it, and tossed them in the bed with the Ford plates.

"Come on, Thorne. We're gonna borrow this nice man's truck."

"I'm not going! That's stealing!"

"Come on, kid!" He reached in for Thorne. "I said get out!" Johnny's wrist wrapped around Thorne's arm, pulling him out of the Hummer. "You're gettin' in the truck, brat!"

"Ouch! You're hurting my arm! Let go of me!"

Johnny opened the passenger door of the Ford and shoved his brother in. "Get in and shut up, or I'll see if I can put some more hurt on you!"

"This is theft, Johnny! You'll go to jail over this."

"Naw! I'm leavin' the guy a fifty-thousand-dollar Hummer and takin' his cheap—" Johnny glanced back and saw lights coming down the road.

He jumped out, grabbed Thorne, and moved the Hummer around to the back of an old tractor shed. Then he waited, but the vehicle made a turn and disappeared behind a windbreak tree line. A few minutes later, he and Thorne switched vehicles again. Johnny backed the new King Ranch out, punched the accelerator, and the vehicle sped back down the dark trail toward the highway.

He drove northwest on a two-lane road. The speedometer tipped out just over ninety-five. Outside the town of Mobeetie, Johnny stopped at a Baptist church, where the parking lot was full and music filtered through the walls of the church. He jumped out and quickly snatched a license plate from a Chevy truck, placed it on the Ford, and headed north for about three miles before turning west again on a county road that took him to the town of Pampa.

At Pampa, Highway 152 took him northwest to the oilfield town of Borger. Thorne wrinkled his nose and looked at his brother. "What's that smell?"

"Refinery. Dad worked there once 'til he got fired."

"What's a refinery?"

Johnny winked. "Where they make gas."

The big dials on the dash flashed repeatedly. "Uh, speaking of gas…"

"Yep, kid, I'm onto it." Johnny pulled into a Conoco Phillips station just outside of town, retrieved his wallet from his rear pocket, and pulled out a credit card—Dan Torgeson's credit card. He slid the card in the slot in the pump and had put in only a few gallons when he heard sirens. He jumped in the pickup and drove around behind the station, took a side street, and circled back to the station after the sirens had passed.

Thorne's voice broke the silence. "You're gonna get caught, and you'll be in a heap of trouble."

The next town coming up on the GPS was Fritch. Still avoiding the interstate, Johnny turned and headed north to the town of Stinnett. From there, he headed west on Highway 152 to Dumas. Just west of town he looked down at the gas gauge. It was hovering just above empty. He switched the digital configuration on the dashboard to miles-to-empty. Thirty-eight miles appeared. "Dangit! Maybe I should turn around and try to find a station back in that town." He looked over at his brother. "What do you think?"

Thorne waited a second. Then he said, "I think you're in charge, dude!"

Johnny drove on, constantly glancing at the miles-to-empty digital reading. The GPS showed nine miles to Dalhart. The miles-to-empty read eight miles.

At Dalhart, he spotted a Mobile station and rolled in on fumes to the pump. The station was closed. Only the security lights illuminated the interior. He grabbed his wallet and pulled out Torgeson's credit card. "You gotta love these kinds of pumps."

"You're a fool," Thorne said. "You're gonna get caught."

Highway 154 straight-lined southwest to Tucumcari. The New Mexico Highway Patrol was waiting with several cars and spike strips across the road. Johnny had no choice. He'd been trying to find a radio station and seen the patrol cars too late, plowing across the strips. All four tires deflated, and as soon as the truck came to a stop, he found a myriad of armed men awaiting him.

"Step outta the truck and put your hands up!"

"Hey, no problem here, officer." Johnny calmly obeyed. "What's this all about?"

Two seconds later, Johnny Barrow found himself plastered to the pavement, spread-eagle, with a Colt .45 pointed at him. The wind howled, and a tumbleweed five times the size of a bowling ball rolled across the pavement in front of him, striking the flat tire on the left front of the Ford.

Another officer opened the door for Thorne. "Hey, buddy, what's your name?"

"Thorne. Thorne Barrow."

"Who was driving the pickup?"

"It was my brother, Johnny, and that truck don't belong to him. He stole it way back in Oklahoma."

The officer took Thorne to the police station and questioned him at length. "So do you live with your brother?"

"No."

"Where are your parents, Thorne?"

"My real dad is in prison, and my mom, I think, lives—is in Oklahoma City."

"So where was your brother taking you?"

"Look, I don't mind answering all these questions," Thorne said, "but first you should call my dad—or rather, my foster dad. He's probably worried." He gave the officer Kirk's cell number.

57

"Mr. Childers, this is Officer Brian Amador with the Tucumcari New Mexico Police Department. We have a kid here who is very anxious to talk to you."

Kirk literally shouted into the phone. "Put him on!"

For a full five minutes, Thorne buzzed out the full details of the trip. There was wind in Tucumcari, a lot of it.

"Thorne, I can barely hear you. What's all that static?" Finally, Kirk stopped him mid-sentence. "Hey, buddy, let me talk to the officer again."

The officer stood with his arms across his chest, grinning. Thorne handed the phone to him. "Mr. Childers, this guy's quite a talker, isn't he?"

"Yeah," Kirk said. "I think he's a little excited. Is he okay? He's not hurt, is he?"

"The boy's fine—not hurt in any way. He's given us some valuable information. The truck his brother was driving is stolen, and Thorne told us where his brother picked it up. Said he left a Hummer there at the farmhouse where he stole the truck. I've called the authorities there, and they'll go out and check it out." Officer Amador grabbed at his hat to keep it from becoming airborne with the latest wind gust. "The boy tells us there was a girl who started out with them, but he said she was ditched out in the middle of nowhere. He said it was somewhere just on this side of the Texas-Oklahoma state line. We'll check that out."

"Man, I can barely hear ya. You on a cell phone?"

"Yeah, let me go inside. The wind is really howling out here. Looks like we got us a nice storm rollin' in."

The officer held the door for Thorne to go back inside with him. "That any better?"

"Oh yeah, much better," Kirk said. "So, Brian, what's the procedure for getting the boy back home? Anything we need to do tonight?"

"He says he was in foster care there with you. Is that right?"

"Yep."

"He'll be returned to the Oklahoma child protective services, or whatever they call themselves there, and then I'm sure they'll notify you."

"Anyway, you'd allow me to come pick him up tonight?"

"Sorry, Mr. Childers, we've gotta follow the rules. He'll be returned to Oklahoma tomorrow morning. Anyway, if you're in OK City, you're probably a good four hundred miles from here."

Katie's ear must have been plastered to the phone also. "Where's he going to stay tonight? You can't just hold him there at the station overnight!" Her voice was escalating. "This is a child!"

The officer held the phone away from his ear and grinned. "Look, lady, he will be okay. Don't worry about him. He's in good hands."

"Well he may be in good hands, but no child should have to spend the night inside a city jail!"

"He won't. I promise. There's not much left of the night anyway, but he'll have a good bed, and my wife will feed him a good breakfast tomorrow morning. He seems like a good kid—won't be no trouble at all."

"I want to talk to him," Katie said. "Put him on, please."

The officer grinned, shook his head, and handed the phone back to Thorne.

The following day, Katie had called Betty Sawyer three times to see when Thorne might be arriving back in Oklahoma City. And for the third time, Betty told Katie she would call her as soon as he arrived. "I'll immediately head your way just as soon as they get here with him."

Katie ended the call and poured herself a third cup of coffee.

Kirk needed to run into town on an errand. "You wanna come with me?"

"Kirk, I'm not about to leave this house! Betty may call anytime now."

"Babe, she's got your cell number…"

"No, I'm not leaving here 'til our boy is home safe with us."

"You know, you should try to get some sleep. You've been up all night!"

"Kirk, how could I possibly sleep at a time like this? That boy of ours is hundreds of miles from home. He doesn't know anyone there. Who knows if they even fed him or not? So, of course, I couldn't sleep! I won't 'til he's back here with us."

58

Tucumcari police found the discarded license plates in the bed of the Ford truck, and the owner was notified.

With an obvious Oklahoma accent, the hard-of-hearing old farmer yelled into the phone, "Yeah, soon as I pulled in here to the front gate, I told the missus my truck was gone. Told her someone's come and stole my brand-new truck. But, get this, whoever it was, they left me this big four-door Hummer. Keys in it. She's a purty thing. Got some bad scratches on the hood, but other than that, she looks brand new."

"Sir," the officer said, "please don't go near that vehicle. It will be used as evidence."

The next day, the Hummer was searched by local authorities. Cocaine was found inside with a street value of a quarter million dollars, as well as a loaded Glock in the glove box. Johnny Barrow would soon be getting back to his home, the one he knew well—Oklahoma State Penitentiary at McAlester.

Katie was watching outside the kitchen window when she heard Betty's car pull up. She ran out and met them at the front gate, threw her arms around Thorne, and kissed him on the forehead.

The next morning, Thursday, Kirk had taken the pickup to town. Brandon grumbled about having to walk up to meet the bus. "No," Katie said, "you guys won't be going or coming from the bus again by yourself."

"Kirk's got the truck," Thorne said. "So how's that gonna work?"

"Guys, if I have to walk up to the gate with you, I will. But this time, I've got a better idea. Come on, grab your backpacks and helmets, and follow me."

Katie walked outside and climbed on the Honda Rancher. The guys just stood there, gawking at her. "Where are we both s'posed to ride?" Thorne asked.

"One of you will get on the back. The other gets on the front rack."

"That ain't right," Brandon said.

"Yeah, is that legal?" Thorne said.

"I don't care what's legal and what's not. My boys are going to be escorted to and from the bus from here on. So come on guys, climb on."

59

After Kirk got back, Katie drove over to the Greyhound terminal. Getting there about eleven o'clock, she sat down with her at the coffee shop around from the bus station and poured forth the entire abduction story as she knew it.

Lana Lou listened quietly, looked down, shook her head, and the deep hurt that only a mother can know was written in her eyes. Katie could see the news of Johnny hurt her. Then Lana Lou said, "What's this done to my baby boy? Is he okay?"

"Sweetie, Thorne is fine. We're so proud of him. He gave the cops exactly what they needed to—" She stopped. "Oh, I'm sorry…"

"No, that's okay. Johnny got what he deserved." Tears started to stream down the woman's face. "Katie, Thorne is all I got now." She took a napkin from the holder on the table and wiped at her eyes. "John's a lifer in some prison, Josh hates me, and now Johnny's gonna be lookin' through them same bars for a long, long time." She ducked her head and bawled.

Katie took her hand. "Sweetie, you've got Thorne—and you've got me and Kirk."

Lana Lou looked up with tears still streaming down her face. "Look at me. My life is a shambles. Thorne can't possibly be proud of his mother. I'm not only an embarrassment to him—I'm an embarrassment to the whole world!"

Katie got up from her side of the booth they were sitting in and moved around to the other side, next to her friend. She put her arm around her, took a tissue from her purse, and wiped the woman's eyes. "Girl, we're going to change that!"

Her biscuit-brown eyes dropped. "How?"

"I don't know, but we will do it. Together, we will do it—we will!"

Lana Lou touched the edge of the table and quivered. "No, even God has given up on me."

Katie pounded the table top and drew a couple of stares from two men seated on the bar stools at the counter. "No! No, baby, God has not given up on you. He has a plan for you. I know He does!"

Lana Lou sniffled, tilted her head, and grinned. "Well, I wish He'd let me in on the plan."

They both laughed and Katie said, "One way or the other, I'm getting you out of here. This street is not your home!"

"Katie," she said, "this is as close to a home as I'll ever have."

Katie reached over and squeezed Lana Lou's cheek. "Sweetie, you're wrong about that!"

At one fifteen, Katie pulled in and saw the Honda Rancher parked by the barn. She killed the engine, got out, and found Kirk inside, bottle-feeding the calf.

"Kirk, I've been thinking…"

Without turning his head toward her, he rolled his eyes her way. "That might be a very dangerous thing to do."

She saw a grin creep out of the corner of his mouth. "Come on!" She tipped his hat forward over his eyes. "Cut me some slack."

Kirk put his boot up on the bottom rail of the stall. He held the bottle in his left hand, and with his right elbow resting on his knee and his hand on his chin, he said, "Okay, let's hear it, Miss Kate."

Katie climbed up on the top rail, held on to his shoulder for balance, and dangled her feet. "I've been wondering what will happen to those two art pieces of Thorne's that Johnny bought. He's in jail now, and if he goes to prison, I want Thorne to have them."

"Well, we can't just go bustin' in where he lived and walk out like we owned them."

Katie was quiet. Then she said, "No, but I know who can!"

60

THE FRONT DOOR was locked, but Lana Lou said she knew the kitchen window wouldn't lock. "In fact, it won't even close all the way." She stared up at the window. "Well, look, that pane—it's been broken. Okay, but how am I gonna get up there? I ain't that tall."

Katie leaned against the wall, stooped down, cupped her hands a foot off the ground, and said, "Put your arm around my neck and your foot right here. I'll push you on up. But be careful. I don't want you to cut yourself on the glass."

Lana Lou did as Katie said, stepped into Katie's hands, and pushed the old unscreened window open.

Just as Katie started to lift the woman up a bit, a voice cracked behind her. "What in tarnation are you two doing?"

Katie let her friend back to the ground, looked around, and saw a size-18 flower-printed dress with a well-seasoned and wrinkled face sticking out the top.

Lana Lou held on to Katie's shoulder and turned in the direction of the raspy voice. "Emma! You scared the crap outta me! What are you doing?"

The woman walked over and grabbed her neighbor's face. "Well, look who's scarin' who. I thought you's probably dead! Where you been keepin' yourself all this time?"

Lana Lou grinned. "No, I ain't dead—yet." Her shoe had come off, and she reached down to put it back on. "Well, Emma, I've been around." She seemed to lose her balance and reached for Katie's arm. "I s'pose this is still my house. Let's hope we ain't breakin' into someone else's."

Emma shook her head. "No, honey, you ain't breakin' into nobody's house but your own. But why don't you just go in the back door? I know where that boy of yours keeps the key."

"You mean my Johnny?"

"Yeah, he's been livin' here 'bout as long as you been gone. That boy's something else! He's got himself a new set of wheels. Calls it a Hummer. I don't know why they would call it that. I thought hummers were little bitty and colorful. This thing looks like a big, black boxcar."

Lana Lou shook her head. "I guess you haven't heard the news..."

"Hey, let's go over and sit down in my lawn chairs out back. You can tell me then. Oh, by the way, who is this pretty lady here with you?"

"Emma, this is Thorne's foster mother. Name's Katie."

Katie stuck out her hand. "I'm pleased to meet you, Emma. You are Lana Lou's neighbor?"

"Yes, I am. I was living here when she and John moved here." She looked at Lana Lou. "What, twenty-some odd years ago?"

Lana Lou laughed. "You said that right, girl!" Her voice cracked. "It was some odd years, all right!"

The three women sat down in the rusted old lawn chairs behind Emma's house. "I guess my Johnny Boy's going back to the slammer. You ain't heard?"

"No," Emma said. "What's that boy done now? I just seen him not three days ago, right out here on the front porch. He was half naked. Course that ain't nuthin' unusual for him, is it?"

It became obvious Lana Lou was having a hard time telling her neighbor about Johnny's latest fiasco, so Katie stepped in. "Emma, Johnny has been charged with the kidnapping of his brother—"

Emma grabbed her chest. "What? You mean Thorne? Well, what in the name of—"

"Yes, he took him from our place and ran clear across Oklahoma, Texas, and they nabbed him in New Mexico. He had switched vehicles—stole one—and when the cops found the Hummer, there was a stash of cocaine in it."

Emma's eyes bugged. "I knew it! I knew that boy was sellin' dope or somethin'. Your house has been buzzin' with activity ever since he moved back in." Emma leaned forward. "So where's Thorne now?"

"Oh, he's back with us," Katie said, "but it was quite a trip. Thorne tried to bail out of the vehicle a couple of times, but he said Johnny locked the doors with the child-lock button."

Emma turned to Lana Lou. "Well, honey, why on earth were you tryin' to break into your own house?"

The woman sat with her head down, and a tear dripped off her cheek. Katie reached over and touched her hand. "It's okay, hon. I know it's difficult hearing bad things about your own child." Then she turned to Emma. "We were told Johnny purchased a couple of Thorne's art pieces, and we've come to collect them. With Johnny put away, Lana Lou didn't want someone breaking in and taking them. The way I see it, they now belong to her. Johnny's sure not going to be able to hang them on his cell wall."

Emma Knutson grabbed the arms of the old chair and pushed herself up. "Well, come on. I know where he keeps the key."

61

"I STILL CAN'T believe my Thorne painted that." Lana Lou had turned around in her seat and was staring at Thorne's first attempt at oils. "I saw the charcoal drawing out there at the museum, but this one is really good too." She looked at her friend. "Are you going to keep these for Thorne? You know I don't have a place."

"Yes, of course I will." She parked the truck just down from the Skirvin Tower. Lana Lou asked why she was stopping here.

"Honey, I want you to see three more pieces your son has painted." The woman looked confused. "Throckmorton Gallery is featuring your son's art. I want you to meet the owner if she is in. Well, actually, it's a husband-and-wife team."

Lana Lou looked down at her wrinkled hand-me-down dress and frowned.

"Don't worry, sweetie, you're okay. They know you aren't one of the fancy city socialites." That brought a super-sized grin from the little woman.

"Are you telling me Thorne's art is displayed in this nice gallery?"

"Yes, that is exactly what I'm telling you. They are in love with his art. Did I tell you that your Johnny walked in here and paid fifty-five hundred dollars cash for those two pieces we absconded with from your house?"

"No! You're kidding!"

"Sweetie, the Throckmortons are telling me they believe your son is well on his way to becoming a great Western artist! They want everything he can bring them."

"College!" she blurted out. "Maybe he can pay his way through college with his art."

"Oh, you have no idea."

Katie opened the door to the gallery for her friend to enter and was greeted by Rhena Throckmorton. She recognized Katie at once and looked at Lana Lou. "Oh, you must be Thorne's mother."

Lana Lou looked embarrassed. "I'm sorry, ma'am." She looked down at her well-worn dress. "I didn't know I'd be coming here."

Rhena took her hand. "Sweetheart, it's okay. I'm so very glad to meet Thorne's mother. You know, this boy is quite an artist. Come on back to my office. I want to show you some of his pieces. I was keeping them back here for my husband to appraise before placing them in the gallery for sale." She unlocked the door to her office and pointed to the one on the floor next to her desk. "Mrs. Barrow, I'd like for you to see this one. I am amazed at how your son got that fog to look so real. And just look at the little angry dog, barking at that bull." She pulled the abstract from behind, turned it around, and quickly placed it on the other side of her desk where Lana Lou couldn't see it. "This one, I'm buying!" She looked at Katie. "Landon has a price in mind. When did you want to get an independent opinion?"

"I really don't know. We are just now getting back to normal around our house." She glanced at Lana Lou. "We've had a lot to deal with these last couple of days. What does Mr. Throckmorton think it should sell for?"

Rhena touched the back of the painting. "We're thinking ninety-five."

Lana Lou's mouth flew open, and she whispered, "Ninety-five dollars? Wow! Let me see it."

Katie stared at her friend. "No, hon, they're talking ninety-five hundred!"

Lana Lou stood perfectly still, obviously in deep thought. She looked at the other painting leaning against the wall. "My boy did this?"

"Yes, he really did," Katie said.

"And this one's worth how much?"

Landon Throckmorton walked in. "Mrs. Childers, it's nice to see you again. And who do we have here?"

"Mr. Throckmorton, this lady is the mother of Thorne Barrow. I'd like for you to meet Lana Lou—"

Landon shook her hand. "You know, we did meet. It was at the museum where your son's charcoal was displayed."

Lana Lou pulled her hand away quickly and hid both behind her back. "You're right."

Landon then walked over to the two pieces beside his wife's desk. "This one Thorne is calling *Sic 'Em* is going on the wall out front today. I'm pricing it at forty-five hundred. The other one probably should be priced a little less than that. But this one…" He grabbed the painting from his wife's hand.

Rhena Throckmorton grimaced. Landon turned the painting around. "This one is a treasure!"

Lana Lou Barrow collapsed into Katie's arms.

"Landon! You shouldn't have…"

Katie quickly moved her friend over to a wingback chair in front of the desk. "Sweetie, are you okay?"

Lana Lou sat limp in the big chair, speechless, staring at her own likeness with the Folgers can. Twin tears were making their way down her cheeks. She put her brown-splotched hand up to her mouth and sat very still.

Rhena Throckmorton pursed her lips and gave a stern look at her husband. "Landon Throckmorton! I can't believe you let her see that!" she whispered. "How thoughtless of you!"

Katie also showed her disappointment as she stood there, staring at the gallery owner. Landon ducked his head and put his hand to his forehead. "I…I just didn't think. I'm sorry."

The big wingback chair was abruptly vacant. Lana Lou marched over to Landon, put her arm around him, and said, "Mr. Throckmorton, don't be sorry. I'm glad I saw that. It's done something for me." She walked over to the painting and gently touched the image of the coffee can. "I'm pathetic, aren't I?"

Rhena, Landon, and Katie all gathered around the shrunken lady, hugged her, and cried with her.

62

KATIE HAD BEEN called to substitute for the first grade teacher in Luther. After all the kids had been loaded on the bus and she'd walked out of the classroom, an idea popped in her head. She walked down the hall to the superintendent's office. The door was open, and she walked in.

"Hi, Katie, we're all glad to see you back here doing what you do best. How'd it go today for you?"

"Mr. Johnson, that's a good class of first graders this year. I had no problems at all. Almost makes me want to re-apply for a class of my own someday."

"First opening we get, Katie, I'm calling you. I won't wait for you to apply."

"I appreciate that, but I've about got my hands full out there on the ranch. The boys aren't much trouble, but that's a big ranch and a lot of work. It takes all of us to make sure the chores get done. But the reason I stopped in was I was wondering if the school might have an opening for a janitor or maybe a cook?"

"Pull up a chair, Katie. I thought you just said you had your hands full out there on that big ranch." The superintendent laughed. "Now you want a job as a janitor or cook?"

"No. No, it's not for me. It would be for a friend of mine."

"As a matter of fact, Jean Carson—you know Jean—just quit. As you know, she's been a janitor here for...well, ever since I can remember. We're just starting to take applications for the job. So who's this friend of yours?"

Katie thought about that question and wondered just how much she should tell him about her friend. "Mr. Johnson, I think you know Kirk and I have been fostering for a few years now. First, we fostered Brandon before we were allowed to adopt him. And now we've had Thorne Barrow, the young man who won your all-school competition in art—"

"Oh, yes. The kid is quite talented. Talk gets around in a small town like this. I've heard a big gallery in Oklahoma City is showing his art now."

"You've heard right. Throckmorton Gallery has three of his pieces now, and they have already sold two others."

"Wonderful. But you were about to tell me about your friend."

"Yes. You see, Thorne's mother desperately needs a job. She is a sweet lady who would probably make a very loyal employee for you."

"She got any janitorial experience?"

"Uh…I believe she has helped neighbors with cleaning. Her name is Lana Barrow, and I've come to know her quite well."

"How do you know her, Katie?"

Katie now felt caught up in an updraft in which she didn't quite know how to get her feet planted back on level ground. "I…I have had many visits with her. Uh…Oh, I might as well tell you the whole story. After all, you did ask."

The man grinned. "Katie Childers, I don't believe I have ever seen you at such a loss of words. This is amusing."

"Well, I'm glad you think so." Katie laughed and shook her head, still finding it difficult to find the right words. "Mr. Johnson, Mrs. Barrow is a homeless person." Then she jumped up. "But… but please…please don't let that scare you. Lana Lou is one of the sweetest people I know. And I believe she would be a very hard worker, if given the chance."

"Katie." He motioned for her to sit back down. "You mean she is one of the homeless who live on the streets somewhere?"

"Lana Lou has been dealt a very sorry deck of cards. She was a victim of spousal abuse." Katie reclaimed the chair she'd been in, even though she would have rather stood. "This lady has a beautiful heart. She loves her son, and Thorne loves her."

"I don't know, Katie—homeless and living on the streets?"

"We could change that," she blurted out. "I mean you could change that. She is a good woman, honest as the day is long. She'll do a good job here. I just know it."

"Katie Childers! If I didn't know you as I do and know what you stand for, I'd think I was out of my mind for even considering such a thing. But I know if you recommend this woman, then I should at least talk to her."

"When can I bring her to you?"

Mr. Johnson ran his fingers through his thinning hair. "Tomorrow after school, okay?"

Katie jumped up from the chair. "Yes!"

"Hon, you've got to understand I'm just talking to her. I can't commit without seeing and talking to her."

"Three thirty! We'll be here." She reached over the desk and shook his hand. "Thank you. You have no idea what this means to me."

Johnson grinned. "Well, if she's a friend of yours, she can't be half bad. See you tomorrow."

Katie turned to walk out the door.

"Uh, Katie." She turned back to him, and he was standing with her heavy key ring wrapped around his index finger. "You might need these, girl."

63

Katie pulled up to the gate, punched in the code, and saw a cloud of dust in front of her. Through the red powdery veil, she saw Kirk on the Honda Rancher with one boy on the back and one on the front rack. She followed behind in the dusty air. Brandon looked back and waved at her.

She pulled in beside him at the ranch house. The boys jumped off, came over, and opened the door of the pickup. Kirk looked at her and said, "I'm sure glad I was in front of you and not behind. We need rain really" bad." He climbed off the ATV, stretched, removed his hat, and ran his fingers over his forehead where a layer of dust had accumulated.

Katie got out of the truck. The boys had both ran inside. "Kirk, come here. I've got something to tell you."

He ran around the back of the truck to where she stood by the driver's door. She threw her arms around him, pushed his hat back, and planted a long and hard kiss on his lips. "Wow! That was something. But what'd I do to deserve that?"

She grinned and pulled his hat forward again. "You probably didn't deserve it, but you got it anyway."

"Kate, I can read you like a book. You got something you're just dying to tell me, so let's have it." He winked. "Unless you'd rather do a repeat of that kiss."

"Kirk, I may have landed a job for Lana Lou!"

"A job? For Lana Lou? I thought you were subbin' today."

"I was. That's where I may have found a job for her."

Kirk gawked at her. "So Lana Lou, the homeless woman with no high school diploma, is going to get a job substitute teaching at

Luther?" He put one foot on the running board of the truck. "Are we talking about the same person? Lana Lou, the panhandler—"

"Shh. We don't need her son to hear that."

"Kate! He's not even outside. Probably in there, pulling out his art supplies and starting on another painting. The kid is on a mission!"

"Honey, I talked to Mr. Johnson—just to see if they had any openings for a janitor or cook or something there at the school. He looked surprised. I think he thought I wanted the job. Then he told me Jean Carson had quit."

"Hasn't that woman been there for coming on a hundred or so years?"

"Well, somewhat less than that. Anyway, I'm supposed to have Lana Lou there at three-thirty for an interview with Mr. Johnson."

Kirk stood there with his arms crossed. "Kate, you just take the bull by the horns, don't you? Have you considered what you're doing?"

"Yes, I have, Kirk. I'm getting the woman off the streets. She deserves better than that."

Kirk removed his hat and threw it in the seat under the steering wheel. "Babe, there's just a whole lot more to it than waltzing in your principal's office—"

"Superintendent, Kirk. He's the superintendent."

"Whatever. What I'm saying is you ought to consider what all that involves."

"Like what?"

"Like, where she would live. Like what clothes does she have to wear to work? Like how that will affect Thorne. Have you even asked her if she would even want to get a job?"

"Kirk, I'm getting her off the street." Katie shoved the pickup door closed. "That is no place for someone like her. I'll find her a place to live, and I'll find her some clothes. And as for how it would affect Thorne, it would be the best thing that ever happened to the kid. He loves his mother, and she loves him."

Kirk moved her to the side, pulled the truck door open again, and grabbed his hat. "Okay, Kate, when you set your mind to something, I know better than to try to change it. But I do think you should ask her if that's what she wants."

"That so? Well, I don't have to ask. I can see it in her eyes. She wants a life, and I'm the only one that's willing to help her get it."

"O…kay." He looked at her, grinned, and shook his head.

"Can you pick up the boys again tomorrow after school? I can run them up to the bus tomorrow morning."

"Yeah, but Thorne says he's gonna grab a pillow to sit on next time. He said the front rack is pretty rough on his bony buns."

At ten thirty the next morning, Katie walked into the thrift shop with her friend. "I'm going to buy you one outfit now, but after you get the job, we'll come back, and I'll buy you several."

Lana Lou was standing by a rack of secondhand jeans. "Katie, do you really think they would hire me?"

"Yes, I do. But we've got to get you all spruced up for your interview." She moved around to the side of the rack until she found the size twos. "Here, you think these would fit?"

Katie held the jeans up to the ninety-five-pound woman's waist. "Maybe we should try a zero." She grinned. "Sweetie, you can't get any smaller. We'll have to go to the children's section if you do."

They found a size zero with decorative stitching on the hip pockets for two dollars. "This pair of jeans would have been very expensive new. They're Gloria Vanderbilt," Katie said. "Now, let's find you a nice top to go with these fancy jeans."

Forty-five minutes later, they were pulling up to the ranch gate. Katie rolled down her window and punched in the code. The little lady in the passenger seat stared. "Where are we going, Katie?"

"I'm taking you up to my house so you can get a shower and clean up. I'll do your hair for you, and I've got some makeup you can borrow. You've gotta be all spiffed up to put on your fancy clothes. Then after you get dressed, we're going to sit down and have a nice lunch. I've already got it mostly prepared."

Katie led her friend through the front door. Lana Lou's eyes were roaming the cavernous room. She walked over and ran her finger over the rock wall, looked down at the hardwood floor, then her eyes turned to the kitchen. "Katie, this looks like a castle! You live here?"

Katie laughed. "I remember that is exactly what your son said when he first was brought to us. Yes, this is our home."

Lana Lou's eyes wandered up to the high ceiling with the big wagon wheel chandelier and then over to the monstrous rock fireplace on the north wall. "My baby lives here?"

"You'd better start calling him your son. He's bigger than you now. I think he'd be offended if you called him baby."

"You're right," she said. "I'll probably keep on calling him that, but not to his face. Just don't tell him. It'll be our secret."

Katie showed her friend the master bath, handed her a big thick terry cloth towel, and said, "I'll have our lunch ready when you get out."

At three thirty, the two walked toward Mr. Johnson's office. The bus students were marching toward the east door to board the busses. Thorne ran toward them.

"Mom!" He took a second look. "Mom? Is that you? Wow! You look—different."

Lana Lou reached out her arms. "Yes, ba—son, it's really me. Miss Katie did quite a number on me, huh?"

The light in the boy's eyes illuminated his surprised but happy face. He placed his hands around her face. "Mom." And then the tears started to roll.

64

"Mr. Johnson, I'd like you to meet my dear friend, Lana Barrow."

Thorne was right by her side with his arm around her twenty-three-inch waist. "And this is my mom!" he said, grinning from ear to ear.

Mr. Johnson reached over to Thorne and produced a tight fist to meet his in place of a handshake, as most of the kids were doing lately. "Hey, guy, would you mind stepping out of the room for a few minutes so I can visit with your mom?"

"No, Thorne should stay," Katie quickly said. "He doesn't get to see his mom often, so I'd like for him to sit here with her." She sat down and patted the chair beside her.

Thorne sat down. His mother did the same, and then she reached her arm around her son and gave a quick squeeze.

There was an awkward silence. The superintendent seemed to be at a loss for words. He looked at Katie, then to Thorne, and finally to Lana Lou. "Lana, first of all, you should know you have a wonderful son. I've watched him progress over the past two years he's been here at Luther. His teacher has high praise for him—and his art. This young man seems to know where he's going in life. His grades are pretty good, his attitude has had a complete turnaround, and he has a talent for art that is amazing. His art teacher says she's never seen anything like it in someone his age."

Thorne suddenly showed a bashful side and ducked his head. His mother reached her other arm over and patted him on the leg.

Mr. Johnson directed his carefully chosen words. "Lana, I believe we can attribute this all to the positive influence of this lady sitting to the left of him. I've known Katie and Kirk for several years now, and DFS could not have possibly chosen a better home for your son. I believe he will be forever branded by the influence of Kirk and Katie Childers. Katie has taught him to read—and read well. She has drilled in manners. And from what I see, Kirk has set a very good example of masculinity for your child. Now the artistic abilities—that's something else—that, I believe, comes from God."

Katie nodded her head in agreement. "You're right. No one can teach that. It is a gift."

"So Lana, tell me what kind of experience you have had in janitorial services."

"I should tell you, I've never worked outside the home, except a time when I worked cleaning house for my neighbor."

"And I understand you are now in a situation where you have no place to call home. Is that right?"

Thorne jumped up. "She *will* have if you give her a job!"

Mr. Johnson grinned. There was a silence. The grin disappeared, and he looked at Lana Lou. "Where would you live if you had a job here at the school?"

"Mr. Johnson," Katie interrupted, "we will have that worked out. She will be living here in town." Lana Lou turned and looked with question marks in both eyes, first at Katie, then at Thorne.

In a gesture only his mother would see, Thorne's hands turned palms up in his lap, as if to say, *Beats me.*

Johnson looked toward Thorne sitting next to his mother. "Uh…I really think it might be best if Thorne would wait out—"

"Please, Mr. Johnson, Thorne should stay here beside his mother," Katie said.

"Okay, well…Lana, I'm having a difficult time understanding your present situation and how that is going to affect any employment you might be getting yourself into. I may have a hard time explaining to the school board that you were"—he whispered—"a homeless person."

Katie started to talk, but Thorne jumped up from his seat and beat her to the defense of his mother. "Mr. Johnson, sir, my mom is as good as you'll get. You could never hire anyone better for this job. I watched her as she kept our house cleaned up for many years, and that was with three of us messy boys and a dad that was an even bigger mess-maker." Thorne sat, nervously gripping the edge of the chair. "You said yourself you saw a big change in me since I've been here. Well, sir, if you hire my mom, we will all see a change. She will have a home, and I'll get to see her. Mr. Johnson, you just have to hire my mom. She will make you proud." He looked straight at the man, stuck his hand up with his index finger pointed toward the superintendent. He paused and then slowly said, "It's the right thing to do."

Johnson leaned forward and looked at Thorne eye to eye. "Young man, I think you have a point. You're not only an amazing artist, but you are quite the salesman. I'm going to hire your mother!"

Thorne climbed over Katie's legs, ran around the desk, and threw his arms around the superintendent in a giant bear hug and held on. "Thank you," he said, "for doing the right thing."

Johnson pretended like Thorne was choking him. "Okay, okay, Thorne!" He laughed. "If I ever need to sell anything, I'm calling on you to help me."

Paperwork was filled out for Lana's employment as a janitor at the school. Katie would have to take her friend back to the old Barrow's house to retrieve her birth certificate and Social Security card, which were the two required documents for employment.

Brandon had taken the bus home, but Thorne rode back in the truck with his mom and Katie. As soon as they walked in the house, Lana Lou questioned Katie about her statement to the superintendent. "Katie, you told Mr. Johnson I would be living in town. I have no money to rent a place. I don't even know how I'll get to work."

"Sweetie, we will have to figure that out. Right now, I'm just thrilled you got the job."

"I got the feeling he really didn't want to hire me."

"That may have been true at first," Katie said, "but your son really is a good salesman. I knew I wanted him to stay in the office with us. I just didn't know why. Your son is quite a kid!"

"Katie, I've got you and Kirk to thank for that. You have been so good to my Thorne. Every child should have parents like you two. But if you were planning on taking me back to the city, we probably should get started." She grinned. "And if not, then I for sure better get going. That's quite a walk for an old woman like me."

"Friend, you are not old! And you are not going back to the city tonight. You will stay right here in this house for the night. I know I'm breaking the DFS rules, but at this point I really just don't care. You are not spending another night out there on the street!"

"Katie, I can't. I don't want to get you in trouble with your caseworker."

"Lana, sweetheart, you might as well donate your Folgers can to someone else. Your son won't have it any other way."

The following morning, Katie took her friend for a walk up to the barn. She was explaining the operations of the ranch to her. "We also have three of our own dairy cows that we milk here. That's where that good rich milk you had last night for supper came from. Brandon usually helps Kirk with the milking and cream separation—loves it. Thorne never has really liked that job. Says he hates those nasty cows. It's a chore to him, so we don't insist he help with that."

Lana looked surprised. "His dad would have blistered his butt and made him get in there and do it anyway."

"No, Kirk understands Thorne helps in other ways. Each child has their own abilities, and we don't believe in trying to push a child toward something they really hate."

"But shouldn't Thorne be required to pull his own weight?"

"Oh, he does. He loves gardening and helps me with it. It's his job to till up the ground for me each spring and again in late fall after we've harvested the crops."

"It sounds like you have a huge garden."

"No, it's just a little patch out behind the house. I grow some tomatoes, cucumbers, okra, and black-eyed peas, and we love our Kentucky Wonders."

"Kentucky Wonders, what's that?"

"That was those green beans you ate last night. Oh, and we've got to have a few watermelons. Thorne knows just how to prepare the hills and plant the seeds. He grows some of the best black diamonds. Thorne knows as much as I do about what grows best here in this soil, how much water it needs, and he never lets the weeds get out of control."

"My son is getting a good education right here on this ranch. I think that is wonderful."

"Lana Lou, Thorne is also quite the fisherman. He'll quite often go down to the pond by himself when Kirk is too busy. He'll always bring back our supper. And another thing, Thorne is always willing to help Kirk with the Angus herd, although it's not his favorite thing to do. He never complains—at least now. He used to."

"My son is a changed kid! You have both been so good to him."

"I guess I'm responsible for his academic change, but Kirk is the one who has really bonded with him. He and Thorne will sometimes spend several hours—just the two of them—cutting firewood, painting fences, or repairing whatever needs repairing. But mostly there is just a lot of horsing around between the two. They sometimes don't get much work done."

Katie noticed the woman shaking her head and looking down. "What's wrong, hon?"

Lana Lou looked up. "What a difference between Kirk Childers and John Barrow!"

As they turned and started back toward the house, Katie grabbed her friend's arm and all but shouted, "I know where you're going to live!"

Lana Lou's dark-brown eyes darted toward Katie. "Where?"

Katie pulled her friend over to the tiny pop-top chalet camper. "This is your new home—at least for a while, 'til we can get you settled into something better."

Lana Lou grinned. "That would sure beat my old tarp behind the tattoo shop."

"Come on, I've got some calls to make. We're going to get you all set up in town, just like I told Mr. Johnson we would."

As soon as the school day was over, Katie called one of her retired teacher friends and asked if they could set up the camper on their extra driveway beside the house there in town. "It would just be temporary. Just 'til my friend here can get a paycheck or two for the first month's rent on something there in town."

When Kirk came in after milking, Katie stuck a fresh-out-of-the-oven cinnamon roll in his mouth. "Go bring our camper up here after supper."

With a mouthful of his favorite pastry, he said, "I thought you hated camping—said you were never going again."

"I'm not." She looked over at her friend. "Lana Lou is."

Katie put everyone to work furnishing the small camper with everything Lana Lou could possibly need: dishes, kitchen utensils, bedding, towels, toiletries, magazines, a radio, and a little black-and-white TV. Thorne attached one of his paintings to the slanted roof above the bed with hook and loop strips. Brandon picked out a few novels and found a place for them in the limited space of the tiny camper. Kirk washed the exterior and checked the tire pressure.

Katie kept handing food items for Lana Lou to find a place for. "Okay," Lana Lou said, "this is surely enough. I've got enough canned goods to last me months."

Kirk pulled the camper to town and parked it on the driveway of Katie's friend's house. He leveled it, hooked up the water and electricity, and took the propane tank and had it filled.

Katie thanked her friend and asked about paying for any electricity and water Lana Lou might use. "Oh, that's nothing," her friend said. "She won't owe me anything. I'm just glad I could help."

It was a one-block walk from Lana Lou's new home to the school. After one week on the job, the woman was smiling again and was making friends with the teachers and cafeteria staff. Life had taken a turn for Lana Barrow. Her son couldn't be happier. He got to see his mom every day at school and sometimes after school, but just as important, he also had Kirk as a father figure to guide him through the teen years. Kirk never failed to compliment him on his latest artwork. Painting was a passion for Thorne Barrow, and Throckmorton Gallery sold his pieces quickly, always asking for more. His college fund was growing.

Anyone who had anything to do with Thorne Barrow—Lana Lou, his teachers, his friends—could easily see the transformation in him. The Thorne Barrow that once sat for hours with his thumbs on the controller of a video game, or the cocky, but insecure Thorne who started playground fights and became the neighborhood bully was amazingly changed. Everyone could see that. Most people attributed that change to two incredible people, Kirk and Katie Childers.

Thorne Barrow had become a popular kid at school, but he chose his close friends carefully. His appearance was changing also. He no longer was the shortest guy in his class.

As she often did, Katie picked up Thorne from school and dropped him off at the camper to spend a little time with his mom. She was starting to leave, and Lana Lou spoke up, "Katie, I've decided to put the house up for sale in the city. I don't think

I'll ever need it again, and I can use the money from the sale of it to buy me a place here in town."

"I think that's a great idea, Lana Lou. I know you can't spend another winter in this cramped box with no insulation."

Lana Lou looked at the walls of the camper and said, "My tarp didn't have any insulation." She laughed. Then the cough returned.

Epilogue

I'm sitting here at my old Remington, clacking out the story of yet another boy God has trusted us to steer into adulthood. I see a picture of a successful young man forming. Lana Barrow's once-obnoxious son is changing even more than any of us could have imagined.

The attitude adjustment certainly has been welcome, but his physical appearance is evolving as well. The sooty-black hair has progressed from the little-boy spike to his naturally straight and free-flowing mop of black silk, always squeaky-clean, lustrous, and trailing down to his shoulders. Kirk liked the spike, but I think Thorne looks the part of an artist. At just under six feet, dark, handsome, and with a mysterious aura about him—that is Thorne Barrow.

I look deep into those beautiful walnut-brown eyes and ask myself where this is all headed. The guy will someday make us all sit up and take notice—it has already begun.

Afterword

SOME PEOPLE SEEM to think a person's value is determined by who their parents are or are not. The truth is, we are all God's children. He cares about us and has a plan for each child.

Hardships at a young age create tough challenges for foster and adopted children to overcome. Most struggle with their own identity. They almost always ask, "Who am I really?", "Why was I abandoned and not wanted, thrown away like trash?", "Do I have siblings?", "Do I look like them?" If these children are fortunate enough to have been adopted into a loving family, they might ask, "Will I hurt my adoptive parents (or the memory of them) if I contact my birth family?"

The stories of these children are often overlooked. I started telling them with my first novel, *Indebted*, and then with the first book of the Normal series, *So, This is Normal?*, and now with this one, *Defying Normal*. I have a third in the series planned. It will be titled *Longing for Normal*.

I'll continue telling stories of foster and adopted kids with many books to come—because I was one of them.

Although this is a work of fiction and no people or incidents in the story are real, the setting for the book was very real. Here are some pictures of the actual ranch:

Milking barn and corrals

John and Lorene Reed, foster parents to fifty-two (52) children while living on this ranch.

Two of the horses on the ranch (one on the left was Dandy).

The author as a teen on Dandy. This character (the horse) was real.

I enjoy hearing from my readers.

You can reach me at eldon@eldonreed.com

Visit and "like" my author page at https://www.facebook.com/EldonReed

Visit my website at www.eldonreed.com

Member: ACFW (American Christian Fiction Writers)

CWG (Christian Writers Guild)

Volunteer: CASA (Court Appointed Special Advocate) for foster children

Reading Group Guide

1. Which character was changed the most in this story: Katie, Thorne, or his mother? Why?

2. Which character was most influential in changing Thorne Barrow, Kirk or Katie? How was this accomplished?

3. Which character was most influential in changing the life of Thorne's mother? How was that accomplished?

4. It is pretty clear that two-parent families are preferred, but sometimes that is just not possible. Single parents often struggle with filling both roles. Discuss the role Katie played as mother of Thorne. How was Kirk's role as father different from that of Katie's? Could one have worked without the other?

5. The simple country life on the Childers Ranch seemed to be good for both Brandon and Thorne. Are there negative consequences to such a simple life for children? How so?

6. How might a child discover his God-given talent? Who can, and should be, responsible for helping a child find his passion?

7. This question is not meant for a written or audible reply: How can you help a child discover his or her passion? As adults, it is our responsibility, in some capacity, to mentor at least one child. That could be forms other than fostering or adopting. Volunteer as a CASA. Use your imagination. Pick a child or children and do it.

Other Books by Eldon Reed

Indebted is about a mother, who watched her son for twenty-five years but was never allowed to speak a word to him—he never knew, and she couldn't tell.

The first novel in the Normal series is about a foster parenting couple's quest to heal and replace the scars of abuse and neglect of five-year-old Brandon. But in the end, will money and prestige trump love and nurturing?

Longing for Normal continues as the third novel in the Normal series.

Kirk's quadriplegia instantly changes everything in Katie Childers' tranquil ranch life. How can they survive with no income and no place to live? Who can she trust? Will their sons stand by them?

In Eldon Reeds' *Longing for Normal*, Katie walks you through this tragedy in her own words. Trusting God is a struggle for her. Will she ever see normal again?